THE STEPMOTHER

SALLY RIGBY AND AMANDA ASHBY

Boldwood

First published in Great Britain in 2023 by Boldwood Books Ltd.

Copyright © Sally Rigby and Amanda Ashby, 2023

Cover Design by 12 Orchards Ltd

Cover Photography: Shutterstock

A CIP catalogue record for this book is available from the British Library.

Paperback ISBN 978-1-80483-516-6

Large Print ISBN 978-1-80483-515-9

Hardback ISBN 978-1-80483-517-3

Ebook ISBN 978-1-80483-513-5

Kindle ISBN 978-1-80483-514-2

Audio CD ISBN 978-1-80483-522-7

MP3 CD ISBN 978-1-80483-521-0

Digital audio download ISBN 978-1-80483-519-7

Boldwood Books Ltd
23 Bowerdean Street
London SW6 3TN
www.boldwoodbooks.com

PROLOGUE

The room was dark, and something hard jabbed into her back. She tried to move, but an unseen weight pressed her down, sending a flood of fear roaring through her body.

In the distance was a dull thud, thud, thud of machinery.

Where was she?

Flashes and images raced through her mind like a freight train, moving faster and faster, making it impossible to decipher what they meant. Just tiny splinters of memory. Crashing waves. The clank of glasses. The scent of him. Him.

She tried to latch onto the memory but the fog pushed it away.

Help. The scream died in her throat and her mouth was coated with the metallic tang of medication.

Had she been drugged and taken to this dark place? She knew it was bad, though the unrelenting haze in her mind couldn't tell her why. Another jolt of fear at the unknown danger flooded through her.

A sob caught in her chest as more images crammed through her brain. A blur of sand, cold and wet beneath her bare feet as she ran. The squeal of car brakes. And then a voice whispering in her ear.

Go to sleep, and soon it will be over.

And suddenly, the fog lifted and it all came rushing back. The truth about what had happened and why she was there.

No one would ever find her.

It was impossible.

Which meant she was going to die.

1

Libby Curtis stiffened as her phone pinged with a new notification. Shit.

A week ago, she would have instantly looked at it. Like a diver, fearlessly breaking through the water headfirst before even checking what lay below the surface. But now... well, now it was different. She waited until the two paramedics at the next table left the staffroom before pushing away her paperwork.

Her shift started in fifteen minutes and she really needed to finish the reports but instead, she let her finger hover over the screen of her phone. Just one touch and the app would open, letting her see Sam's latest post. It still astounded her that the same seventeen-year-old boy who could barely give monosyllabic answers at home didn't seem to have any problems sharing his life online.

It was how she knew he'd ditched school on Monday to go surfing, not to mention the four bottles of cider he'd drunk in his room last week, and the furious rants that sporadically appeared as he raged against the world.

She could only presume he had no idea his parents would be watching.

And of course, Nathan wouldn't.

That wasn't his style. Even after everything that happened six months ago, Nathan still trusted his son to make good decisions. But Libby had quickly discovered she wasn't cut from the same cloth. Then again, Sam wasn't really her son.

Well, not her biological son. Her husband's first wife had died while giving birth to the twins, leaving Nathan to raise two babies on his own. And that's what he'd done until he met Libby almost eleven years ago.

She'd always known they were a package deal. Love me, love my kids. And oh, how she did. She'd been there for all the school reports, grazed knees and night terrors. And in return, she'd been able to bask in the sunshine of raising two thoroughly adorable children. She cringed at how smug she'd been back then. With her wall charts and calendar schedules and the large tote bag filled with everything an organised mother should have with her. She was Instagram perfection without even knowing it was a thing.

Until six months ago, when it had all come undone. It still made her blink at the speed of the implosion. One minute, Sam was in love with Andi, his first real girlfriend – even letting that love spill over into the house – with his spontaneous hugs and long conversations. And then it was all over. Andi and her family were moving to London and she wanted to concentrate on school.

Sam had taken the breakup badly and after storming up to Andi's house, only to be refused entry, he'd caused seven hundred pounds of damage to their front garden as he'd kicked it to pieces.

It had been an exhausting couple of weeks as Libby and

Nathan had met with Andi's parents before finally convincing them not to report him to the police. It had cost a lot more than seven hundred pounds, but at least it meant it wouldn't completely ruin his future.

However, Sam didn't see it that way, and from there had come the parties and the drinking and the arguments.

The terrible things he'd flung at her.

Piss off, Libby.

You're not my real mother.

I might as well just kill myself.

It was the last one that really cut. Not that Sam would've known that. No one did except Libby's brother, Todd, who was no longer alive to tell the tale, and their mother, Angela, who'd been at the heart of it all. But Angela couldn't say anything now, trapped as she was in the dementia that had claimed her mind, but not yet her life.

And so, Libby had taken the hit, knowing that no matter what he said, she wouldn't let him fall.

He'd been equally savage with Nathan, but nothing had seemed to stick to him. After all, he was Sam's father, from the matching curve of their mouths and slant of their jaws, through to their athletic prowess. They belonged together in a way that didn't make Nathan stay up at night questioning what he could have done differently. Done better.

Then, because there was no show without punch, Sienna, Sam's twin sister, had suddenly quit her rowing team, turned her back on her old friends and started dressing like a Victorian widow as part of her own more subtle rebellion. Strangely, that was the one that had concerned Nathan more. *Bloody hormones. It's like my little girl disappeared over night.* But at least Libby understood Sienna's deflection.

It was the one-two punch she knew well. The flap of the

butterfly's wing that eventually resulted in a tornedo. After all, that's what happened to her. And to Todd.

And now she was here. Trying to help the two people she loved more than life itself. But they'd both shut her out. Her spreadsheets and planning, and the large tote bag full of snacks, no longer worked. Leaving Libby stranded on the other side of a river, without a bridge to get back across.

It's what had led to her new, unexpected side hustle as a digital detective.

She rolled her shoulders, trying to get comfortable in the ancient staffroom chair. It had been far too easy to set up a new profile and become friends with some of the girls in Sam's year. That had shown her quite enough of his feed but then he'd accepted her own request and given her full access to his life.

Anything to help find a way back to Sam.

Until he posted the video.

A thirty-second clip that she'd pressed, assuming it would be another one of his rants against something seemingly innocuous. But it wasn't.

It was filmed at night, the blue-black sky going in and out of focus as branches and trees appeared and disappeared. There was no commentary, just the heavy crunch of shoes on the ground, the rustle of the branches, and his increased breathing as he jogged. Then he came to a stop at a picnic bench and his face abruptly appeared, his features blurred from the flashlight, eyes almost glowing as his mouth flattened out into a manic smile.

Libby closed her eyes, trying to push the image from her mind, but it was lodged there, along with the comments. *Get her. You're the man. Predator.* On and on they went. Some of the girls even told him how hot he looked. Except he didn't. He looked *other*. A blur of features that somehow combined the six-year-old boy she'd first met and this seventeen-year-old stranger.

'Great, you're here. My shift just ended but I wanted to catch you before I leave.'

Libby jolted up and forced the dark images from her mind as Denise joined her at the table. They'd worked together for the last eight years as paramedics and had become fast friends, thanks to having kids of a similar age and a great love of wine.

'Just finishing up a health and safety report.' Libby put down her phone. She'd check the notification later. When she was alone.

'Don't suppose you want to do mine?' Denise flashed her a smile. She was short, with a silvery blonde buzz cut and the kind of cheekbones that Libby had long given up hope of ever getting. 'I bumped into Danny yesterday and asked if he'd heard from you.'

Libby blinked, remembering last week's conversation about the maths tutor who'd helped Denise's daughter back on track. It had come after one of Sam's teachers had bluntly told him to pull his finger out or kiss goodbye to any chance of getting the rowing scholarship to Florida that he'd all but been promised by a visiting scout last year. Not that she wanted Sam to move to the US, but everyone at the club had assured her that with his talent, it would be foolish not to do it.

Now she suspected it was the least of his problems. She plastered on an apologetic smile.

'It's been a crazy week, and when I mentioned it to Nathan, he wasn't keen. Unsurprisingly, neither was Sam.'

'Becca was the same, but once she met Danny, things seemed to click, and now she's going into second year at Bristol. He's worked with a few other kids from school and helped them as well. And try not to take it personally. You're a great mother, Lib.'

'Sam and Sienna would disagree.' She sighed, wishing she could take Denise's advice to heart. But it was hard not to blame herself. Had she been trying too hard? Or not hard enough? It was the never-ending question that plagued her these days. It wasn't like she was one of those helicopter mothers who wanted their kid to study medicine at Cambridge or anything. She just wanted them to have options and to make the most of the opportunities they were given. And then there was her obligation to Julia.

Libby had never met Nathan's first wife and yet she owed her everything. Julia been the one to decorate the house that Libby now lived in, to give birth to the kids she now loved and to help Nathan become the man he was.

Yet, if Julia hadn't died, Libby *never* would have changed her mind about wanting children. She would have gone through her entire life trapped within the wounds of her past, without experiencing the purest love. To not feel the press of soft, dimpled arms around her neck and the rhythmic breathing as a child slept in her arms. To not experience the ability to sit with them at night and watch their tears retreat as the world turned to right, just because she was there.

It was a gift that she didn't take lightly. She was the surrogate mother Nathan had chosen, and she not only owed it to him and the twins, but to the dead woman whose shoes she now filled.

'Yeah, well, despite what they think, kids don't know everything. And that's why you need to call Danny. He's brilliant,' Denise said as Jonathan walked in for his shift and grinned at them both. At forty-eight, he was still handsome in a hippy kind of way with faded blond hair that permanently seemed to need a cut, wide brown eyes and a scattering of freckles across his nose.

'Comparing war stories?' He lifted an eyebrow, well used to their conversations. Like them, he was a paramedic, though despite having a procession of girlfriends, he'd never settled down, which meant he found their domestic details and complaints endlessly fascinating.

'You know it.' Denise got to her feet. 'Anyway, I'd better go and make myself pretty for date night. Still can't believe I have Saturday night off.'

'Lucky for some,' Jonathan said though there was no malice there. Then he turned and checked the time on his phone. 'Think I have time to grab something to eat before we do the vehicle check? I'm starving.'

'Probably... though I do have a cruffin,' she admitted, reaching for her large tote bag. She'd stopped on the way to work to get Nathan's favourite sourdough bread for tomorrow and had been lured to the pastry counter with the intention of eating her feelings.

But the guilt had caught up with her, along with the reminder that in four weeks' time, she, Nathan and the kids would be in Tenerife to celebrate her forty-sixth birthday. And while she wasn't going to wear a bikini, she did want to go swimming without hating every moment of it. Then again, considering how tense things were, she wasn't sure she'd get the kids on the plane.

His eyes lit up as she pulled the paper bag out. 'Is that from Maples? God, I love those things. Are you sure?'

'It's all yours.' Libby handed it over. At least someone still appreciated her ability to produce treats from her bag. She then watched in fascination as he casually demolished it with no thought of calorie calculations at all. Once it was gone, he rolled the paper bag up into a ball and aimed it at the rubbish bin.

'Thanks, Lib. You're a lifesaver.' He dumped his backpack into a locker and Libby did the same with her bag before they headed for the door. 'Everything okay at home? You were looking tense there. How's Sam?'

Libby rubbed the back of her neck. 'Last week, he didn't say two words to us, but yesterday, he sat at the dinner table and had an in-depth conversation about Sea of Thieves.'

'Of which you probably only understood one word in ten.' His mouth twitched with amusement.

'It's like a foreign language,' Libby admitted. Not that she hadn't tried in the past, but gaming was just one thing that wouldn't stick in her head. Thankfully, Nathan didn't mind sitting down with a controller in his hand, and then there was Jonathan, who not only volunteered to do it, but seemed to enjoy it.

'Let me know if you want me to have a chat with him. Believe it or not, I know a thing or two about flunking out. I'm the ultimate cautionary tale. Maybe I could scare him with my years in the wilderness with no cell phone or TikTok.'

'Hopefully it won't come to that, but I'll keep you posted.' Libby managed a weak smile.

Jonathan had only moved to Bournemouth eight years ago, and after discovering he didn't have any plans on his first Christmas, she'd invited him along to their place. And despite Nathan and the kids not being happy at having a stranger crash their day, they'd soon been won over. The kids because Jonathan had visited so many countries and followed the same YouTubers they did, and Nathan because Jonathan was always happy to assemble any flatpack furniture or help with minor repairs.

He was like the forty-eight-year-old man-child they never knew they needed.

'Make sure you do. He's a good kid. They both are,' he said as they reached the garage and made their way over to the last ambulance in the bay. 'Right. Let's get everything checked and book into dispatch, and then we'll see what the afternoon brings.'

'It's all we can ever do.'

She'd been working for the ambulance service for the last fifteen years and knew that no matter how prepared you were for any event, it was impossible to know what lay around each corner.

It didn't take them long to get into a familiar rhythm and while Libby checked the medical equipment and drugs, Jonathan checked the tyres, oil, and fuel level. Once everything was prepared, they updated central dispatch, and their first call came through within minutes.

It was to a dance school where a student had suffered a seizure and hit their head. The Saturday afternoon traffic was light thanks to the lull between lunch and afternoon activities and Jonathan carefully pulled out of the station and headed along Fairmille Road. An hour later, the young student was in the hands of the hospital team, and they were on the way to pick up an elderly patient who needed some tests doing, when the radio sounded with a new call.

Libby immediately answered.

'I need you to head to Steamer Point. A young girl, around seventeen, has been found with serious bruising, dehydration, and possibly still under the influence of drugs or alcohol. There's no phone or identification so we don't have any medical history. Police are there. It's a possible failed abduction,' the operator said before giving them the address and the time the girl was found. Libby managed to do all the necessary things and then leaned back in the seat.

As always, it started with a buzz in her ears and then the roar of nothingness, as the world disappeared and the dreadful darkness of the past rushed through her, stripping her of the last thirty years and taking her back to *then*.

She closed her eyes and clenched her fists.

Not now.

Not now.

Not now.

The words were like razors, slicing through the oblivion that was trying to drag her down. Over the years, she'd mastered the technique, and while she couldn't control the triggers, she knew how to push it back into the compartment where it needed to go. At least until her shift was over.

'Hey, it's okay.' Jonathan put the sirens on and turned the ambulance back the way they'd come. It was always high risk travelling with the lights on and he carefully navigated the traffic on their way to the Christchurch nature reserve. 'I've got this. You check on her.'

The *her* was Sienna.

They always checked on their own families if they were sent to an emergency where it was possible they might be related to the victim. Especially for something like this. Libby shook away the last vestige of the darkness and flicked through the calendar on her phone, trying to remember if Sienna had anything planned.

But the slot was blank.

Of course it was, because these days, neither of the kids told her shit.

Her chest tightened and she took a shuddering breath.

She could text, but she doubted Sienna would pick up, thanks to their latest argument about a concert in Austria that Sienna had been desperate to go to. Libby had – what she considered quite reasonably – refused to hand over five hundred pounds and since then the atmosphere had been frosty. Which meant the chances of Sienna replying were slim to not going to happen.

'Hey, I know what you're thinking, and you need to stop it.' Jonathan turned left and slowed his speed on the narrow road. 'I might not have all of Denise's Yoda-like wisdom, but you have great kids, Lib. Sienna's careful. She doesn't take chances.'

'I know,' she said, but the words scraped along her raw throat. Because she didn't know. Not any more. How had they reached this place where she had no idea what her kids were doing?

She called Nathan but it went through to voice mail and there was no time to leave a message before Jonathan reached the reserve. Which meant she was going in blind.

2

Steamer Point was a nature reserve flanked by the beach and sea on one side and a golf course on the other. But the endless views of the southern coastline were marred by the two police vans parked outside the entrance to the reserve. The sun was dipping and Libby shivered as Jonathan turned off the sirens. Several walkways had been cordoned off and one of the officers walked towards them. The police would have been called at the same time as the ambulance and it was up to them to make the scene safe for the paramedics, and ensure that all relevant evidence had been collected.

'You can go straight in.' The officer nodded to a cluster of trees near the cliff. Libby hurried over, leaving Jonathan to gather up the equipment they might need. One of the officers had put the girl into a recovery position and she was lying on her side, long hair clumped together with sweat and dust.

It was brown. Nothing like Sienna's freshly dyed, black hair. The relieved breath was out of her mouth before she could stop it. Shit. What right did she have to be pleased it was someone else's daughter lying in front of her? The poor family probably had no idea the teenager was even missing. All the same, relief flooded her as she dropped to her knees, trying to take in as much as she could.

There was no sign of vomit, but the girl's face was covered in dirt and grime, along with thick, black eyeliner that had smudged into two heavy shadows. A tangle of gold necklaces hung loosely around her throat and she was dressed in a tiny bustier and a pair of baggy jeans. Judging by what Sienna and her friends wore, the outfit suggested a Friday night party rather than a Saturday morning trip to the high street.

Did that mean she'd been out all night? Another stab of guilt rushed through her. A reminder of how little she knew of what her own kids were up to. When they were younger, Libby had designed complex routines for Nathan to follow, helped by his mother, Eloise, so that someone was always with them when she was working a shift. But as they'd started high school, she'd relaxed the regime, wrongly assuming that enough trust had been built between them all to be honest.

Underneath the bustier was the faint rise and fall of her chest.

'Hey, sweetheart. I'm Libby, and I'm a paramedic. Have you taken any pills?' She put her gloves on and felt for a pulse. It was there, but very erratic. The girl's eyes were closed and Libby clicked her fingers. The girl didn't respond.

'Can you hear my voice?' She rubbed her knuckles into the girl's sternum. Still nothing. Libby turned to one of the officers. 'Has she been conscious?'

'Yes. She keeps drifting in and out, but we can't get much from her. Not even her name. She just keeps talking about a shed. Do you think it's concussion?'

'It's always a possibility.' Libby clapped her hands close to the girl's face. A muscle around her mouth pulled down, as if the noise had reminded her of a terrible memory. And then her eyes flew open and she let out a choked wail.

They were wide and brown and the pupils were dilated.

Definitely drugs.

'Hey, it's okay. Stay still.' Libby leaned over, ready to restrain her if she tried to stand up too quickly. The wail increased and tears leaked down her face. Hell. Poor kid. The girl's breathing was coming in short gasps, and Libby swore. Was she going into cardiac arrest? That wasn't good. Libby immediately began CPR and her own heartrate spiked as she counted her compressions then blew into the girl's mouth. By the fourth round, the breathing had become steady, and Libby rested on her haunches so she could study the girl.

There was a cut across her jaw, a scattering of freckles on her nose and a small dimple on one cheek.

Libby stiffened and ice spread through her veins. She knew this kid.

Hayley Terrace. She'd been on the same rowing team as Sienna and Libby had watched them, through sleep-deprived, bleary eyes, at five in the morning from the comfort of her car while the girls had trained and rowed and goofed around as the sun had barely smudged the sky. Strong, determined seventeen-year-old girls with their muscular legs and strong shoulders, more concerned about their resting heart rate than what they looked like. And now Hayley was here, in a crumpled heap. Her clothes ripped and torn and who knew what else.

It wasn't right. She was too young. Too much like Sienna.

Too much like me.

Tears stung her eyes but she pushed them aside, the same way she always did. It was the only way to do her job.

She beckoned the officer over just as Jonathan arrived with the gear. 'She's a friend of my daughter's. Her name's Hayley

Terrace. I don't have a phone number, but her mother's name is Adele, and they live on Dingle Road. I'm not sure what number the house is.'

'The one from rowing?' Jonathan asked in surprise. He'd been around the house enough times to have heard Hayley's name mentioned.

'Yes.' Libby nodded. 'Hopefully, the police can track down the parents.'

'We'll make sure we do.' The officer looked at the prostrate figure. 'The poor sods. They probably thought she was at the library or down the high street with her friends.'

'It's a shit way for them to find out.' Jonathan unpacked the bag as Libby gave him an update on Hayley's condition and then leaned closer to the young girl.

'Hayley, this is Libby Curtis. Sienna's mum. I'm going to help you, but you need to tell me what you took.'

Hayley didn't answer, just let out a soft whimper. Libby rechecked her pulse and temperature before nodding to Jonathan to give Hayley naloxone to stabilise her. While he worked, Libby did a quick visual. There were no signs of bruising on her arms or the exposed part of her stomach and while that didn't mean she hadn't been sexually assaulted, Libby was hopeful.

Once Hayley was on the trolley and strapped in, they carefully pushed her to the ambulance. A couple of journalists had appeared, one of them was talking to the officers who'd greeted them when they'd first arrived. Fiona Watkins was a local crime reporter and Libby quickly looked away. They'd had several encounters lately and none of them had been pleasant.

Hayley was starting to respond and colour had returned to her cheeks. She moaned, and she managed to grasp Libby's arm. Her fingers were covered in mud and where there had once been five pink acrylic nails, one had come off, leaving behind a ragged stub that had been chewed down to the quick.

'Please. Let me out. I don't want to be here. I want to go home. Where's my mum?' Her speech was slurred as she opened her eyes. Her gaze was unfocused and she let out painful sob. 'Don't hurt me.'

'It's okay, sweetheart. You just need to rest. Your mum's waiting at the hospital. You'll be with her soon.'

'Let me out. I want to go home,' Hayley whimpered, not seeming to hear Libby at all. Her heart ached for the girl, and while her physical injuries appeared minor, apart from the drugs, it was impossible to say how long it would be before the trauma went away. If it ever did.

Jonathan turned to the police officer who'd accompanied them.

'Will you be travelling with us?'

'Chance would be a fine thing. We're too short staffed but we've contacted the parents and they're heading straight to the hospital. Once Hayley's stable, we'll take an official statement. If she mentions anything, please make a note of it. Meanwhile, we're searching Steamer Point and the surrounding area to see if we can find the shed that she kept talking about.'

'Good luck.' Libby glanced around as Jonathan moved to the other side of the trolley so they could push it up the ramp. She doubted there'd be anything in the woods, and if there was, the local kids would have pulled it to pieces or covered it in graffiti, making it easy to find. Which left the surrounding suburbs. Or one of the nearby beach huts that Bournemouth was so famous for. But how did Hayley get back to the reserve in her condition? It was an open space with only the wind-blasted trees and a couple of picnic benches dotting the—

Picnic benches.

No. It couldn't be the same one.

'Okay, you ready?'

'Yes,' she said, her voice sounding far away.

Jonathan pushed the trolley but Libby's hands wouldn't work and they fell away from the rail, causing the whole thing to jolt. He swore and immediately tightened his grip to stop it from rolling back down the ramp.

'Libby. Hey, what's going on?' His voice was sharp and sweat had beaded on his forehead as he strained to hold the trolley in place. She stared at her hands in horror as she realised what had almost happened.

'S-sorry.' Instinct took back over and her fingers curled around the rail to help take the weight of the trolley. Jonathan's jaw was clenched as he locked eyes with her, his gaze demanding as he asked the silent question.

Was she okay to continue?

She swallowed, grateful that she didn't have to try and speak, she gave an emphatic nod. *I'm okay. I can do it.*

'On three,' he said coolly as he counted them in. This time, Libby kept her focus on Hayley and the job she was there to do. He didn't speak as they locked the trolley into place and Libby prepared an IV, but she knew there would be questions later.

And he had every right. A loss of focus could mean making a bad situation even worse and they weren't there to put anyone's lives in jeopardy. She had screwed up big time and they both knew it.

Once it was done, Jonathan gave her another questioning look.

'I'm fine. I promise,' she said.

'Okay.' He moved to the front of the ambulance and Libby stared at Hayley, who looked impossibly fragile on the trolley. Then she peered out of the tiny window at the picnic bench.

The one that looked almost identical to the one in Sam's video. Of course, the days didn't match. That video had been posted over a week ago and yet it didn't stop the question from forming in her mind.

What had her son done?

3

Pale morning sun streamed into the bedroom, and Libby rubbed her eyes. She'd had the dream again. The dark room. The shadows. And then *him*. It was the same one she'd had for years, but over time it had morphed and grown, absorbing newer parts of her life. But when she woke, it was always the same unsettling tightness in her stomach.

Something was coming.

She sat up and swung her legs out, letting her bare feet touch the floor. It was a way of grounding herself back to the now, forcing the tendrils of the dream away. Libby fumbled for her phone. It was almost nine in the morning and Nathan's side of the bed was empty. It wasn't a surprise. He'd never been able to sleep past six, even on a Sunday.

By nature, she was more of an owl than a lark, but usually tried to get up with him. However, it had been midnight by the time she'd arrived home and raced up the stairs to check on her own kids.

Sienna's door had been slightly open for the cat, and Libby had peered in, relieved to see a figure asleep in the bed. Sam's door had been shut, with only a pale glow spilling out from the crack at the bottom and a clatter of computer keys to let her know he was inside. Except it hadn't given her the comfort it usually did.

What was he doing in there?

Earlier, in the car park, she'd looked at the video again, desperately studying the picnic bench. But it was too dark and unclear to see if it really had been the same as the ones at Steamer Point. Which meant that after she'd showered and crept into her own bed, sleep hadn't been quick to arrive.

It didn't take her long to get ready and she made her way downstairs as the ding of the washing machine sounded. The cycle had finished. Libby lifted an eyebrow. Despite an ongoing campaign to domesticate her family, she was the chief officer when it came to laundry. Curiosity piqued, she detoured to the small room at the end of the hallway.

The washing basket was sitting on the floor and she knelt to open the front loader. In there were two old towels that she usually kept in the garage, in case anything leaked, and a pair of Nathan's jeans, along with a white T-shirt. The clothes were now covered in a fine layer of lint thanks to being washed with towels, but it didn't explain why they were there. Especially since there was still a full hamper of dirty clothes that also needed to be done.

Frowning, Libby got to her feet and carried the basket back through to the kitchen, which led out to the back garden. There was no sign of Nathan, and she quickly pegged the washing on the line, before leaving the basket on the potting table and returning to the house.

They'd renovated several years ago, taking down the wall between the kitchen and dining room, and extending out into what had once been a patio. A giant skylight had been added and the whole space opened out into the back garden through huge, bi-fold doors.

The kitchen counter showed signs that Nathan had been there. The old-fashioned coffee grinder and Italian expresso percolator were by the gas hob, and the Sunday papers were folded up on a tray, along with a slab of butter and a jar of Stone's Ginger Marmalade, all waiting to be carried out to the wrought iron table and chairs at the far end of the garden.

It was the same ritual he did every Sunday: coffee, toast, and a quick scan of the papers before he went for a jog or a surf, depending on the weather. So where was he? She retrieved her phone from her pocket. He hadn't left her a message but there was a missed phone call and two texts from the reporter, Fiona Watkins.

Her stomach dropped, though after seeing her yesterday, she wasn't really surprised.

Their paths had crossed several times over the years when Libby had been attending any major crimes or accidents. But she'd never even considered giving her any kind of statement. Until the whole thing with Sam had started. What she hadn't realised was that while Andi's parents had been content to let Libby and Nathan pay for the damages and keep Sam away from their daughter, one of the neighbours had taken it on themselves to send in a photograph of the carnage to the local paper.

Sam had been in the local sports pages enough times over the years to be well known there, and when Fiona came and showed Libby the photograph, she'd done everything in her power to convince the journalist to not run the story. Especially since his schoolwork was already suffering; it might ruin his chances of the scholarship.

Fiona had immediately agreed and Libby had mistakenly

thought she was doing it out of the goodness of her heart. She'd quickly learnt otherwise.

Sighing, she read Fiona's message.

I heard that Hayley Terrace is a friend of your daughter. What was Hayley like, and how you would describe her condition in the ambulance? The police are refusing to issue any information but the public has the right to know. Especially since it's been confirmed Hayley was at a bonfire on Friday night at Highcliffe. I'd love a quote. We have a great photo of you at the scene. Call me!

Libby swallowed.

Call me! It was the third time Fiona had contacted her since the photograph and Libby knew that it wasn't a request; it was a command. She reluctantly sent her a text to say she'd be in touch later in the day. After she'd had coffee.

She reached for a cup when Harriet, a tortoiseshell cat with amber eyes and a 'you are beneath me' attitude wandered in and casually jumped up onto the bench, as if that was something she was allowed to do. It wasn't, and Libby scooped her up and deposited her back on the floor, before heading over to the fridge to get some cat food.

A note was pinned up on the door with a magnet.

Just going to Maples to get bread.

Oh, no. The bread she'd bought for him yesterday was still sitting in the car, forgotten, along with her work bag and jacket. She swore again and walked away from the fridge. Harriet gave an angry meow, which would have been more effective if she didn't already have a bowlful of dry biscuits.

'I won't be long.' Libby hurried into the hallway.

A jumble of coats hung from the wall and there was a small stand with a wooden box where they kept all the car keys; Nathan would occasionally joke that they might as well make it easier for thieves to steal them. And while he was right, they'd yet to come up with a better way to manage the long, narrow driveway that contained three cars that constantly needed to be moved.

Keys in hand, she stepped outside. The bright light stung her eyes and she winced as she waited to adjust. Her car was parked in its regular spot at the far end of the driveway and she retrieved the loaf of bread, which was now stale thanks to a night in the back seat.

She locked her car and stepped onto the lawn to collect a random chocolate wrapper that must have blown in from the street, which was when she noticed the tyre track across the neatly trimmed grass.

Not again. She didn't need a forensic expert to come in and analyse the tread. It was from Sam's car, which was drunkenly parked, with the front wheel on top of the stone edging that Nathan had laboriously cemented in the previous spring. And to really finish off the job, one of the solar powered lights that dotted the lawn had been crushed on the way through.

Libby let out an irritated sigh. It was the third one he'd run over, suggesting he'd learned to drive from a notorious rockstar rather than the reputable instructor they'd hired to help him pass his test two months ago.

Had Nathan seen it before he'd gone out? Probably not, since she hadn't heard him wake his son up, but she doubted Sam would be so lucky the second time around.

Then there'd be another fight.

Libby rolled her neck. Unlike the picnic bench, which she could easily push to a tiny part of her mind, this was something she could fix. Especially if she wanted to convince Nathan about getting a tutor. But if she moved the car and replaced the damaged light with one of the spares from the garage, would she just be enabling Sam's refusal to act responsibly?

Maybe. But at least there wouldn't be an argument.

She gathered up the damaged light and replaced it with a new one from the garage before dumping the stale loaf of bread on the hallstand and picking up the car keys.

Sam's car was a silver Fiat that had belonged to Nathan's mother before she'd been forced to stop driving thanks to arthritis. But while the outside hadn't changed much from its time as a One Lady Owner, the inside had undergone a transformation.

It was now permanently filled with an array of sports gear, muddy boots and discarded food wrappers and empty carrier bags. She opened the door and winced as the dank smell of wet towels and rot hit her.

She opened the window and reversed the car, careful not to hit the new light, all while trying not to breathe. How could he keep it like that? Shuddering, she reached for a carrier bag and gingerly scooped up a half-eaten hamburger along with a pile of napkins and several scrunched-up shopping receipts. Sam was going to owe her.

Tucked under the passenger seat was a dirty sock and she reached it to pick up. As she did, something flashed in the light and then a single, bright-pink acrylic fingernail fell into her lap.

Libby picked it up and blinked.

She knew that nail. But—

No. Suddenly she was back in the ambulance, leaning over Hayley's shaking body as she clutched at Libby's arm. And the four pink fingernails acting like neon lights, all pointing to the spot where the fifth nail had once been. Except now it was interposed with Sam's face almost glowing against the dark sky in the video.

Don't hurt me. Icy pain slammed into Libby's chest, so hard and heavy that she slumped back into the seat. It couldn't be Sam. He wasn't that kind of kid.

Well... up until six months ago, he hadn't been.

Back then, he'd much preferred playing sport and staying at home and gaming with friends than going out. *But now?* It was a question she couldn't answer.

She swallowed hard. Think. She had to think. Whatever had happened to Hayley had most likely taken place on Friday night. She shut her eyes, trying to remember the day. Her shift had started at two in the afternoon so she hadn't seen either of the kids since breakfast.

All she knew was that Nathan had gone around to Eloise's house on his own because the kids had both refused to go with him. Which meant Sam could have been anywhere.

Including a Friday night bonfire.

Bile burned her throat. She was going to be sick. Clamping her hand over her mouth, she stumbled out of the car, only just making it to the downstairs toilet in time. She hadn't eaten since the previous evening and after gagging several times, she finally straightened up and stared at herself in the mirror.

Her dark eyes were glassy, and her thick hair, usually so hard to control, was hanging limp around her face. She looked such a mess. She cleaned her teeth three times and then splashed some water on her face before finally looking down at the fingernail that was on the side of the sink where she'd put it.

How she wished she'd just left Sam's car where it was. Let him tidy up his own mess. At least it wouldn't have put her in this terrible position. If it was proof that Sam at least knew about

Hayley being attacked, then it was something the police needed to know.

Except how could she do something that might implicate her son?

Besides, it was just a nail. There were a hundred reasons why it could have been there. For all she knew, there were four more matching nails in the back seat that had belonged to one of the many girls he knew. Hope raced through her. Of course. She hadn't even bothered to look in the back seat or the boot.

She needed to search the rest of the car.

She slipped the nail into her pocket and hurried into the hallway just as Nathan walked through the open door, holding onto the woven market bag he always used. Behind him, she caught a glimpse of his black Audi parked in the driveway.

Hell. Libby pinched the flesh of her inner arm. The jab of pain was almost a relief and helped clear her mind. Whatever was going on, it wasn't something her husband needed to know about.

At least not yet.

Besides, it might be nothing.

'You're back,' she managed to say.

'And not a moment too soon.' He glanced over at the hall table while clutching his heart with mock hurt. 'Do our vows mean nothing to you?'

Libby blinked and followed his gaze.

Oh. The stale bread. It seemed like a million years ago that she'd come out to get it. But, like an actor waiting for the next line, his eyes were locked on her, a reminder it was her turn.

'What can I say? All's fair in love and bread,' she bantered back, the way they'd always done. It was one of their things. Bad jokes that carried on for days until the kids would beg them to stop. But now her heart wasn't in it. All she could think of was Sam.

'Look at you, trying to get a rise out of me.' He opened the bag for her to inspect the contents. As well as a loaf of bread, which looked much fresher than the one she'd bought for him, there was the all too familiar aroma of a Dorset apple cake. 'For you. And to think I was going to share.'

'You don't play fair,' she protested as he reached her. They were the same height, and so their noses brushed as his mouth found hers. Usually, she loved kissing him, but as the familiar scent of citrus and wood enveloped her, all she could think was that he'd know she'd thrown up.

Then he'd ask why, and—

Stop it. She was overreacting. This had nothing to do with Sam at all. It was just the delayed shock of last night. It was always the same when she was reminded of her own past. And that's all it was. Her past. Nathan and the kids were her future. Her now.

Nathan slowly broke the kiss and ran a lazy finger along her arm. Despite herself, her stomach fluttered, and Libby let out a soft sigh They'd first met at a party eleven years ago. Back then, he'd been lean and gorgeous, with thick, long hair that had been tinted blond from years of surfing. He was so far out of her league that she'd been strangely uninhibited. Especially when she'd discovered that despite his rockstar looks and chiselled body, he was quite reserved.

It was to become just one of the many contradictions she found so endearing.

And what had started with a slightly one-sided conversation had ended with him coming back to her small flat and staying the night. Even then, experience had taught her that men with muscled bodies didn't want a second or third date with someone with a rounded figure, towering height and a preference for low-key dinners rather than nights at a club.

But there had been a second date. And a third. Then he'd introduced her to Sam and Sienna, and somehow, her life had changed in a moment.

Her mouth tilted into a smile as they walked into the kitchen. These days, his leanness had given way to a more rugged physique and the long, sun-kissed hair had been cut short, emphasising his beautiful, sculptured face and piercing eyes framed by dark lashes.

Still achingly handsome, and still the man she loved. And she knew he loved her as well... though not quite in the same way. His was a love built from the need to have a mother for his kids – someone to help give them all the things he couldn't – and he'd picked her. And in a way, so had Julia and the kids themselves.

All of them had somehow found her worthy of being a mother. It wasn't something she took lightly.

'I didn't hear you come in last night.'

'I tried to be quiet,' she said, despite knowing he had the ability to sleep through anything. Still, the fact he was a heavy sleeper lessened the guilt of working shifts and coming in at all hours of the night. She liked to think it meant they were a perfect match.

'I wouldn't have minded being woken,' he teased as they reached the kitchen and he put the shopping onto the counter. 'By the way, you missed Jonathan. He dropped off some timber to finish building the storage units in the garage and decided to join me on my morning jog. He said you sleep too much and are missing out on life.'

'Why am I destined to be surrounded by early risers?' she asked. The two men had formed a genuine friendship that no longer required her presence. Which was good because early morning jogs and talking about building storage units weren't really her thing.

'You're just lucky.' He rubbed his eyes. Maybe he should have stayed in bed longer too. Then she noticed the deep lines around his mouth. He was worried.

Which could only mean one thing.

'Did he tell you about Hayley being attacked?'

His eyes clouded over and he gave her a grim nod. 'I can't believe it. How are you feeling?'

She swallowed. Libby had never told him about her own attack. It had happened so long ago, and the tangle of guilt and shame were still so intertwined with everything else that followed, she'd never found a way. Plus, she didn't want him to look at her like she was damaged. Less than. A victim.

'I'm okay.' She knew it was a terrible answer. The kind that they always told the kids not to use. But these weren't the kinds of emotions that she could ever talk about with Nathan. Or even herself. 'But it was still a shock.'

'Is she okay? Do we know what happened? Jonathan was light on details.' He put the percolator on the hob and started slicing the fresh loaf. What would he say if she told him about the pink nail in Sam's car that might, or might not, be identical to the one Hayley was missing?

'She was cut and bruised and her clothes all ripped – and was severely dehydrated. There were drugs in her system, but I'm not sure what.' She pulled the toaster out of the cupboard and plugged it in, ready for the bread. Then she leaned against the bench and studied him. 'She was at a bonfire at Highcliffe beach on Friday night. What did Sam say he was doing? Did you see him before you went out?'

Nathan shook his head. 'No. He was getting a shower when I

left, but he was heading out to play Dungeons and Dragons with Chris and some of the guys. Why?'

'No reason,' she said quickly. 'It's just that these parties seem to be getting more and more out of control. And Hayley was clearly on something. I'm worried.'

'And that's what makes you a great mother.'

Libby winced. Was she? After all, she'd worked on Friday night, which meant she really didn't have a clue what Sam or Sienna had been doing. It could have been one of them she'd found yesterday instead of Hayley. The video of Sam running through the woods flashed into her mind, as if trying to remind her of another alternative.

The one where her child wasn't the victim at all.

4

Enough. Libby had to stop thinking about it. If Sam had told Nathan he was spending the evening playing Dungeons and Dragons, it was her job to believe him. One fingernail did not a crime scene make.

The low hiss of the coffee percolator cut her off and Nathan went and stood guard over it, a tea towel slung over his left shoulder like an old-fashioned barman.

Which reminded her about the laundry she'd discovered.

'Did you put the washing machine on this morning?'

'Oh, yeah. I managed to stand on the drain hole while I was having a shower and almost flooded the bathroom. It was stupid.' He didn't meet her gaze as he carefully lifted the lid to make sure the coffee had finished percolating.

'Nothing I haven't done,' Libby said, suddenly feeling like an overbearing wife. 'And thanks for sorting it out.'

'I figured it was one less thing for you to worry about,' he admitted as she put the toast onto a rack and carried it outside, along with the tray of butter and jam. Nathan followed several seconds later with the coffee, cups, and a carton of oat milk.

They ate in silence and Nathan was buried in the paper when Sam wandered out to join them. At six feet, he was like a taller version of his father. His brown hair was bleached at the ends from hours of surfing and rowing and his physique was lean but muscular. He was dressed in boxer shorts and a faded T-shirt for a local real estate agent and his eyes were currently obscured by a pair of sunglasses, making Libby suspect he'd hardly had any sleep.

Or because he had something to hide.

'You'd better not have used all the milk,' he announced by way of greeting, then picked up the carton and lifted it up to his mouth. He drank noisily before collapsing into a nearby chair, as if the effort of standing was unbearable.

Libby had learnt long ago to pick her battles; and milk cartons and teenage lethargy didn't even make it onto her top twenty list. But next to her, Nathan let out a frustrated sigh as he put the paper down.

'Seriously, Sam? How many bloody times do I have to tell you to use a glass?'

'It's nearly finished anyway.' Sam ran a hand through his scruffy hair. 'What's wrong with you two? Looks like someone's died.'

Libby stiffened at the word and Nathan's mouth flattened into a straight line. 'One of your classmates was badly injured yesterday.'

'Oh yeah. Hayley. It's all over Twitter.' He shrugged, as if they were discussing the best way to wax toe hair. Something so inconsequential that he didn't need to have an opinion on it.

Dread pressed down on her chest, taking her breath away.

Where had his attitude come from? She knew he wasn't heartless. There had been too many times over the years when he'd cried upon finding an injured bird or dead hedgehog.

Which either meant he had nothing to do with it and didn't understand how serious it was. Or, because he was trying to distance himself from it?

'You don't seem very bothered.' Nathan frowned, obviously also picking up on his son's indifference.

'I guess that's what happens when you get off your face at the beach and walk into the woods.' He drained the rest of the milk, his face partially concealed behind the container, making it impossible to see his expression. He let out a long burp.

'You were there? I thought you were playing Dungeons and Dragons with Chris.' Libby worked hard to keep her voice calm, but it was hard. He was meant to have been somewhere else. With an alibi. She inwardly shuddered at the fact she was even thinking about alibis.

Sam's whole body shifted, as if donning invisible armour. Shit. She'd always been good at reading people, or so she'd thought. But she'd clearly missed how close to the edge Sam was. The fact he wasn't as indifferent as he made out should have made her feel better. Instead, it increased the thumping of her heart.

'What business is it of yours? You're not my mother.'

Libby's hand went up to her cheek, his words like a slap. Next to her, Nathan bristled, and her own panic increased. Most of the time her husband was placid but he did have a short fuse, which had become increasingly noticeable in the last few months.

'You will not speak to her like that. Apologise immediately.'

Sam's jaw went rigid, a storm of emotions sweeping across his face. But finally, his shoulders dropped, and he rolled his neck. 'Sorry. I shouldn't have said that.'

'Thank you.' Nathan's own posture softened but he didn't seem to notice that Sam hadn't used the word 'mum'. A hollowness gathered in her stomach, leaving her weightless. Untethered. It was as if every look and word Sam said to her was a knife, cutting away the maternal strings that she'd spent years weaving.

Her fingers curled around the arms of the chair to stop herself from flying away.

'Whatever. I'm going back to bed.' He stood and stalked back towards the house, casually drop-kicking the empty oat milk bottle towards the recycling bins by the shed.

Nathan glanced from his son's retreating back to Libby.

'Has he said that to you before?'

Libby rubbed her temples, not wanting to make the situation worse.

'Only a couple of times. Denise said it's a rite of passage to push away from the parents and leave the tribe.' The hollowness increased and she clenched her stomach muscles, trying to keep herself in the chair.

'You should have told me. I know he's dealing with a lot... but there's no excuse for him to behave like that.' Nathan ran a hand through his hair, his mouth still in a troubled line. 'But it's not like you to interrogate him. What's going on?'

Libby shut her eyes. Asking him to clarify where he'd been on Friday night was hardly an interrogation, but sometimes Nathan could be as sensitive as his son, so she shook her head. Besides, she could hardly tell him that she suspected Sam was involved in something so heinous, she could barely even say the words.

And what right did she have to make allegations?

If she was wrong, it could destroy Sam's life. And their family. Everything she worked so hard for would be gone in a flash.

Just like last time.

As if on cue, Todd's face appeared in her mind. At fifteen, his upper lip was dark with the beginnings of facial hair and his skin still bore the faint scars of acne, but as he lay on the bathroom floor, the length of his neck was concealed by the thick leather belt pressing into his windpipe.

All she'd been able to do was stare at him, incapable of moving or thinking. Of course, now was different. Now she would be able to save him. To fix him. To make him better. But back then, she'd just been a stupid girl who stood there staring at her brother's dead body.

And it was all her fault. She'd made a terrible mistake and Todd had paid the ultimate price. She refused to let it happen again. Then she blinked and realised Nathan's gaze was fixed on her. She clenched her hands together. She needed to focus.

'Nothing. Sorry. I'm just worried. Especially with his grades.'

'I talked to him last week and he was up to date with his homework.'

'He also trained every night after school and you know what he's like when he's tired. He probably opened a book and shut it again,' she said in a careful voice. Nathan was smart and had flown through university without too much effort. And despite Sienna's current phase of dressing in black, she also had no problems with exams. But Sam had always needed to work hard for his grades and she wasn't sure Nathan realised his son wasn't like him.

'What are you saying? That rowing is interfering with his schoolwork?' Nathan's brows met and his mouth straightened into a grim line.

She shook her head. Though it had often worried her. Once, she'd found Sam crying over a homework assignment when he was twelve, too tired to properly understand what he was meant to do. At the time, she'd floated the idea of cutting back on sports, but it was Nathan who'd looked more horrified than Sam.

'Denise gave me the name of a tutor who's meant to be a miracle worker. I think we should talk to him. Otherwise, I can't see how Sam will even pass, let alone get a scholarship to Florida.'

Silence hung between them and something crossed Nathan's face. While he never spoke about it out loud, he revelled in Sam's abilities, and he'd been the one to suggest Sam seriously consider studying in America. He rubbed his jaw and finally nodded.

'If you think it will help, I'd like to meet him. Sam won't be happy, though.'

'Hopefully, he'll thank us one day. Should one of us go and talk to him?'

'Let's wait until tonight; I've got to be at the golf course in an hour. I don't want to keep Tom waiting.'

Libby winced. Yet another thing she'd forgotten about. But it also explained his short fuse with Sam and the tired lines under his eyes. The kids weren't the only ones who'd been causing them sleepless nights.

TLC Manufacturing produced roller doors and premade industrial sheds and was almost a Bournemouth institution. Nathan had only planned to work there as a summer job but had fallen for the boss's daughter, Julia, and stayed on once they were married.

Then, in a terrible year, his father-in-law had been killed in a car accident, and six months later, the still-grieving Julia had started haemorrhaging while giving birth to the twins and had died before even seeing her two babies. Leaving Nathan as the reluctant owner of the business. He'd been there ever since.

But a recent increase in orders from a large property developer in Birmingham had left the business stretched, stuck in the position of not being able to expand fast enough to meet the demand. *The irony of success*, Nathan had called it, though his voice had been grim.

He'd never involved her in the business side of things and she hadn't pushed. After all, it was part of his life from *before*. What right did she have to question him? So, when he'd announced that he was going to move part of the manufacturing arm up north where the rents were cheaper, and they were closer to their clients, she'd agreed. But for that, he needed investors.

Hence the meeting with Tom Wallace. The man owned a building company in Poole and had wanted to buy out Nathan several years ago. At the time, Nathan had refused, feeling the offer was far too low. So now he was trying to encourage him to come in as a silent partner. Except Tom was a notoriously bad golf player, which meant Nathan – an adrenaline junkie – would have to work hard not to beat him by too much.

'How do you think it will go?'

'I'm confident. He wants our market share to expand his own business,' Nathan said. 'It's a win/win. I can protect Adrian's legacy and expand it for Sam and Sienna.'

'The fact you've kept it running through everything that's happened over the last few years is amazing. Tom must respect that.' Libby brushed his arm. She knew how guilty he felt about taking over the business that his father-in-law had built from scratch. And how personally he took his obligation to make it succeed.

It was another reason why Sam's night of rampage had been unwelcomed. Not to mention the large jump in car insurance now that he was driving. Just another layer of worry for them both.

'Let's hope so. I'm not sure what time I'll be home.'

'Will you see Eloise on the way back?' she asked. Visiting his mother was part of his Sunday ritual, but he shook his head. This time, a flicker of something crossed his face. Probably guilt. He loved his mother but was struggling to work out a way to get her to move out of the family home, which was far too big for her. It was a losing battle and one that had kept him up at nights, worrying.

'I doubt it will still be light by the time Tom reaches the final hole. I visited her on Friday evening, so she won't mind. Unless you can swing by.'

'I wish I could,' she said truthfully. Eloise Curtis was the quintessential homemaker who'd dedicated her life to her son. And while sometimes Nathan found her a bit overbearing, Libby loved getting a second stab at the family dynamic. Compared to her own mother, who had openly blamed Libby and Todd for everything that had gone wrong with her life, Eloise was wonderful. 'Denise and I are on volunteer duties down at the park. A day of weeding is in my future.'

'Of course.' He nodded, though it was obvious he'd forgotten. 'I'd better go, but I'll text you when I've finished.' He gave her a kiss and jogged back to the house. It was Nathan's way. Ever since she'd known him, he couldn't sit still. Though for once, she understood the sensation, and while usually she would spend longer on her coffee and flipping through the newspaper, the pink nail in her pocket made it impossible to relax.

She needed to search the rest of the car.

Five minutes later, the sound of Nathan's engine let her know he'd left. Libby got to her feet. Upstairs, she could hear the murmur of voices, which meant Sam was playing a game online. The chances of him looking out of his window, let alone opening the curtains, were slim to none.

For once, she was pleased, and she hurried out to the front of the house.

Her pulse hammered. She'd always sworn she wouldn't be that kind of parent. The one who monitored their kids and followed their social media accounts. *Shared values lead to high trust.* That's what she'd always told Nathan.

Except now she'd done exactly that. She'd broken her own rule and spied on his online life, destroying both his trust and hers. *Once you see it, you can't unsee it.* The phrase hammered through her mind as she opened the back door of the car.

The smell had lessened and she pushed through the rest of the food wrappers and discarded sports gear that Sam seemed to have forgotten even existed. But there were no more nails or anything else to incriminate him. Just smelly, teenage rubbish.

'What the hell are you doing?'

Libby stiffened and awkwardly slipped out of the driver's seat to where Sienna was standing. She was the opposite of her twin brother, with a slender figure, soft, brown eyes and straight, auburn hair. Well, it had been auburn until last month when she'd dyed it black to match her current wardrobe. She was cool winter compared to Sam's warm, summery glow. But the dark kohl under her eyes couldn't conceal the swollen lids and red rims. She'd been crying.

Oh, no.

Libby wanted to wrap her arms around her, like she'd done when Sienna was younger. But that was no longer an option. Along with the black clothing had come a prickly outer layer that acted as a warning.

'You know about Hayley? Are you okay?'

'Why wouldn't I be?' Sienna snapped. Her voice was high pitched and her eyes were glassy.

'Because what happened to her was terrible,' Libby said, hoping for a way in. A tiny slither of light to let her know that the door was open.

'I don't want to talk about it.' Sienna folded her arms in front of her ruffled, black shirt. Entry denied. And yet, she couldn't just leave it. For the last six months, she'd been floating on the outside of the family, too scared to do or say too much in case it pushed the kids even further away. But it couldn't go on.

'I know it must be hard. Did you go to the party?'

Sienna's eyes filled with loathing. 'Do I look like someone who would go to a bonfire?'

'I just want you to be safe.' Libby flinched. She hadn't really been expecting a proper answer but it still hurt.

'Well, you can relax. I was safely stuck in my bedroom. Unlike the rest of the family,' she retorted, her eyes narrowing. 'And what are you doing? Sam will go ape if he knows you're touching his precious car.'

'It won't be precious for much longer if he doesn't clean it,' Libby said, not wanting to get drawn into the ongoing argument between the pair of them about the car. And since she could hardly admit the real reason she was there, she held up the carrier bag she'd started filling up. 'I'm going to wash the towels and throw away the rotting food.'

Sienna studied her for several moments, then she shrugged. 'Let me know if you need a hazmat suit.'

Libby swallowed. It was the most they'd talked since the argument last week. Though Sienna's body language had let Libby know that she was still on notice. Responsible for crimes that she didn't even know about. Which was the hardest part of it. How could she defend herself and make things right if she didn't know what it was she'd done?

You're not my mother.

Sam might have said the words but everything about Sienna's body language echoed it. Libby's body ached from the pain of it as she watched her daughter saunter into the house. Finally, she turned back to the car and gathered up the aforementioned towels, as well as the football kit and grey hoodie that had seen better days. One of the sleeves was covered in orange paint from a long-ago art class and the cuffs were frayed from where Harriet had chewed them.

Maybe, instead of washing it, she should throw it away. But she knew she wouldn't. Sam loved it and she still loved him. Sighing, she dumped them on the driveway and climbed back in, gathering up the discarded coke cans and Subway packaging. It was disgusting.

And yet it was so normal. So, Sam. He was bright, funny, smart. And a total slob. But none of that made him capable of hurting someone.

She stared down at the nail. It was nothing. A speck. A piece of plastic that she'd somehow attached a meaning to. But what if she hadn't been the one to take Hayley in the ambulance? If she hadn't seen the girl's missing nail, Libby never would have noticed this one. It would've been a piece of debris in the sea of rubbish. But she had and now it signified something more sinister. It was telling her that Sam might have a darker side. One she didn't know anything about. The idea rocked her. She'd seen enough darkness in her own life.

The buzzing started again, and Libby's whole body stiffened as she leaned back against the car, bracing for what was to come.

She was sixteen, and suddenly, he was there. On top of her. Her mother's boyfriend, Alan was a drunken pig, but he'd never done this before. He reeked of beer as his hands tugged at her jeans, pushing them down. No. She'd tried to scream but the shirt he'd shoved into her mouth stopped her. Tears leaked from her eyes and—

Then there was a thud and his head rolled back before he fell to the floor of her bedroom. Libby whimpered and pulled the gag from her mouth as she stared up at Todd. He'd only just turned fifteen and was still skinny for his age, but he'd played cricket since he could walk, and the bat in his hand was now covered in blood. Alan's blood.

Todd had only done it to save Libby. But what neither of them had expected was Angela's fury. She blamed Libby for lying and Todd for ruining her life. It didn't subside and their mother's continual abuse and taunts sent Libby's sweet, caring brother first into drugs and finally into taking his life.

Libby had been so wrapped up in the aftershock of what had happened that she'd barely noticed her brother was falling... until it was too late.

No. Her fingers tightened around the nail and she pushed it into her pocket and walked to the house, carrying the laundry.

She wouldn't let it happen again.

She wouldn't turn her back on family.

She wouldn't become her mother.

5

Sienna wasn't sure what she hated most. The blue and white tartan skirt of her uniform, the refusal of the school to even consider letting them wear trainers, or the fact that unlike most of her friends, her parents expected her to make her own way to and from school. And that meant cycling.

It was so unfair. Sam had passed his own test five months ago and had immediately been given their grandmother's car. Yet he refused to let her touch it, despite the fact she'd just passed her own test two weeks ago. He hadn't even offered her a lift. Not that she'd take it, anyway. He'd been born twenty minutes before her and still needed to always come first. Such an arsehole.

Which brought her back to her current problem. Her fingers trembled as she tried to slot the key into her bike lock. Her mind had been so full of what had happened to Hayley that she hadn't been paying attention this morning when she'd snapped it on, and now she was almost in a sitting position, trying to get the key in.

It just about summed up the awfulness of her day.

All anyone could talk about was what had happened.

Including Mrs Taylor, the head, who'd decided to turn it into a messed-up talk about the perils of alcohol and drugs. Victim shaming much. But even that couldn't stop the rumour mills. It was a combination of stuff from the newspaper and from the kids who'd been at the bonfire.

She'd clawed her way out of a shallow grave.

She'd woken up and one of her kidneys was missing.

She'd been abducted by aliens.

It was all stupid stuff but the one thing everyone seemed to agree on was that Hayley had been attacked, drugged and was still off her face when she'd been found the next day by some guy and his dog.

Tears jabbed her eyes. Hayley would hate that everyone was talking about her. Especially people she despised. Which, thanks to *the* fight, now included Sienna. Sometimes Sienna wasn't even sure that they'd ever really been friends. Maybe she'd made it all up? After all, Hayley was so beyond her touch. So effortlessly popular, and beautiful.

But they'd both been on the same rowing team and discovered a shared love of K-Pop. Even then they'd never talked at school. Just in the early-morning and late-afternoon training sessions that had bookended each day. It had been nice. A real friendship.

Until everything had blown up.

And now Hayley was recovering in hospital with no memory of what had happened that night. At least that's what the police said. None of it was helped by the fact Libby had been the first responder. There was something about the way she looked at Sienna yesterday that wasn't right. Had Hayley said something to her? And why was Libby going through Sam's car yesterday? Had she been searching for something?

'Get a move on,' someone complained from behind her.

'Or what?' she retorted, not bothering to look up. The only other kids who rode bikes were the Year Eights and Nines. And if they were giving her lip, they probably hadn't been at the school for long. Finally, the key slid in and the lock clicked open, allowing her to remove the D-shaped piece of bar.

'Or what?' the voice mimicked. A spike of irritation ran along her arms and she narrowed her eyes. Being wound up by a little smart arse was the last thing she needed.

She slowly turned around, her gaze taking him in. He only came up to her shoulder, with a freckled face and several cow licks. His mouth was set into a mocking sneer. Clearly, being irritating was a full-time job for him.

'Are you serious?' She raised an eyebrow at him.

The kid smirked and opened his mouth as if preparing to mimic her again. But quickly shut it, as his eyes widened in alarm.

'Um, no. Sorry. It's no big deal.' He took a step back, his limbs contracting in on themselves, as if he was a transformer. 'Er, hi, Sam.'

Sienna let out a long breath as her twin brother appeared beside her. Now the kid's reaction made sense. While she was lucky to hit five foot five on a good day, Sam was six foot and had been rowing and playing rugby and football since he was a kid.

'Is he bothering you?' Sam asked, not looking at the kid, who was shaking. Not such a smart arse now, was he? Irrationally, it just made Sienna more annoyed. Why did the little shit think it was okay to get in her face when her brother wasn't around? Except if she said anything, Sam, who didn't have good impulse control, would do something stupid. And since he'd used up all his Get Out of Jail Free cards after Andi dumped him and he lost his mind, getting into another fight wasn't a good idea.

'He was just leaving,' she said as the kid plunged back

through a group of students and disappeared behind the red brick administration building. She turned back to her brother. 'What are you doing here? I thought you had the afternoon off.'

'Gotta see a man about a horse.' He gave a vague shrug as his eyes scanned the playing fields, which were still dotted with groups of seniors. He nodded to a couple of guys from his old rowing team and one of them made a whooping noise. 'And figured you might want a lift home. Two birds, one stone.'

'Sure, you got enough clichés in there?' Sienna couldn't hide her surprise. They'd been back at school for three weeks and he hadn't offered her a lift once. Or even acknowledged her presence when they were outside the house.

'If you don't want one, far be it from me to do something nice,' he said, just as it started to rain.

'What about my bike?'

'It will fit in the back,' he said with the kind of certainty that came from overloading the car with friends, surfboards and scooters on a regular basis. 'You coming or not?'

Sienna chewed her lip. Her brother didn't usually do things without wanting something in return. And the bike ride might be a good way for her to clear her head.

'Oh my God. I can't believe someone would do that to Hayley.' A shrilly voice drifted over and Sienna stiffened. Zoe Perkins was Hayley's ex-best friend – the ex-part coming when Zoe had slept with Hayley's boyfriend, Tate, and then ended up dating him. 'She's the sweetest, best person I know. And poor Tate. So ridiculous that he had to go down to the police station like a criminal because he was at the bonfire with his ex-girlfriend. But we were all there. It's not *his* fault she ran off.'

And now Zoe was somehow trying to get sympathy for pretending that she cared, while at the same time rubbing in the fact that Tate was hers. Sienna's fingers tightened together. It was unforgivable and Sienna had to restrain herself from punching Zoe in the face. Or, at least telling her what a complete bitch she was.

'Tick, tock.' Sam tapped his wrist despite never having worn a watch.

'Yeah. Thanks.'

'Cool. I'm over in the teacher's car park. Wait there while I go see someone. And if anyone tries to make you move, tell them to chill out.' He threw the car keys at her and jogged to where Zoe and her friends were huddled. At the sight of him, Zoe peeled away from her group and joined him by the fence.

Bile rose in Sienna's throat.

Why was Sam talking to her?

He'd never had any time for Zoe in the past, and it had only become worse after she started dating Tate, who'd been his rival in pretty much every sport they'd ever played. Then again, Sam had changed so much in the last six months. Since the breakup, their parents simply thought he was messing up at school, but it was other places as well. He was drinking too much and his social media posts were creepy as hell.

She leaned forward, wishing she could lip read. What were they talking about? Was it Hayley? Despite her past relationship with his arch enemy, her brother seemed to have a soft spot for Hayley, and there was a hot moment when Sienna thought Hayley might've had feelings for him as well.

It still didn't explain anything. His shoulders were tight and his fists were clenched. Whatever they were discussing, it wasn't good.

Sienna's grip on her phone tightened.

Was it about the party itself?

Sam hadn't said where he was going on Friday night but that was nothing new. And he might not like Zoe and Tate much but from what she could gather, they often ended up at the same places on the weekend. Either way, he'd left the house not long after their dad, when a friend had come to collect him in a pimped up 4WD, leaving Sienna alone to spend yet another boring Friday night trawling YouTube.

She watched them speak for several more minutes before admitting defeat. She pushed her bike towards the teachers' car park. It was strictly out of bounds for both students who could drive and parents doing the school run. But apparently not for her brother.

Sucking in a breath, she scanned the thinning crowds to make sure no one was around. It was almost three thirty and while most of the teachers were still in their classrooms, the place was emptying out of students.

Cautiously, she pushed her bike onto tarmac and used the key fob to unlock the car. Her arms were strong from her own rowing days but it still took several attempts to get her bike into the back of the car and she was sweating when Sam came jogging over.

Without speaking, he held out his hand for the keys.

'You could always let me drive home,' she said hopefully.

'When pigs fly,' he retorted, seemingly determined to use every cliché in the book. 'Come on, let's get going.'

She climbed into the passenger seat. Sam fired up the engine and reversed out onto the street, tyres squealing before she even had her seat belt on. Scrambling, she buckled herself in and studied her brother's profile. His jaw was set in a stubborn line and his knuckles were white as he gripped the steering wheel. What had been so important that Sam was speaking to someone he despised? But she could only think of one reason.

Her mouth was dry.

'Were you two talking about Hayley?'

'No,' he said a moment too quickly. 'Why would we be?'

'You weren't home on Friday night so I figured you must've been at the bonfire. Maybe you and Zoe were trying to piece together what happened?' Sienna said in a careful voice, knowing what he was like once he got into a mood.

'This isn't a stupid detective book. I don't give a shit what happened to Hayley or about trying to help Zoe. And I wasn't at some lame bonfire.' He let out a bitter laugh. 'I bet you're pleased Tate didn't pick you.'

'What's that meant to mean?' Sienna choked, the air pushing out of her lungs as if he'd physically punched her. It wasn't just that he could so casually dismiss what had been the worst time of her life, but that he could bring it up now, as if they were talking about the weather, instead of what—

She broke off, refusing to let herself think about what Hayley had gone through.

'Gee... let me think. You and Hayley both had a crush on him at the same time, then he picked her, and you fell into deep, goth-core despair. Should've listened to me. I told you he was a dick.'

'You can't seriously think he'd hurt Hayley. They're not even dating any more.'

Sam kept his eyes on the road and just shrugged. 'The prick scissor tackled me and broke my leg when I was ten. So, yeah. Sure, I think I he could do just about anything.'

'That's not funny.' Tears prickled in the corners of her eyes and she wiped them away. Sometimes, she really hated her brother.

He must have noticed she was upset because he let out a sigh.

'Shit. Ignore me. I'm just being a dick. I don't really think it was Tate. But I hope whoever it is, they catch them.'

'Me too,' Sienna said, as Sam pulled up at a red light. 'So, if you weren't at the party, where were you?'

'Did Dad and Libby put you up to it?' He raised an eyebrow, but he didn't seem angry. At least not at her.

'God no.' She frowned. Like she'd act as a go-between between Sam and their parents. Not that Libby was technically their mother, but up until last year, Sienna had thought of her as such. But lately, Libby started becoming more and more annoying. 'Why would you think that?'

'They were grilling me about it yesterday.' He shrugged, taking a sharp right. 'I already told them that I was playing Dungeons and Dragons. It's like I can't do anything right. Can you believe they want to get me a tutor?'

Sienna wasn't sure why he was so surprised. He'd bombed his exams last year and unless a miracle happened, he could kiss a rowing scholarship goodbye. As far as she could tell, he needed all the help he could get.

She wisely kept her thoughts to herself and they made the rest of the trip in silence. Sam pulled into the driveway, not seeming to care that he'd drifted across onto the grass. Sienna raised an eyebrow but he just climbed out and headed into the house, not bothering to help her with the bike. Obviously, he was back to being a prick again.

Sighing, she opened the door as her phone pinged with a text message. She looked at the screen but there was nothing there. Okay, that was weird. She double checked her apps before catching sight of Sam's battered old iPhone sitting in the car console, where he'd tossed it. It beeped again, and Sienna stared at it.

It would serve him right if she left it there and saw how long it took him to retrace his steps. Of course, she wouldn't. He might be irritating as hell most of the time, but he was still her big brother, who occasionally acted like a human being.

'You so owe me,' she muttered as she picked up the phone. It beeped for a third time and despite being locked, the notification came up on the screen.

It was from Hayley.

We need to talk.

Her stomach churned and Sienna leaned forward, hoping to push away the rising nausea. Shit. Shit. Shit. If Hayley sent Sam a message, it could only mean one thing.

That she remembered what happened.

6

'Thanks so much for making time to meet me.' Libby took a sip
of her peppermint tea. The café had managed to resist the urban-
ising lure of white subway tiles and light wood tables and still
had mismatched furniture and a selection of retro paintings and
mirrors covering the walls. Not to mention the most amazing
custard tarts, but Libby's appetite had deserted her, and she
waved them away. Unlike Danny, the tutor Denise had recommended, who'd ordered two.

He was in his early thirties and after eight years teaching
maths at an inner London comprehensive, had moved down to
Bournemouth with his girlfriend. Libby could already see just
why Denise had raved about him. He had brown, curly hair, a
laid-back attitude and a ready smile. Then there was the fact that,
academically, he was brilliant and he'd already helped several
wayward locals across the line and into university.

'No problem. I was out this way to buy the most expensive cat
food known to man. Seems I own the fussiest furball on the planet.' Danny finished off the first of the tarts.

'Only because you've not met Harriet yet. She hates the smell of bacon and claws the cupboards every time someone tries to cook it. So, we buy bacon butties at the shop around the corner and make sure we eat them at least half an hour before we go home,' Libby said.

'Fellow minions, I see.' Danny teased.

'Guilty,' she admitted. 'Sam's the worst of us all. He dotes on her.'

'Great. Sounds like we'll have something in common. Well, I did also row for a few years, though not at the same level,' Danny said before tilting his head. 'What I suggest is that instead of booking me in for the semester, I'll come around and meet him first. Because if he isn't committed, then all the tutoring in the world won't make a difference.'

Libby reluctantly agreed. Personally, she just wanted to lock Sam in a room until he *did* commit, but realistically, she knew that wouldn't work. She also knew that even if Danny could work miracles, it wouldn't solve everything. Far from it. But after no sleep last night, she decided that taking some action was better than just crossing her fingers and hoping things would just go back to normal.

It helped that the papers didn't have much of an update. Just that Hayley still hadn't remembered anything but police had found the lock-up where she'd been held. For some reason, it had given Libby hope. A lock-up sounded like something an adult would do. Not a teenager. She'd also been checking Sam's social media feed non-stop, but there were no new posts, and he'd decided to take down several of his most recent videos. Including the one where he'd been running through the woods at night.

'Sure. What does your schedule look like?'

He opened an app on his phone. 'I'm out your way next Monday afternoon. I could do 5 p.m.'

'Perfect.' She didn't bother to check her own calendar. It was only Pilates – which was where she was heading to after their meeting – and she was always happy to miss a class. Not that she didn't trust Nathan to make sure that Sam was on his best behaviour, but she wasn't convinced either of them understood how important it was. How much Libby needed a win. Even if it was a small one.

'Great.' He put the details straight in just as her own phone rang.

Libby turned it over and looked at the screen. It was Dalton Towers Care Home in Hull. The place that looked after her mother.

Libby squeezed her eyes shut as the guilt raced through her. It had been fifteen years since Angela's stroke had resulted in a fall down the stairs, which had confined her to a wheelchair. The vascular dementia had followed several years later. And despite everything Angela had put Libby through, she still felt like a bad daughter for not trying to move her mother closer to Bournemouth. Then again, it had been Angela who insisted on moving to Hull just weeks after Todd's death, dragging a devastated Libby along right in the middle of her GCSEs. All because she'd met a guy online.

The relationship had failed within a month, just like they always did, and Angela had stayed on, growing more and more bitter, while Libby had only waited until she was eighteen before moving down to London and making a life for herself without her mother.

Which is what she was still doing. Though despite everything, she couldn't bring herself to cut Angela off completely. And so, she dutifully visited once a year and did the occasional video call as well as getting a monthly update from the staff.

Which is what this would be.

She quickly declined it. Her mother had stubbornly clung to life for years; Libby doubted she was going anywhere in a hurry.

'Sorry about that.'

'No problem. I don't mind if you want to answer it. You said you were a paramedic. It could be work.'

'It's my day off,' she assured him.

'In that case, I'll let you get on with your afternoon.' Danny stood up and held out his hand. 'Don't worry about Sam. I have a way with kids who don't want to learn. I'm sure we'll get along fine. And say hi to Denise for me. I'm pleased to hear how well Becca is doing. Looks like all her hard work paid off.'

They exited the café together and then Libby followed the curve of Old Christchurch Road towards the first-floor Pilates studio. Her phone rang as she reached the crossing.

It was Nathan's mother.

'Hi Eloise. How are you?' she asked, trying not feel guilty about answering her mother-in-law's call but not the one from Dalton Towers. Then again, if Angela had even tried to act like a decent human being, it might have been different.

'Good as always.' Eloise said in a bright voice. 'I hope I'm not disturbing you, dear. I know how busy you are.'

'Don't be silly,' Libby chided as the walk light flashed green. 'You know I'm always here. Is everything okay?'

'Yes, yes,' she said before letting out a small groan. 'Well, almost. The silly man who delivers the food put in the wrong kind of apples and when I called they refused to swap them. I tried to explain why it was necessary, but they wouldn't listen.'

Libby bit back a smile. She'd explained numerous times to Eloise that she couldn't ring the main number for Waitrose and expect them to come out every time her Friday delivery wasn't quite right.

'Why didn't you give them to Nathan when he was there on Friday night; he could've swapped them over for you.'

'Because he had that thing on and didn't visit. I can't remember what it was called. I did ask Fredrick next door to take them back but he said he was busy. I do hate being a nuisance.'

Libby frowned. She was sure Nathan had mentioned going around there. But why would he lie? And where had he gone instead? Then she recalled the laundry he'd done on Sunday morning. Two towels and a change of clothing.

Ice prickled her skin.

'What thing?'

'Goodness, I can't remember. But it was terribly important and now I'm stuck with the wrong apples. What's to be done?'

Libby's fingers tightened around the phone. Part of her longed to press Eloise more and demand an answer. But her mother-in-law tended to hyperfocus on things and until the apples were exchanged, Libby doubted it would do any good. Which meant she'd have to wait until at least tomorrow before she tried again.

It's probably nothing. 'How about I bring you more around tomorrow. I can drop them off before work.' Libby mentally adjusted her calendar to make sure she had time.

'Are you sure? I hate not being able to drive,' Eloise said, a hint of frustration in her voice. Libby didn't blame her. Her mother-in-law had raised Nathan on her own and wasn't used to relying on people. One of the reasons they'd encouraged her to give Sam the car was in case she took it upon herself to drive again.

'It's not a bother.' Libby reached the Pilates studio. 'I've got to go to my exercise class now but I'll see you tomorrow.'

She finished the call and brought up Nathan's name on her phone. Her finger hovered over the green button. She should talk to him. *To say what?* That she knew he hadn't visited his mother on Friday night? And to double check why he suddenly decided to do his own laundry?

No. It was ridiculous. And she was probably just trying to borrow trouble. Tomorrow, she'd ask Eloise again and, in the meantime, she would try and forget it. Feeling better, she walked over to where Denise was waiting, along with Petra, who'd left the ambulance service to start up her own homeware business. The three of them had remained friends, and one night over a bottle of wine, they'd realised that when it came to exercise, it was safety in numbers. Because if they went on their own, they'd be far too likely to not turn up.

'Well? Did you get him?' Denise demanded as they climbed the narrow stairs in single file. The Pilates studio itself was a huge space with gleaming wooden floors and large windows to let in the afternoon sun.

'He's coming around next Monday to meet Sam, and if they can build up a connection, Danny will take him on.' Libby sat down on the wooden bench that ran the length of the wall. There was still ten minutes before it started, so, on the pretence of warming up, Libby stretched out her legs. 'I just hope he can get Sam to pass.'

'Try not to fret.' Petra grabbed her hand. 'The teenage years are torturous but you'll get both your kids through it. It probably doesn't help what happened with that poor girl. Denise said you were the first attending.'

'Yeah, it wasn't pretty.'

She hadn't been back into the hospital to see how Hayley was doing but she'd been following the reports online and it was alarming. Physically, she seemed to be improving, though her memory hadn't come back.

According to several sources, she'd been with a group of

friends at a bonfire but had wandered off. The friends had all been drunk and hadn't even realised she was gone until the following morning. Libby closed her eyes, once again imagining if it had been Sienna who'd been so easily overlooked by her supposed friends.

'I assumed the bonfire would've been tame. What did Sam say?'

Libby's body stiffened and her jaw loosened. 'What do you mean?'

Petra looked at her in surprise. 'Nothing... it's just Hank saw Sam's car there. He knows it from when Eloise used to double park it next to the bookstore every Friday.'

'A-are you sure?' Libby's throat was tight and the dots in front of her eyes began to blur. Petra's husband, Hank, was a detective constable who'd grown up in Bournemouth and cared for the community like they were his own kids. 'Was it definitely Friday... not Saturday night?'

'Hank wishes.' Petra let out an undignified snort. 'He spent all week trying to swap shifts so he could avoid coming to my mother's birthday party on Saturday. Still, they're hoping to find who was behind it soon. There are so many photos and videos on social media these days that it's better than any CCTV footage. Police are working through them all now.'

Videos from social media? Her mind returned to Sam's channel. Was that why he'd taken down the video? The thought left her dizzy.

'Are you okay?' Denise's eyes widened with concern.

'Of course,' Libby said, more and more questions coming into her mind.

Why was Hayley's nail in Sam's car? Why had he taken down the video? And why was he lying? She tried to push the questions away. There were lots of people there that night. It didn't mean they'd all done something bad. And it was the same for Sam. Just because his name kept coming up didn't mean he'd done anything.

But it didn't mean he hadn't.

She wanted to be sick.

Brrrring.

Fiona Watkin's number flashed up the screen.

Crap.

She'd tried to contact the journalist but it had gone to voicemail and she hadn't left a message. The woman was the last person Libby wanted to talk to. Especially now there was a tenuous connection between Sam and the party, not to mention that terrible video. Even if he'd removed it, that didn't mean it couldn't be found. Didn't they always say that once something was online, it would never go away? What if Libby accidently said something she shouldn't?

But if she didn't answer, Fiona might just be spiteful enough to run the photograph of Sam, standing in the ruined front yard of his ex-girlfriend, a look of fury in his eyes.

Her nausea turned to ice-cold fear.

That photo could do so much damage. Especially if Fiona started digging. Which meant Libby could no longer sit on the side lines.

'Sorry, I have to take this,' Libby mouthed to her friends and awkwardly threaded her way past the rest of the class until she reached the small landing. Once she was on her own, she answered the call.

'About time you picked up,' Fiona said in a sharp voice. 'I was beginning to think you'd forgotten our deal.'

Libby leaned against the wall, hoping her knees wouldn't give out. 'What do you want?'

'You know what I want, Libby. A story. And I really hope you're the person to give it to me.'

Libby shut her eyes and nodded, even though Fiona couldn't see her. 'Fine. I'm at Pilates on the Old Christchurch Road. Where do you want to meet?'

'There's a wine bar around the corner. Meet me in fifteen minutes. Don't be late.'

Libby gritted her teeth. Hating that she didn't have a choice.

7

Gemma Harrington tapped her finger against the side of her glass. There wasn't enough wine in the world to get her through what was about to come. In the far corner of the pub Stu, her boss, was waving a karaoke microphone, while two of her co-workers were arguing over how to convince customers to buy the premium support package for the terrible computer software the company sold.

She was thirty-seven years old, single, and stuck at a monthly team bonding night with people she hated. How had this become her life? But she already knew the answer. There was only one thing she cared about and that wasn't something that paid the bills. In fact, all it did was cost her money and keep her stuck where she was.

And yet, she couldn't let it go.

Wouldn't let it go.

A squeal came from the microphone and the opening bars of a Whitney Houston song came on. Several more of her colleagues let out a loud cheer, and one of them knocked

Gemma's glass of wine, sending the half glass of pinot noir splashing down the front of her white blouse.

Not one to look a gift horse in the mouth, she let out a startled cry and got to her feet.

'Shit. Sorry, Gemini,' a male voice slurred. 'My mistake.'

Gemma bit her tongue. She'd long ago stopped trying to remind her manager what her actual name was, mainly because if she did, she might also tell him to piss off. And right now, she couldn't afford to lose her job.

'It's fine. I'd better go and wash it before it stains,' she said and, without waiting for an answer, she headed for the bathroom before peeling off and slipping out of the front door of the pub and onto the street outside.

There was a bus stop around the corner and she trudged towards it. She'd much prefer to book a car but the red wine on her blouse now looked like a crime scene and she doubted any driver would want to let her in, considering the stench of alcohol.

Thirty minutes later, she climbed down from the bus and reached her tiny studio apartment. It was the top floor of an old, converted house. The bathroom and kitchen were squashed onto one side of the gables, while the other half was large enough for a bed at one end and a couch and dining room table at the other.

She slid the deadbolt across and walked over to the large cage that took up most of the floor by the window. Thelma, her Rex guinea pig, poked her nose out of the hideout, but Louise was asleep in the corner. Gemma lowered herself down to have a chat with them, careful not to get too close. Despite having them for a year, they were still nervous around her, but that was just because they'd had a tough life in a research lab before she'd adopted them.

After feeding them, she had a quick shower before shaking salt onto her stained blouse and then letting it sit in soda water.

Her hair was wet, but she couldn't be bothered to dry it, so wrapped it in a towel and busied herself in the galley kitchen. Once she had a pot of peppermint tea, she settled down at the second-hand dining room table which doubled as her desk.

It was currently covered in newspaper clippings and photocopied articles as well as the pages and pages of handwritten notes that she'd taken from the last trip to Yorkshire where she'd spoken to Alan Ryman's family. It had been forty years since the eight-year-old boy had gone missing, and while the family had lost hope of finding him alive, they were as anxious as ever to find the person responsible.

Not find, she corrected herself. Because they all knew who had been responsible.

Colin Wallace.

The problem was proving it was him, especially now he was dead.

He'd only ever been convicted of one crime, back in 1984 when he'd abducted eight-year-old Wayne Mason and held him prisoner in a lock-up connected to a rundown block of flats. It had been Wallace's wife who'd found the boy and the evidence recovered from the gruesome scene had been enough to put him away for life.

But while Wayne Mason and his family got the justice they deserved, Colin's conviction was no relief for the twelve other local families who were still frantically searching for their own sons, who'd all gone missing over a five-year period. The most terrible part was that on the night of his arrest, Wallace had talked at length about the young boys, all aged between six and ten. He mentioned names and hair colour, and even birth marks, as well as alluding to the fact the lock-up he'd used to hold Wayne Mason wasn't the only one he'd rented.

The following day, after speaking to a lawyer, he retracted

the statement and refused to give any details, thereby destroying any hope the devastated families had. But there had been a smugness to him all through the trial. His wide mouth curled into a mocking smile. As if he fully understood the pain he was causing, and liked it. That by denying the families answers, he was also denying the police a reason to keep searching for evidence.

And so it had continued until his death five years ago.

Even now, the unfairness of it made her chest ache. Which is why she'd spent the last ten years researching Colin Wallace and writing a book on him. But thanks to his refusal to help the police, he wasn't considered a serial killer, and it had been impossible to find a publisher. So, she'd self-published it and set up her own website. But, unlike so many of the true crime influencers out there, Gemma had no interest in exploring any other cases. She was interested in Colin Wallace alone, which meant she only had a small audience and no revenue from it.

But it wasn't enough to stop her.

Colin Wallace was an animal, and while he would never receive the punishment he deserved, she was determined to get to the truth. Because that's what those lost boys deserved. The ones who never came home and whose stories weren't told. All twelve of them. Including her own brother, Lucas.

Gemma woke with a start. Her neck hurt and her arms were cold. Then she groaned as she lifted her head and several pieces of paper fell away from her cheek. She'd fallen asleep at her desk again. Shivering, she fumbled for her phone to see the time. It was four in the morning and she knew from experience she wouldn't get back to sleep even if she tried.

It was always the same when she thought too much about her older brother.

Lucas had disappeared before Gemma was born but she felt like she'd always known him. His shadow was the marker she used to judge her life. And up until age ten, it had been easy. Lucas loved swimming, so she did too. Lucas visited the pet shop every weekend, and so did Gemma. It got a little tricker when she turned eleven and there were no more of Lucas's milestones or interests to aim for but she'd always tried her best.

Unfortunately, it had never worked.

She'd been born for one reason. To be the plaster that would heal her parents' shattered lives. Instead, she'd made it worse. She was just a reminder that Lucas was no longer there. They lost a son and in return all they'd got was... *her.*

Her parents divorced and not long after her father committed suicide. While her mother – already old in spirit by the time Gemma was born – shrank in on herself, leaving Gemma alone to try and navigate her way in the world. And as far as she could tell, she only had one job.

Find out what happened to Lucas.

She rolled her shoulders, trying to shake out the cramps. Her shift didn't start until ten so she stood up and made herself a pot of English Breakfast before returning to her work. She was halfway through doing a new blog article and this would give her a chance to get stuck into it. She yawned and turned on her computer but instead of opening her document, she found herself clicking onto the low-tech message boards that she'd first stumbled across back in high school. Looks wise, they had hardly changed in the last twenty years, making them out-of-date compared with more modern sites or the slew of online bloggers who had moved into the true crime space.

But apart from not having to listen to a YouTuber talking

about their theories about real-life murders while putting on their make-up, the other advantage of the SK Boards was that they were like finding friends hiding away in the stacks of the library; she could always stumble upon live threads at any time of the day or night.

Down one side was a list of people currently online and she recognised a few familiar names. There was a discussion around a Netflix documentary and how it tackled racial profiling and she dipped in to read a couple of comments before bouncing across to an argument about a case that was going through the courts right now.

Gemma yawned. She should really get started on the blog post. She was about to flick it off when another thread involved a headline from a newspaper article that someone had posted.

Girl Escapes from Monster's Sick Trap.

She gave a shudder. With that kind of sensationalist headline, there was only one newspaper the story had come from. Most of the comments were in disgust at the way the clickbait shock value of the article didn't seem to care about the dignity and well-being of the victim.

What started as a small party to celebrate a friend's birthday, down at a popular Bournemouth beach, resulted in A-Level student, Hayley Terrace, waking up to find herself trapped in an old lock-up that had once belonged to a block of flats, with no recollection of how she got there. She was lucky enough to escape, but has this happened before? And more importantly, will it happen again?

The world stopped and Gemma's body seemed to shut down. As if it was too scared to move or do anything until she'd had time to digest what she'd just read. This time, she pored over every word until she got to the end, and then rubbed her chin. She hadn't been mistaken.

The girl had been held in a lock-up that was near some abandoned flats.

A setting that was almost identical to where Wayne had been found.

Gemma scanned the rest of the thread, her heart pounding rapidly in her chest. A few long-time members had also brought up the Colin Wallace connection but most had dismissed it, apart from Agatha in Southport, who was concerned it might be a copycat murderer. In response, Agatha's long-time nemesis, Stuart from Wolverhampton, had informed her that a copycat wouldn't take a seventeen-year-old girl.

He was right.

The terrible paraphernalia and pornography that had been found in the lock-up had suggested that Colin Wallace was a paedophile who targeted young boys. But that didn't mean Agatha wasn't right as well. It could still be a copycat who was trying to mix things up.

Gemma took a sip of tea and settled into her chair. Reading Agatha and Stuart as they battled it out was so much more relaxing than going to work events. These were her people.

She scrolled further down to where someone had posted another article about the case. It was almost as trashy as the first one, except instead of a photograph of the lock-up Hayley had escaped from, there was one of a paramedic leaning over the girl, who was wrapped up in a blanket. It was written by a journalist called Fiona Watkins and this article was focused more on the first responders and the hospital. Gemma sighed. It clearly meant there were no new leads and so they were trying to create a story out of nothing.

Forty-five-year-old paramedic, Libby Curtis, said, 'Seeing the victim in that state was heart breaking. I have kids about the same age. I hope they find whoever's behind it.'

The article moved to the ongoing problems associated with beach parties and the dangers of too much alcohol and drugs on the young adults of Bournemouth. But Gemma ignored it as she stared at the woman in the photo. There was something familiar about her.

She blew up the image to try and get a better look but it had been taken at a distance and was heavily pixelated. Damn. Libby Curtis. Curtis? Why was it familiar?

Chewing her lip, she brought up another screen and searched LinkedIn. There was no photo, just a timeline of her work history, along with a couple of posts to support paramedics who were after a pay rise. There was a husband called Nathan Curtis who ran some kind of company but nothing else.

Gemma sighed. Clearly, it was time to get off the Internet and start working on her blog before she had to leave for work. No doubt Stu would have something to say about her leaving early last night.

She picked up the unlined notepad that she preferred to write in and studied her notes. Her brother, Lucas, had disappeared on his way home from the local shops as he'd walked across a playing field and, according to the interview she'd recently done with the Ryman family, Alan's aunt lived not far from the playing field. Although there was a year between when the two boys disappeared, Libby wanted to investigate it further.

All her old street maps were on the bookshelf and she quickly found the one she needed. Over the years, she'd methodically marked in every landmark and house number that she came across, hoping it would give her a better picture of things.

There was software that could do it as well, but Gemma found that by working with her hands, it somehow kept her connected to her brother. And to her mission.

As she returned to the table, her leg brushed one of the folders she'd hastily jammed into the bookshelf. It fell to the floor, sending out the loose-leaf sheets of paper, landing everywhere.

Pages and pages of notes fanned out around her feet.

Okay, maybe there was *something* to be said for using software to store some of her research. Sighing, she dropped into a crouching position and gathered up the mess. Most of them were from her first trip to Yorkshire, back when she first started looking into her brother's disappearance. There were pages of interviews with the few neighbours who were still living in the same street where Wallace's family home had been. She'd also found several other people who'd known the family and been happy enough to talk to her.

She messily thrust them back into the folder when a name caught her eye.

Marion Curtis.

The words danced on the page as Gemma's entire body went stiff. Curtis was Marion's maiden name before she'd married Colin.

Gemma snatched up the piece of paper, scanning through her old notes. The interview had been with one of Marion's co-workers, who'd gone into great detail about how Marion was from money and that her family had never approved of the marriage, believing that Colin Wallace, who'd been working as a labourer when they'd first met, wasn't suitable.

How right they were.

Over the years, Gemma had spent a lot of time researching Marion's history because after the court case, she'd gone to live in

Spain, along with her five-year-old son, Ian, before the pair of them seemed to disappear off the face of the earth. Over the years, there had been a lot of speculation about where they might be, but no definite sightings.

Until now.

But was it too much of a coincidence that a teenage girl had been kidnapped in Colin's signature style and that someone with his wife's maiden name was involved? A cynic might say yes, but Gemma had been doing this for a long time. Months and months of her life without even a hint of a way forward.

Her skin prickled and she hurried back to her computer to find out more about Libby Curtis. This time, she went deeper into her history and bookmarked page after page. There were two children in high school, and the husband, Nathan. And while she couldn't get into any of their social media accounts, there were several newspaper articles over the years, mainly for sports. Some just with the kids winning medals and once with Nathan and Libby dressed up for an art deco ball.

Gemma's heart thumped like a drum as she stared at the photographs of the whole family. They looked happy. But that didn't mean anything. All families had secrets. Question was, did the man in the photo have the kind of secret she was looking for? Was he the missing son of Colin Wallace?

She widened her search and found a couple of mentions of the mother, Eloise Curtis, but there were no photos. It wasn't such a surprise. While lots of older people did use the Internet, there was still a large number who avoided it.

A buzz of dopamine blasted through her and Gemma scrolled through her phone to see when the next train to London was going. Because if Marion and Ian Wallace really were down in Bournemouth, possibly living under a different name, she needed to find them. To get justice for the many families whose lives had been destroyed by the monster. And revenge for the brother she'd never met.

* * *

'Can I just remind you that this is a terrible idea?' Stephen said an hour later as he pulled to a stop outside the station. It had started to rain and he flicked on his wipers before turning towards her.

At forty-four, he was five years older than her, with the first sprinkles of grey streaking his dark hair. It suited him more than the soft brown of his student days when they'd first met. But unlike her, he'd gone on to finish his degree and now worked as a lawyer, while she'd dropped out after a year and had jumped from one dead-end job to another. He also lived five minutes away and was the only one of her friends that Thelma and Louise weren't scared of. And while he'd immediately agreed to look after them, he'd also insisted on driving her to the station. No doubt with this in mind.

'No, it's not. This is the break I've been waiting for. It could change everything,' Gemma reminded him.

'Or it could be a wild goose chase that costs you lots of money. Not to mention that you have no holidays left. What did your boss say?'

Gemma swallowed. Stu hadn't taken it well but had grudgingly agreed to let her take a week off. But if she wasn't back at her desk by the end of next week, then there would be trouble. But that was a problem for another day.

'He said it's fine. We're not that busy,' she said. Steven raised an eyebrow as if her feeble excuse wasn't even worth cross examining.

'What if you *do* find Marion and Ian? They've obviously gone underground for a reason. Trying to start a new life without the shadow of Colin Wallace hanging over their heads. What right do you have to expose them to the world again?' he said.

'What about the rights of the grieving families to know where their loved ones are?' she countered, her gaze holding his. Finally, he shrugged, just like she knew he would. Gemma gave him a grateful smile and leaned over to kiss his cheek. 'Thank you for the lift. And for agreeing to feed the girls.'

'You say it like I had a choice,' he said, the worry still deep in his eyes. She swallowed back her guilt. They'd slept together several times over the years and she had the feeling he wanted more. Maybe she should have just asked Edith in the downstairs flat to feed the guinea pigs instead? 'Just make sure you check in with me every day while you're down there, so I know you're safe.'

'Safe from what? Colin Wallace is dead.' Gemma reached for her small travel bag and opened the car door. 'I'm only chasing the bones.'

'No, Gem, you're chasing ghosts, and sometimes that can be worse.'

8

Libby's phone buzzed as she stopped at the roundabout. She let out a groan. It was probably another colleague or neighbour asking if she knew about the article in yesterday's paper.

So far, she'd been polite with her answers, but it was wearing thin.

Fiona had been all smiles when they'd met on Monday night, but each of her questions had been loaded with tiny barbs, just waiting for Libby to get tangled up in. Trying to navigate through them without showing any of her concerns had been far more exhausting than any Pilates class. And that was without Fiona knowing anything other than Libby had been the first attending and that Sienna and Hayley had been friends.

At least the article hadn't been too dreadful, mainly focusing on Libby's role as a mother and the concern she had over her own kids. Though if Sienna's icy glare at breakfast was anything to go by, she didn't agree. Libby couldn't really blame her. If her own mother had been quoted in the paper spouting out maternal concern, Libby would have probably ripped the thing up. And even Nathan had lifted an eyebrow and said he'd been surprised by her judgement in speaking to the press.

That had stung. Especially since Libby had been all but forced into meeting Fiona because of the damn photograph and her previous attempt to stop Sam's rampage through Andi's front garden ruining his chances of a scholarship.

She also had no doubt over how much harder Fiona would push if she ever caught wind that Sam might be involved.

The traffic eased and she pulled into the car park of the private hospital where Hayley had been transferred to, at her parents' request. Libby had been surprised at the move but it was Fiona who'd explained that the family were trying to hide out there and avoid the press. Libby couldn't blame them.

She turned off the ignition and leaned back in the seat. She wished she could just trust that the boy she'd spent the last ten years raising wasn't involved, and that all her worries were just a result of too little sleep and over-anxious maternal instincts. But no matter what she did, the niggle remained. What if it *was* Sam?

Which was why she was here. Even if Hayley didn't have any memory of what had happened, she presumably still had her fingernails. And if they weren't a match, then Libby could finally relax.

Brrrring.

Her phone went again and she rolled her eyes. Okay, she'd relax as soon as she knew that Sam hadn't been involved in anything *and* when her fifteen minutes of local Bournemouth fame was over.

She ignored the call and walked between a Lexus and an oversized Toyota. Despite the late summer, some of the deciduous trees had decided to start shedding their coppery leaves, which caught in the wind as she reached the front entrance of the recently built facility.

She'd never been to the clinic in a work capacity because they didn't have an accident and emergency department, but she had no trouble finding her way to the second floor, where Fiona had told her Hayley's room was. The journalist hadn't tried visiting herself because the family had already refused to speak to her. It made Libby uneasy about what kind of reception she'd receive.

She needn't have worried. Before she'd even reached the waiting room, a woman with bright-blonde hair and unnaturally smooth cheeks gasped in recognition. Libby didn't know Adele Terrace very well but they'd exchanged numerous nods of recognition as they'd taxied their daughters to and from the brutally early morning rowing sessions. It had been almost like a badge of honour. The brigade of mothers who suffered through the endless procession of practices and competitions in the hope that it would do... *something*. Libby wasn't even sure what that was meant to be. Make their kids better, stronger, more capable?

Definitely not this terrible alternative of Hayley lying in hospital and Adele Terrace's eyes rimmed with red from crying too much.

'Libby.' She hurried towards her; arms outstretched. 'I've been wanting to thank you for everything you did. If you hadn't recognised her so quickly, it might have taken hours, or even days more—'

Adele broke off, her mouth trembling, no doubt going over whatever terrible scenario her mind had come up with. And then she dragged Libby into a tight embrace, enveloping her in a perfume of stale coffee, sickly sweet berries from vaping and despair.

Libby's throat tightened with guilt as she realised too late Adele thought she was here to offer comfort and support to them. *I am*, she reminded herself. Of course she was. It was one of the main reasons she was a paramedic. To help people in the most practical and immediate way that she could.

But she also needed to help *her* family.

'Sorry. I didn't mean to pounce. You must think I'm crazy.' Adele dabbed underneath her eyes with her fingertips that were barely visible behind her long, acrylic nails. They were painted silvery grey with several small diamantes dotted on them. Like mother, like daughter.

'Not at all.' Libby lightly touched her arm. 'I can't imagine how horrific it's been. I hope I'm not intruding but I wanted to see how Hayley is.'

'You're definitely not intruding.' Adele led her over to the small waiting area. It had padded armchairs in slate-grey velvet as well as several orange sofas, making it seem more like a frequent flyer lounge than a hospital. 'The nurse has taken her for an X-ray and Trev's gone home to shower. We can't thank you enough.'

'You don't need to thank me. It's my job. Though this part isn't. I don't usually follow up with a patient once we've done our part, but...' she tailed off, not wanting to say the words that floated between them.

It could have been my daughter.

'You don't need to explain.' Adele once again tapped under her eyes, as if to stop more tears. 'She's physically okay. A few scratches and bruises. Whatever they drugged her with has worn off and she's rehydrated. We're hoping to take her home tomorrow.'

'That's good.' Libby pressed her lips together, knowing she had to ask the question, even if she didn't like the answer. 'And has she remembered anything? Do the police know what happened?'

Adele closed her eyes, the true depth of her fatigue evident in the tiny lines trying to inch their way around her smooth, Botoxed skin.

'No. She can only remember tiny flashes, and every time she tries, it ends in tears. As for the police...' Her voice darkened and her eyes narrowed, suddenly alert and lit up by anger. 'They keep feeding us the same old bullshit about keeping their lines of enquiry open instead of arresting the bastard who did this.'

Libby clutched her hands together as a dull buzz sounded in her ears. Was this why Adele had been so welcoming? Because she wanted to get her alone? To make Libby turn on her own son? She sucked air into her belly before letting it out in a long breath. It helped calm down her pounding heart. She repeated it twice more before allowing herself to speak.

'You know who it was?'

'Oh yes.' Adele's mouth tightened. 'Tate Raymond. That boy is the biggest piece of shit I've ever met. I warned Hayley at the time he was trouble. I went to school with his father and he was the same. Bloody apple doesn't fall far from the tree, does it?'

Libby let out a soft gasp as the buzzing sound retreated and the world came back into focus. Tate was the same age as Sam and they'd had an ongoing rivalry for years in cricket and football, first to get on the teams and more recently for making captain.

She was also certain he was the boy responsible for the rupture between Hayley and Sienna once he'd started dating Hayley. Though the relationship hadn't lasted long, as Sam had gleefully announced. Two months was all it had taken for Tate to show his true scumbag nature by cheating on Hayley and breaking her heart. And while Sienna's face had turned to stone at the announcement, Libby had been relieved that her daughter had dodged a bullet.

But the fact Tate might have gone from being a serial arsehole to something so much worse was a shock.

And a relief.

'I *know* it was him.' Adele's eyes glittered with anger. 'Not only did he cheat on Hayley and start dating Zoe, but he's been privately messaging her, saying he made a mistake and she needs to take him back. That he can't live without her, and if she won't talk to him, he might be do something like kill himself.'

'Have you shown the messages to the police?'

'It was the first thing we did. They haven't found her phone yet; thankfully, her account was also on her laptop. That's why they interviewed him but then they let him go because of lack of evidence.'

'You still think it was him?' Libby hated how hopeful she was. Hopeful that some other boy had gone down such a dark road, if only it meant that her son hadn't done anything. And yet, she couldn't help it. She needed to know that Sam was safe.

Adele gave a vigorous nod. 'We've spoken to her friends who were at the bonfire. They all said Tate was acting strangely and that he'd started dabbling in steroids a few months ago.'

Libby shivered. She'd seen first-hand how violent people could become on steroids. But before she could reply, the familiar squeak of a wheelchair filled the air and a nurse appeared, pushing Hayley down the corridor. Her dark-brown hair was now clean and hanging over her shoulders, and there were several scratches on her face, as well as a purple crescent of a black eye.

At the sight of her daughter, Adele's anger faded and was replaced by concern. She turned to Libby. 'Sorry. I need to go. But thank you for coming by. And for caring. It's nice to know there are still good people in the world.'

'Of course,' she said, her eyes dropping to Hayley's hands,

which were sitting limply in her lap as if she'd forgotten what she was meant to do with them. Some of the scratches had faded but Libby barely noticed.

All she could see was the pink acrylic nails that were still adorning nine of her fingers. And the tenth fingernail was still chewed down to the quick, as if signalling that something was wrong. That somewhere was a single nail that had been lost and needed to return home.

All the relief she'd felt at the mention of Tate's name was gone and nausea rose up in her throat. She wrapped her hands around her torso to stop from shaking. There was no denying the colour and shape of the other nails now. They were the same as the one she'd found in Sam's car.

She continued smiling as Adele hugged her goodbye before disappearing with her daughter and the nurse. Then she let out a breath.

Shit.

* * *

There was no sign of Nathan's Audi when she pulled up to her house twenty-five minutes later but Jonathan's old Toyota was there. It had once been navy blue but now there seemed to be more rust marks than anything. However, he refused to replace it until it stopped working, which was proving an impossible feat.

She followed the trail of power tools and piles of plasterboard into the garage and found him squatting down with a pencil clasped between his teeth, holding a spirit-level on a piece of wood.

'Ah, the media star appears.' He stood up, his brown eyes filled with amusement.

'Don't you start.' She tried to muster up an air of calmness.

But it didn't work and her heart continued to pound in an agitated rhythm while the acrylic nail dug through the pocket of her jeans into her skin like a rose thorn. A constant reminder of the wrongness of everything.

Jonathan's mouth straightened out into a concerned line. 'Everything okay? Was it a tough shift?'

'Always,' she said before letting out a breath. She'd long ago learnt to separate out parts of her life so that she didn't bring her work home. But not only had Jonathan been with her when they'd gone to Steamer Point, he was almost part of the family. 'I went to see how Hayley's getting on. I spoke to her mother.'

'Ah.' He let out a soft whistle of understanding. 'That must've been tough. We'd better go put the kettle on.'

Unexpected tears prickled Libby's eyes and she found herself mimicking Adele and using her fingers to gently tap them away as she followed Jonathan out of the garage at the side of the house and through the large, bi-folding doors into the kitchen.

A discarded sachet sat on the counter, along with an empty ramen cup and a pair of chopsticks. It was Sienna's afternoon snack of choice and Libby didn't even have the energy to bitch about the mess. Jonathan guided her to one of the mismatched antique wooden chairs dotted around the dining table while he bustled about making a pot of tea. He even went straight to where she hid the emergency chocolate Hobnobs, tucked behind a large jar of brown lentils.

Once he'd finished playing mother and she had a steaming cup of tea with a splash of milk, just the way she liked it, he gave a punctuated nod as if he was turning a programme back on.

'Tell me everything. How's Hayley doing?'

'Physically, pretty good, but she has no memory of what happened and Adele was beside herself with worry.' Libby wrapped her hands around the porcelain mug, letting the heat seep into her fingers.

'Can't blame her for that. That poor bloody family. Things like this don't just get healed. It must be hell not knowing who was responsible.'

'Absolutely.' Libby swallowed, trying to focus on the sweet pungent aroma of the tea. 'Adele's convinced it's Hayley's ex-boyfriend.'

'Tate?' Jonathan's eyebrows flew up. He'd spent enough meals with them to know about the soap opera type drama of Sam and Sienna's lives and the names of the cast. Usually, it appealed to him, but there was no hint of amusement now. 'The idea of kids hurting kids is hard to swallow.'

As if on cue, the front door crashed open and Sam appeared several seconds later. His hair was still wet and stiff from salt and his shoulders were high and stiff with tension.

'Hey,' Jonathan said with an easy smile. 'Any decent waves?'

'What do you think?' Sam glared at the unmoving weather-vane Nathan had installed at the far end of the garden. His dark expression was almost an accusation, as if the lack of breeze and therefore swell, was somehow their fault. Then he spied the packet of Hobnobs on the counter and emptied half of them out into his hand before stalking off.

'Woah.' Jonathan turned to Libby once Sam's footfall had stopped echoing out from the staircase. 'What terrible crimes have you and Nathan committed now?'

Libby swallowed at his word choice. 'That tutor that Denise recommended will be here on Monday. Sam's still... processing...'

She tailed off, her mind too full of tangled thoughts to know how she felt. Her body, on the other hand, had no problems letting her know and she began to shake. Jonathan reached out and gave her hand a squeeze.

'He'll come around. You and Nathan are great parents, even if Sam doesn't see it yet. He's bloody lucky you're here to stop him from going off the rails.'

Stop him from going off the rails.

The words jabbed at her as Todd's face flooded her mind. It was getting harder to remember the details now and she hated that his image more resembled one of the few photographs she still had of them both. There weren't many left. Angela had burnt most of them after Alan's death in one of the furious outbursts that had so much been part of their lives.

Libby should have done a better job of protecting her brother from their mother's vicious tongue and cutting words. Of the way she tormented him over Alan's death. She hadn't stopped him going off the rails at all. She'd just stood by and let it happen.

And it was something she'd never forgive herself for.

The shrill sound of Jonathan's phone broke her thoughts and he studied the screen before softly swearing.

'I've got to take this. Try not to worry about Sam. He'll come right. I'm sure of it.' He walked back out towards the garage and the half-built storage units.

Libby rolled her shoulders and stood up. Finally, she could do the thing she knew she had to do. She'd known it from the moment the nurse had pushed Hayley out in a wheelchair and Libby could properly see the colour of her fingernails.

No longer could she pretend it was a coincidence. Or that it was a different colour. A different nail. A different girl.

Hayley's nail had been in Sam's car. Fact.

Guilt coiled in her stomach, sharp and unforgiving.

It wasn't fair. Like Todd, Sam was a good kid. Bright and funny. And just because there was a chance he'd lost his way didn't mean he should be punished for the rest of his life. Yet surely Hayley had rights too. Libby squeezed her eyes shut. This wasn't about Hayley. She had her own parents to take care of her. To fight in her corner and make sure she came through it.

But Libby had to stay on Sam's side. Make sure that he was okay. That nothing happened to him. Not now, or in the future.

Taking a deep breath, she took the single acrylic nail out of her pocket and studied it.

The glossy colour still pristine bright despite all it had been through. What if Hayley never remembered what had happened? Did that mean the nail was the only piece of evidence linking her son and Adele's daughter? It seemed a lot of responsibility for something so inconsequential.

But it wasn't Libby's job to solve crimes. It was her job to help people. And that's what she was doing.

She walked to the counter and dropped the nail into a shallow pottery bowl before reaching for the spare matches they always kept in the drawer.

It took three attempts to strike it across the side of the box before the sharp scent of sulphur filled the air and a tiny, orange flame danced on top of the stick. Libby didn't bother to admire it. She held it above the acrylic nail, slowly lowering it down until the flame jumped onto the new surface. It burnt away to nothing, as the article on the Internet had said it would.

And then there was nothing left.

Libby took a deep breath. She might have let her brother down but she wouldn't make the same mistake twice. Whatever was going on with Sam, she would protect him from it. That's what good mothers did.

9

Gemma held up her hands and squinted at her phone, trying to follow the progress of the taxi that was meant to be collecting her. But the late-afternoon sunshine made it almost impossible to see her screen. The wind nipped at her ankles, bringing with it swirls of sand that had already covered her once-clean, white trainers. Finally, she gave up and thrust her phone back into her pocket.

She'd reached Bournemouth two hours ago after a hideously long train trip down from Manchester. And while part of her wanted to collapse onto the hotel bed in the accommodation she'd booked, she'd refused to allow herself the luxury.

Her meagre savings wouldn't go very far and she didn't doubt Stu would fire her if she didn't return to work in a week. Which meant she had a ticking clock. She tapped her foot. She hadn't told Stephen the full extent of her plans because she knew he wouldn't approve. But then again, he hadn't been through what she had. Hadn't seen how it had destroyed her parents and ripped apart the other families.

And if she wasn't going to be in Bournemouth for very long,

she had to do everything she could to find the answers she needed. And that meant taking risks.

Another gust of wind swept past her and a group of tourists several feet away yelped as their thin, cotton clothing moulded to their shivering bodies. But Gemma, who hadn't bothered to change out of the jeans and jacket she'd been wearing when she left Manchester, didn't flinch. Instead, she rubbed her eyes and cursed.

Why hadn't she asked the driver to wait while she walked around Steamer Point nature reserve where Hayley had been found earlier in the week? Instead, she'd assumed she could easily call another one when she was ready to head over to the lock-up where Hayley had allegedly been held.

It had been relatively easy to trace the lock-up owner back to a man called Stan Butcher, who owned a block of nine, two of which were currently available for rent. She was due to meet him in half an hour before he flew out to Los Angeles, which was why she'd come there first instead of trying to hunt down Libby Curtis and her husband, Nathan.

If her lift ever arrived.

She turned to a grassed area to the left of a picnic table. There was no sign of the crime-scene tape that had barricaded the area, but thanks to numerous photos both in the papers and online, Gemma had been able to pinpoint it. She shivered at what Hayley Terrace might have gone through before she'd escaped. And the worse fate she would have avoided.

It seemed wrong for it to happen in such a beautiful location with the beach and sea below and trails of gorse leading into the woods surrounding the area.

Her phone beeped and the app flashed to let her know her lift had finally arrived. The wind picked up and it almost pushed her back across the reserve to where a white Honda had appeared.

She jogged the last few feet, no longer caring about the state of her trainers, which were covered in a fine layer of sand and dust. Thankfully, the driver didn't seem inclined to talk as he drove out of the car park and through an older estate with well-kept houses before coming to an empty lot off Lymington Road.

It had once housed a block of flats. But they were long gone, leaving behind only the concrete pad, which had been partially covered by weeds. Further back was a row of nine identical lock-up garages that would've once belonged to each flat.

Her skin prickled.

The lock-up where Wayne Mason had been found had been pulled down as soon as the trial was over, and a petrol station now stood there. Gemma had visited it once, hoping it would somehow give her the answers she longed for. But there had been nothing to indicate the lock-up had ever existed.

But this was different.

This was where Hayley had been taken last Friday night.

She rubbed her arms and looked across the vacant lot to where they stood. The police hadn't officially released any details about the location. But thanks to all the people who'd felt compelled to take selfies and record videos of themselves there, Gemma had found it with a quick internet search. The dark fascination people had with crime and criminals wasn't a new thing to her.

After all, wasn't that why she was here?

But that wasn't quite true. For so many of the people she met online, it was like a puzzle to be solved, or the need to confirm their own goodness by judging the evil of others. But Gemma didn't have the luxury of that kind of detachment. Her brother's disappearance and probable murder was a living, pulsing force inside her that never rested. It whispered in her ear, waking her at night and pushing her forward.

There could be no silence until it was over.

The air was dank and the breeze whipped around her hair as she walked across the vacant lot. It was desolate, covered in beer bottles and fast-food remains from where kids had used it to party. Had they been there last Friday night when Hayley had been taken? Had she tried to scream, only to be drowned out by whatever music they'd been listening to?

Gemma shuddered and looked around, holding up her phone to take as many photos as she could. She'd learnt the hard way not to overthink it. Take the photos and then wait until she was calmer before going through them all. She took several more and continued walking.

There were signs of the recent police investigation. The grass had been trampled and there were a series of tyre tracks on the dirt driveway.

The lock-ups were all connected and had been well maintained, with identical black aluminium doors that were hinged from the side, making them easier to open. And to conceal things from prying eyes.

Crime-scene tape still dangled from one of them, and an extra padlock and security camera had been installed, making it easy to identify as the one where police had discovered Hayley's denim jacket and one of her shoes. But no identification had been made about who'd rented it. Or, if it had, the police hadn't released it.

Spots danced in front of her eyes and Gemma took a few calming breaths before the dizzying sensation left her. Even though the lock-up where Wayne had been held was long gone, she'd spent hours studying the photographs, staring at the stark interior that had been custom fitted with a camp bed, as well as wrist and ankle manacles.

The rest of the space had been laid out like a nineteen sixties living room, with brown floral carpet and clashing wallpaper. There had been an orange sofa and a standard lamp, as well as a vintage record player and a single record of Verdi's *Requiem*, 'Dies Irae'. But worst of all were the tiny ticks that had been carved into a wooden beam. Forty of them.

Was that what the police had found in this lock-up? Had they even known to look for carvings? After all, they had no reason to suspect a copycat. Colin Wallace had refused to ever discuss the confession he'd retracted, which meant in the eyes of the law he'd only ever abducted one boy and not killed anyone.

Which made him even more of a monster in Gemma's eyes. To die without giving any relief to the suffering families was cruel. Goosebumps prickled her arms, like they always did when she thought about him for any length of time.

She had to get inside that lock-up to see what was there. If there was anything that the police had missed.

'All right, my luv. Are you the one from up north?' A short man with a bald head and handlebar moustache appeared at the side of the lock-ups. Gemma's spine stiffened and her pulse increased as he walked towards her. Stan Butcher was about sixty and was sweating profusely, despite the breeze. And while he didn't look remotely dangerous, she should've been more vigilant.

'Yes, that's right. Gemma... Waverstone.' She straightened her posture, making sure to show her full height, while her fingers bunched into a fist, the way Stephen had taught her. 'Thank you so much for seeing me at the last minute.'

'Never hurts to be nice to a pretty girl.' He panted, pulled an old-fashioned handkerchief from his pocket, and wiped his brow. She unclenched her fingers and relaxed her shoulders.

'Except you didn't know what I looked like,' she reminded him. Not least since she'd given him a false last name, so even if he'd tried to find her, he wouldn't get very far.

'Guilty.' He didn't appear remotely bothered that she'd called him out. 'Let's say it never hurts to be nice to anyone who might want to do business with me. So, tell me, Gemma, what would you be wanting one of the lock-ups for?'

'I'm moving down here for a job and need to store my furniture for at least six months,' she said, using the prefabricated story she'd come up with on the train journey.

'I see.' His eyes swept across her, as if trying to decide whether to believe her. 'And how did you find out about them?'

'They're listed on several sites and a community page,' she said in what she hoped was a casual voice. He gave a small nod, as if accepting her story. She quickly moved on before he could change his mind. 'Are they still empty?'

'Yes.' He fished a large key ring out from his trousers. 'I've got number two and number five available. They might look old, but there's no mould or damp in them, and we're above the flood zone.'

'Great,' she said as he led her over to one at the far end. She stopped and pointed to the one with the recently added lock and camera. 'Though I'd prefer that one. It looks more secure.'

'Sorry, that one's not available. But I can promise these are all safe as houses.'

Gemma pressed her lips together. He might not be physically threatening but he was as slippery as an eel. 'So why does that one have a security camera?'

He narrowed his eyes, all pleasantries gone. 'You want to know what's behind there, you ask the police. And if you think of coming back again, you might find someone a lot less agreeable than me. Now, unless you want to waste more of my time, I have a flight to catch. We clear?'

Gemma's heart hammered and she tried not to think of Stephen warning her not to go looking for trouble.

Stan smirked as a second man appeared from behind the lock-ups. He was a lot taller and fitter than his boss and had a sleeve of rent-a-villain tattoos down one arm.

'Clear,' Gemma agreed, sweat beading along her collarbone as she carefully backed away until she reached the road. Stan and his goon continued to stare at her. Her original plan had been to try and retrace how Hayley might have found her way from the lock-up, through the reserve and out to the look-out at Steamer Point, where she'd been found. But she was going to have leave that for now. Unless she wanted to risk being followed.

Her hands shook as she pulled up the app to book another lift, and it wasn't until half an hour later, when she was safely back in the hotel, that she let out a frustrated growl. What a colossal waste of time that had been.

Irritation prickled her skin as she thumbed through the photos that she'd taken, trying to see if there was another way to go back. But even the other units, without the extra padlock, still looked secure with their new doors. Unlike the lock-up that Wayne Mason had escaped from, where the old wooden door had been prised open with a crowbar.

The downside of progress.

She dragged her finger across the screen to expand the photo so she could see the locks. She'd never tried to pick one before, but then again, that was hardly a problem these days, and she was sure a quick tutorial on YouTube might be able to help. *Except for Stan's friend*, she reminded herself.

Sighing, Gemma rubbed her eyes before catching the maker's logo in an oblong circle under the handle.

TLC Manufacturing.

She dropped the phone as if it had just given her an electric shock. She knew that name. She'd come across it when she'd first researched Libby Curtis and her family. TLC Manufacturing was owned and operated by Libby's husband, Nathan. The man who was possibly Colin Wallace's son, Ian. And there was a grandson as well. She closed her eyes until she recalled her notes. Sam Curtis. Which meant there were potentially two generations walking around with Colin Wallace's blood pumping through their veins.

Gemma leaned back as the grim reality pushed down on her chest.

Her gamble to come down to Bournemouth had been right. There was some kind of connection between what had happened to Hayley Terrace and the man who she believed to be responsible for her own brother's disappearance. A new sense of purpose raced through her. No longer was she chasing ghosts. The connection she'd been searching for was here and she wasn't going anywhere until she got the answers she needed.

10

Libby rubbed her eyes and stared at her computer screen, but the words were blurring together, making it hard to proofread her report. It had been a long day that had ended with a trip to the emergency room with a patient who had a serious case of peritonitis.

None of it was helped by her lack of sleep. Her dreams were filled with policemen turning up to reconstruct the pink nail from the tiny blob of black smoulder that had been left behind, before dragging Sam away from the house.

No. She'd screamed at them, *I have to keep him safe. You don't understand. It's my job. That's why Nathan married me.*

But her voice was muffled and she'd been forced to watch the police car disappear down the road. She'd woken up covered in sweat, and by the time the dawn had pushed through the half-drawn curtains, she was exhausted and on edge.

Which was nothing to how she felt now.

She swallowed, her mouth thick with the aftertaste of coffee and the headache tablets she'd taken earlier. Sighing, she went back to the beginning and read over it before uploading it and signing out of the network. Then she picked up her own phone and refreshed the local news feed. But it was only showing the same article that had been there in the morning. It was a vague report that police were still investigating and wouldn't be making any further comments until they knew more.

Did that mean it was over?

She hoped so. Burning the nail had been so instinctive, so right, that she'd done it before she could fully consider the ethical implications. Which was probably for the best. Besides, it didn't really matter what she ethically thought; it only mattered what her actions had been. The actions of a mother looking after her kid.

I did the right thing.

'You still here? I thought your shift finished an hour ago.' Jonathan appeared in the doorway of the staff room. Libby jumped to her feet, a combination of worrying that he could somehow read her thoughts, and the caffeine that was still pounding through her veins.

'You scared me.' The words were out of her mouth before she could stop them, and he raised an eyebrow, his gaze racking over her.

'It's three in the afternoon and I was whistling as I walked in. If I scared you, it's because you're running on empty.'

She swallowed. It was clear by the concern in his eyes that he hadn't forgotten about the mistake she'd made with the trolley. The back of her knees buckled and she swayed slightly.

'Of course not. I'm fine... just a little tired.'

He folded his arms across his chest, mouth in a grim line. 'You're not fine. You look exhausted. When was the last time you slept properly?'

'When is the last time any women in their forties slept properly?' she said but he didn't laugh.

'I know there's been a lot going on at home with the twins. But you need to look after yourself. Not just for your own sake, but for your patients as well.' This time, he held her gaze. Libby pressed her lips together, hating that he was right, but grateful that he was a good enough friend to be honest.

'It's okay. I promise I've got things under control. And it's only three weeks until the trip, which means I'll get a proper break.'

He continued to study her; before he could answer, Denise walked in and grinned.

'My favourite two people. I just bumped into Nancy and there's a quiz night next Tuesday at the Albatross. I put our names down. Team Don't Ask Us Any Cricket Questions can ride again. You both in?'

'Sure. Sounds great,' Libby quickly said, pleased for the subject change.

'Sorry, no can do.' Jonathan shook his head. 'That's when our darts team will be claiming victory in the final. We were cheated last year, but this time around, we'll be wiping the floor with them.'

'I forgot all about it,' Denise admitted. 'Lib, does that mean you'll be going to cheer Nathan on?'

Libby swallowed, not wanting to admit she'd also forgotten about the local team that Nathan and Jonathan had joined a couple of years ago. They'd started going as a joke but had both become competitive with it.

'I don't want to put him off his game,' she said in a light voice.

'Fair enough. Quiz night it is,' Denise said before wrinkling her nose. 'And by the way, weren't you meant to finish an hour ago?'

'We were just discussing that,' Jonathan said. Libby held up her hands in defeat. The conversation was going from bad to worse.

'I know when I'm beaten. I'll see you both tomorrow.' She picked up her bag and coat before she was given another lecture on working too hard. The temperature had dropped, making her glad she had her jacket on. She followed the path that led down to the car park and climbed into the driver's seat.

Nathan was stuck at work, Sienna was studying with a friend, and Sam wasn't showing any signs of changing his mind about speaking to her, so she was on her own. Usually, she hated the empty house, but after the last week, the idea of being alone was almost a relief.

She pulled out her phone and brought up the number for her favourite Indian restaurant, but before she could dial, a car nearby reversed and straightened up, the headlights flashing into the front of Libby's own car.

Did they realise they had their full beam on? Tiny dots danced in front of her eyes and her vision blurred as the car in question came to a halt, effectively blocking her in.

Libby's pulse quickened as a shadow emerged from the driver's seat. Her mind emptied out, leaving her effectively stuck in the car unable to move as the figure reached the window.

It was Fiona Watkins. Her dark hair was pulled back off her face and she was wearing a very well fitted wool suit, complete with heels.

What did she want now? Had she heard about Libby's visit to the hospital yesterday? Her nerves jangled as she stared at Fiona through the glass. She longed to turn on her engine and drive away but that was no longer possible. She'd crossed the line when she'd destroyed the nail. Which meant whatever Fiona wanted was probably something Libby needed to know about. Foretold was forearmed.

She reluctantly let down the window. 'What's going on? Have the police caught someone?'

'Not that they've told me,' Fiona's voice was cool. Libby hadn't really expected a different answer but all the same, her breath quickened. She just wanted this whole thing to be over. 'But we need to talk.'

'I've already told you everything I know. I wasn't the only one there.'

Fiona scoffed. 'The police officers were both in uniform and seem to think they'll be viewed as traitors if they even open their mouths and you were the first attending.' Her mouth softened, though it seemed more from victory than compassion. 'It's important. And I'll buy you dinner.'

She gritted her teeth. 'Fine. But I can't stay long.'

'Great. The Fox and Fen pub is around the corner. I'll park my car and we'll walk. You're doing the right thing.'

Libby didn't bother to answer as she climbed out of the car and tightened her jacket against the cool night breeze. She might be doing the right thing, but who was it right for?

* * *

The Fox and Fen had been refurbished several years ago. The dark wooden panels had been replaced by pale wallpaper and the heavy wool carpet had been lifted to reveal wooden floorboards. They also did great food and Libby often came with Denise after work. However, what little appetite she'd had, disappeared on the walk over with Fiona.

It was clear the journalist had something on her mind and Libby's anxiety was thundering through her body like a drum. The pub was noisy and the sharp buzz of conversation and the clink and clash of glasses and cutlery swept through her. Several of her colleagues were in the far corner and Libby forced herself to plaster on a smile and wave on her way to the bar.

'I'll get the drinks and food if you want to grab us a table. What will you have?' Fiona asked. Libby swallowed. Usually, she'd only have a soft drink when she was driving, but the overwhelm of Fiona's intensity and the pub itself were muddling her thoughts. She needed to calm down.

'A glass of Pinot Gris, and wedges, thanks,' Libby replied. Fiona raised a pleased eyebrow, no doubt hoping the alcohol might make Libby more talkative. She just hoped it would help her calm down and not do anything stupid, like go running out of the place.

Libby made her way through the busy public bar, bypassing her colleagues, until she found a quieter table. She sat down and tried to regain some composure. And by the time Fiona appeared several minutes later holding the drinks and a table number, Libby was able to give her a polite smile.

'I ordered wedges with sour cream and sweet chilli sauce for both of us.' Fiona slid a wine glass towards her. It was a large one. Libby picked it up and took a sip, letting the alcohol course through her nervous system. Then she met Fiona's eyes.

'What's this really about?'

'I had a call from one of my sources. He said that yesterday, a woman turned up at the lock-up on Lymington Road where Hayley had been held, asking lots of questions. Blonde, in her thirties. Was it you?'

'Are you serious?' Libby pointed to her thick tangle of dark curls. Not to mention the fine lines around her eyes.

'There are such things as wigs and men can be idiots.' Fiona gave a dismissive snort and narrowed her eyes. 'Are you sure?'

'Yes, I'm sure.' She frowned. She had driven past the place a few times but hadn't dared get out of the car. 'Why would I go there anyway? You're the one who's interested in the story, not me.'

'Exactly, and if it wasn't you, then it might mean another journalist is sniffing around. Have you been approached by anyone else?'

'No. And even if I had, I wouldn't have spoken to them,' Libby said, emphasising the last words. They both knew there was only one reason she was here.

'Good,' Fiona retorted, impervious to the dig. 'There's a story here and I want to find it. No way am I going to let some out-of-town journalist or YouTube true crime influencers get in my way.'

'What do you mean?' Libby's mouth went dry and she picked up her wine glass again, finally understanding the implications of what it meant. Someone else was asking questions.

'I mean that not everyone's as scrupulous as I am,' Fiona said without irony. 'You have no idea how many corners some of these hacks cut. And it's only going to make the police close ranks and give us even less information. Not that they seem to be doing much.'

'Does that mean they're no longer investigating it?' Libby tried to drop her shoulders and pretend it was just a casual question. But it was at odds with the rapid beat of her heart.

'Not with any urgency. It seems the lock hadn't been tampered with, which means Hayley wasn't being held against her will. So, when she woke up, she simply opened the door and walked out.'

'What?' Libby's eyes widened and this time she didn't try and hide her surprise. 'That wasn't reported in the papers.'

'Of course not. They can't print it without implying that Hayley had been making the whole thing up.'

'But you don't think that's the case?'

Fiona's lips tightened. 'No. My source told me that forensics couldn't find any prints or hair follicles in the lock-up apart from Hayley's. That's not the kind of thing an amateur could get away with. I mean, it's more than just wearing gloves. It takes planning. A *lot* of planning.'

'So why did they spend so much time planning it and then forget to lock the door?'

'My question exactly. All I can think is that whoever was responsible *did* lock it and someone else came along later and unlocked it.'

'You think someone else knew what was happening and wanted to stop it without anyone getting in trouble?' Libby caught her breath.

'I do, and I intend to find out who. The prick gave her ketamine. No wonder she was so out of it.'

'Shit.' Libby shuddered, horrified at the fate that might have awaited Hayley and surprised at just how much Fiona knew.

'Exactly. Which is why you're here.' Fiona tapped the screen of her phone. 'There was a CCTV camera outside the lock-up but it wasn't filming. However, a nearby neighbour had installed the cameras to stop kids vandalising his rubbish bins. His place is on one side of the private road leading up to the lock-ups, so it's not clear if this is the right person, but it does fit the timeline.'

What?

A thousand volts of electricity raced through her. The sound of it hummed in her ears, pushing away the outside world, and she wasn't sure if she remembered how to breathe. But she had to. It was bad enough that Fiona had dragged her into this but she couldn't afford to let the journalist suspect Libby knew any more than a regular paramedic who had turned up to do a job.

'D-do they know who it is?' Sweat beaded on her collarbone.

'Not yet. Which is why I wanted you to see it. You were at

Steamer Point when Hayley was found. Was there anyone else around? If there is a chance you can identify them, it will be a big break through. Here. Have a look.' Fiona thrust the phone at Libby.

No.

Whatever it was, she didn't want to see it.

But it was too late, and her traitorous eyes focused in on the image. The photograph had been taken at night and wasn't much more than a blur of black and grey pixels. Still, she couldn't look away, and as her vision adjusted, she managed to pick out a shrouded figure. It was from the back and their head was covered in a hoodie, making it even harder to identify who was beneath it.

Libby's throat tightened. On the sleeve were several white dots, as if someone had dripped a paint brush down it. Ice trickled down her spine. The whiteness was brighter than the rest of the photograph. Almost as if the paint had been luminous. Or orange. From a senior school art class. Barely daring to breathe, her gaze dropped down to the cuff, already knowing that would be frayed from an overzealous cat.

Her vision blurred and she looked away. But it was far too late for that. The image was burned into her brain and something in her chest broke open. No. It couldn't be true.

Ever since she'd arrived at Steamer Point and seen Hayley's crumpled body, Libby felt like she'd been thrust into a never-ending nightscape. But that had been nothing compared to the terrible ache that was now creeping into her limbs.

It couldn't be true.

And yet it was.

Because she might not recognise the figure beneath but she knew exactly where the hoodie had come from. She'd last seen it in the back of Sam's car, before she'd washed it and left it in the laundry, waiting for Sam to fold it up and put it away.

'Do you know this person?' Fiona leaned forward, clearly hopeful.

'No.' Her voice was hoarse and raw and she gripped at the table to steady herself. She was melting down. Crumbling. All her years on the job, facing untold horrors, and none of them had prepared her for this. For having to consider that the boy she loved so very much could possibly have done something so terrible.

It swept over her like a wave, pushing the air from her lungs. She had to get out of there. Away from Fiona's sharp eyes and the implications that hung in the air, like fairy lights, flashing in front of her, refusing to go away.

Fiona's phone rang and the journalist swore as she checked the number. 'I have to take this.'

'O-of course. I need to go anyway.' Libby reached for the half empty glass of wine, swallowed it in one long gulp and lurched to her feet, grateful for the chance to escape. Fiona gave her a quick nod then turned away.

Somehow, Libby managed to stay on her feet as she wove her way through the crowd. Once outside, she sagged against the wall of the pub and tugged at the collar of her blouse. She booked a car to collect her, knowing that even without the alcohol, she was in no fit state to drive. Once it was done, she stared at her hands, which were shaking. They were the same hands that Sam had clung to when they were crossing the road. That had washed his hair when he was getting a bath and that had clapped when he'd collected yet another rowing medal.

But now that seemed like a hundred years ago. Another lifetime. And—

Stop it.

She straightened her spine and pushed away the dark thoughts. They weren't helping anyone. Sam was still her son. She was still his mother and that meant she had to get home and find the grey hoodie she'd taken out of Sam's car last weekend. Back when all she had to worry about was a fingernail.

11

TLC Manufacturing was based in an industrial building that had been plonked down in the middle of a farmer's field. Or that's what it looked like to Gemma, who'd been forced to park the rental car further up the laneway, tucked alongside an overgrown hedge. She'd decided that after the Uber incident, a rental car would be a better option, although she hadn't planned on being stuck with a bright-green Fiesta. Not ideal for undercover work.

Still, it didn't seem like the employees who worked for Nathan Curtis had any interest in her or the car, as one by one, they pulled out onto the main road to make their way home for the night. Lucky things. Gemma's legs were cramped, and she longed to get out and stretch, but she didn't dare. She glanced at her phone. It was almost five, but according to the phone call she'd made to Rita, TLC's office manager, the workshop didn't close until seven when the second shift of workers finished.

Of course, Rita didn't know that she had been talking to Gemma. Instead, she thought it was regarding a maintenance request for one of the machines. It had all been a little too easy and Gemma had to assume that the place was poorly run. As for getting Rita's name and number, it had all been there on the company website.

Now Gemma just needed Nathan Curtis to go home so she could try and talk to some of the workers. All part of plan B.

Her original idea had been to confront him about the roller doors that his company had supplied to Stan Butcher for his lock-ups and take it from there.

And she'd almost done it as well. She'd driven up to his beautiful family home first thing in the morning and waited across the street, determined to make him give her the answers she needed. But then a good looking, middle-aged man with short hair suddenly appeared in a pair of shorts and an old T-shirt. He stopped in the driveway to do a couple of stretches before taking off and jogging down the road.

It was him.

She'd seen several photographs of him online but nothing prepared her for her body's visceral response. It was like a knife carving deep into her gut, trying to drain away her life force. Despite herself, Gemma had clutched at her stomach and leaned forward, desperately trying to catch her breath.

It had taken fifteen minutes before she'd managed to compose herself and by then he was long gone. Part of her knew how stupid it was. Even if Nathan Curtis really *was* Colin's son, it didn't mean he was responsible for his father's crimes. After all, Ian had only been five when Colin was caught.

And yet her skin had still crawled at the idea of talking to him.

Was this how victims felt in court when they watched their assailants get sentenced? Gemma had no idea but it was clear she couldn't face him. And so she'd gone back to the hotel and doubled down on her research, looking for everything she could find about Nathan and his mother. But there hadn't been a wealth of information. Just a few photographs of them at public events which had ended up in the newspaper, along with several of him, Libby and their two children, Sam and Sienna.

Ironically, she'd had more luck finding information about Nathan's father-in-law from his first marriage. Adrian Fuller had been a successful sailor, at first making sails before branching out into building industrial warehouses and sheds. Nathan had started working there not long after getting married to Adrian's daughter, Julia, and then eighteen years ago, double tragedy had struck.

Adrian had been killed in a car accident and six months later, Julia had died while giving birth to the twins, leaving Nathan sole heir and owner of the business. Which is why she'd decided to speak to some of his employees in case they had insight into Nathan and his background.

The pitch of her ringtone made her jump and Stephen's name flash up. A jab of guilt nudged at her. She'd sent him a brief email last night and then put her phone on silent. He'd left several messages, each more concerned than the last. If she didn't talk to him soon, he'd probably do something stupid like come down after her.

'Are you determined to give me anxiety? What happened to calling every day?' he said by way of an answer.

'I know you had a busy day at work. I didn't want to bother you.'

'Correction, you knew I'd tell you to come home. Your life is up here, along with your job and your guinea pigs. Who both miss you, by the way. The run in you had with the landlord yesterday could have ended badly. You can't go digging through people's lives based on a theory.'

'It's not a theory. I know what Colin Wallace did.' Her

knuckles whitened as she gripped the steering wheel. The urgency of the situation was echoed by her pounding heart. She knew he meant well but it wasn't his life. His history. It was hers. And she wanted it to be over.

'But the bones were never found,' Stephen reminded her. 'No matter how likely it is on paper, without forensic evidence to link Wallace to the other missing boys, even posthumously, he can't be called guilty.'

Gemma swallowed. She knew he was right. Just as much as she knew even if Nathan was Colin's son, it didn't mean he'd been behind the attack on Hayley. Yes, there was research to suggest certain genes could lead to violent inclinations. But the genes weren't enough. Epigenetics had proven what a difference upbringing and environmental factors made as well. And for most of Ian's life, he'd been away from his violent father.

But... that didn't mean he was innocent.

And it certainly didn't mean she could turn her back on what she'd found. But before she could tell Stephen any of that, a black Audi slid out of the driveway and turned right onto the road. The coast was clear.

'Sorry, I've got to go,' she said and finished the call before Stephen could protest. She waited until the car had disappeared before opening the door.

Show time.

The grass was wet and hadn't been cut in a while and her plain white sneakers were soon covered in muck as she trudged down the road and crossed over to the large industrial building. There were at least ten cars and vans parked up there and the giant doors were open so that light spilled out, along with the screeching sound of metal being cut.

It was still light enough to see two guys in their early thirties standing at the far end of the building, their faces highlighted by the bright glow of cigarettes. They were deep in conversation and judging by the lace-up shoes and button-up shirts, she guessed that they worked in sales instead of on the factory floor. Neither of them had noticed her so she turned towards them.

It seemed as good a place as any to start.

'I wouldn't.'

Gemma cautiously turned to where a small woman wearing a large blue apron was standing, tucked into the side of the building, as if she was hiding. Her grey hair was in tight curls around her head and her legs were covered in thick, gravy-coloured stockings, reminding Gemma of the dinner lady at her old school.

'Wouldn't what?' Gemma walked towards her, nerves giving way to curiosity. The woman was holding her own cigarette between two fingers but didn't seem in a hurry to light it. Instead, she let her gaze drift down to Gemma's ruined sneakers and back up to her denim jacket. Then she shrugged.

'Ask them for a job. They've already done the interviews. And while women might have worked in the factories during the war... this lot have never hired a single lass ever since Mr Fuller passed.'

The dark glare the woman aimed in the direction of the two men suggested that they were only a step above grave robbers. Gemma couldn't blame her. She didn't have any intention of applying for the position but the fact she couldn't because of her sex seemed outdated.

'That's terrible,' she said, trying her best to look disappointed. 'I guess that means you've worked here a long time?'

'Too long.' The woman put the unlit cigarette into the pocket of her work apron and picked up the large, plastic bucket filled with cleaning products. Her break was clearly over. 'Anyway, sorry you wasted your time. You could try the hardware in Poole. My sister-in-law heard they were looking for staff.'

Gemma swallowed as the woman walked away. Then she glanced at the two men again. They were still deep in conversation and hadn't even bothered to look over. And it was clear that the woman had a gripe against Nathan Curtis.

Decision made, she hurried after her, sifting through her thoughts. She'd worked in sales and telemarketing for long enough to know that the best lie was the one closest to the truth.

'I'm not here about the job. I'm writing a book on... *sailing*, and want to speak with people who knew him as part of the research. Is it right that his son-in-law owns this place now? Do you think he would talk to me?'

The woman snorted but didn't slow her pace as they reached the office block. She had a lanyard around her neck and fumbled with the swipe card. 'Him that is too special to get his hands dirty? You'd be lucky if you even got past the door. His secretary is like a bulldog. Thinks she's so far above the rest of us just because she has some fancy degree. Well... if she's so fancy then what the hell is she doing working in this dump?'

It was clear this woman didn't like the place, or Nathan, for that matter. Perfect. Gemma rubbed her chin and feigned disappointment.

'Sounds like there are a few *challenging* people here. What a pity; from what I've discovered, Adrian Fuller was considered a local legend. What do you think he'd say if he was still here?'

'The shock would probably kill him all over again. Believe it or not, this was once *the* place to work, but over the years, I've watched it descend into hell. I'm the only one left from back then and the reason they don't fire me is because I was once known as the TLC girl. They used me in all the advertisements. Of course, that was back when I had a waist. Tiny, I was. Anyhow, as much as I hate it, without my Stanley, an old bird like me can't afford to just walk out. Then again, the way things are going money wise, it might be me who needs that job in Poole.'

The scorn in her voice sent a shiver through Gemma's spine. When she'd come up with the plan to talk to some of Nathan's employees, she hadn't quite expected to hit paydirt so quickly.

'Is it really that bad?'

'Worse.' The woman peered around and then lowered her voice. 'Mr Fuller never wanted his daughter to marry Nathan Curtis. He always said there was something about him that he didn't trust. But she wouldn't hear any of it. She'd fallen for him, hook, line and sinker. Then he died and something changed.'

'What do you mean?' Gemma's voice was urgent as she leaned forward. The thud, thud, thud of her heart sending her whole body on high alert as the evening birdsong and chorus of insects all faded away. Something rippled across the cleaner's face and her eyes darkened.

'Julia loved her father but something changed in her... and not just from the grief. It was like she couldn't bear to be near her husband. There was an incident at the funeral where he put an arm around her but she pushed him away. I was there, and I know what I saw. His wife feared him.'

Gemma let out a startled gasp. 'Did she blame Nathan for her father's accident?'

'It's not for me to say.' The woman fiddled with the lanyard. 'But nothing was right with those two after it, and then when she died while still in the hospital... well suddenly Nathan Curtis, who hardly knew his arse from his elbow, was the owner of this place. The fact he's managed to keep it going for so long is a minor miracle but I can't see it lasting.'

The implication was clear and Gemma's thoughts began to

swim. She'd come down to Bournemouth in the hope of getting answers for herself and the other families whose lives had been in limbo for so long.

But now... this was something even darker. Had Nathan somehow been involved in Adrian's accident? Was that why Julia had tried to distance herself from him? More importantly, did it mean that Nathan had inherited his father's darkness?

Gemma swallowed but before she could say anything else, one of the guys she'd seen earlier walked around the corner. Up close, she knew she'd guessed correctly about his job in sales. He had the smarmy look that so many of them got when they thought they were the king of flogging off whatever roller door or computer software that they'd been hired to sell. And it created some kind of dark, competitive spirit that usually saw them stab their colleagues in the back for any kind of advantage. In other words, they tended to massively suck up to the boss.

Gemma gritted her teeth as his smug gaze narrowed as he took them both in.

'Mo, your break finished ten minutes ago, and who the hell are you?' He turned to Gemma, mouth in a flat hostile line. Yup, definitely a suck up.

'She came about the job. I told her it was filled,' Mo said in a tart voice as she folded her arms in a battle stance. She was quite formidable and suddenly Gemma had no doubt how she'd managed to stay at the place for so many years. 'She's just leaving.'

'Yes. Thank you for your time and for telling me about the place in Poole that is hiring.' Gemma plastered on what she hoped was a jobseeker smile. Then she walked across the car park out to the road where her rental car was waiting. But the whole time her mind refused to slow down.

Nathan Curtis was in financial trouble and at least one person – Mo – seemed to think his father-in-law's death was suspicious. And that his first wife feared him.

12

It was dark when Libby climbed out of the Uber and unlocked the front door. It wasn't often she was in the house on her own. Regardless of what time it was, Nathan or one of the kids would be there somewhere working, gaming, or doing Zoom classes, while occasionally shuffling in and out of their rooms for food. And normally, Libby loved it like that. Her family were the heartbeat that gave her life meaning, and without them there, it took her back to her own fractured childhood. But tonight, she was relieved to have the place to herself.

On the ride home, she'd let herself sink into the dark corner of the back seat as the waves of panicked emotions swirled through her. And all she wanted to do was run a bath and calm down her jangled sympathetic nervous system so that she could work through her tangled thoughts. None of which she could do until she retrieved the hoodie before the police found it. Or Fiona uploaded the CCTV image for everyone to see.

Harriet was lying in wait in the hallway, ready to herd whoever came home in the direction of her food bowl.

'Sorry, you'll have to give me five minutes,' Libby didn't even stop to pet the outraged cat, let alone take off her jacket as she jogged down to the laundry. As well as the usual pile of dirty clothes and towels, there were two baskets of clean washing that needed to be folded and put away. One for Sam and one for Sienna.

It was something she'd instigated last year after realising that most of the washing she did ended up on their floors and would then come back for another wash simply because they were too lazy to put it away. Nothing much had changed but at least the clean washing no longer got done twice.

Her hands were clammy as she reached Sam's basket and sifted through the unfolded pile of T-shirts and jeans before finally reaching the hoodie. It was still there. Her shoulders sagged with relief that Sam hadn't put anything away.

She brought it up to her nose and closed her eyes, breathing in the scent of washing powder, the salt of the sea from all the times he'd thrown it on after surfing, and a faint hint of body odour that never quite came out. It was him. Sam. All the things she loved about him were tangled up in the tattered old piece of clothing.

And it could also be his downfall.

At least the duelling, internal fight she'd been waging with herself was no longer there. It wasn't about whether Sam did or didn't do anything. It was making sure she kept him safe and sometimes that meant being proactive. Like hiring Danny or destroying a nail.

Libby took in one more breath and reluctantly put the hoodie down on top of the washing machine to flatten it out. What was she even looking for? An alibi to prove it wasn't the same hoodie the police had in their files?

She studied the splotches of orange paint and the frayed cuffs, but they appeared innocuous, as did the lint ball of tissue that hadn't been removed from the pocket before the wash. And whatever other evidence that might have been found had now been washed away. Which wasn't a bad thing.

The question was, what did she do with it now?

She quickly dismissed the idea of burning it or dumping it into random skip. But what else was there? Frowning, she retrieved her phone from her handbag, which she'd dumped on the floor by her feet. Maybe there would be—

The sound of the front door creaking open was followed by the dull thud of someone dropping a laptop case on the bottom of the stairs. Nathan. Libby stiffened and snatched up the hoodie as the front door shut, quickly followed by the rustle of fabric as her husband shrugged off his coat the same way he did every night.

All thoughts of destroying the hoodie were gone and she quickly bent down and opened the cupboard under the sink, pushing it right to the back where she kept all the cleaning products. She doubted the rest of the family even knew the cupboard was there. Then she straightened up and went to walk out to greet him but stopped as his voice echoed out down the hall.

'What do you mean she was gossiping with someone tonight? Christ. You know how much she hates me.'

Libby's skin prickled at the low growl in Nathan's voice. He sounded angry.

Who was he talking to? It sounded like a work call but even that wasn't like him to sound so aggressive. And why was he taking the call inside the house when he knew she was at home? He tended to keep the two parts of his life separate. Her pulse spiked as she looked down at the handbag by her feet and her own jacket that she hadn't bothered to take off.

And her car was still at work, waiting until she collected it tomorrow.

He doesn't know I'm here.

'Jesus. Do you think it was a creditor? Rita's been fobbing them off for the last two months, but if someone managed to get Mo talking, there's no telling what she might have said. I should have fired her years ago.'

Creditor?

What kind of creditor would go to a workplace at night and talk to a cleaner?

Libby's heart hammered and she wrapped her arms around her chest. It didn't make sense. She knew that finances had been tight at work, but that was because of how rapidly things were expanding. And even though he'd been looking paler than usual, there had been nothing to suggest it wasn't more than a short-term cash flow problem.

But that wasn't how he sounded now. *Because he thinks he's alone.*

She pressed herself against the wall of the small room, unsure what she was meant to do now. She'd left it too long to step out now, but if she didn't, it would seem like she'd been spying on him. Abruptly, the call ended and his footsteps echoed into the kitchen. The hum of the fridge door being opened, and then the crack and hiss of a beer top, was quickly followed by the wide, glass doors leading to the backyard being pulled open.

He was going to the table at the back of the garden where he always sat. Libby swallowed, pulse still hammering in her ears as she waited until the creaks of the house returned to normal before cautiously stepping back out into the hallway. In the distance were the familiar faint shouts of a commentator and the roar of a crowd. It meant Nathan was watching a football match on his phone.

Harriet was still in her spot at the bottom of the stairs and glared as Libby shrugged off her coat. 'Come on.' Libby nodded for the cat to follow her through to the kitchen so she could feed her.

Everything felt wrong. Like the time her year four teacher made her play a sunflower instead of the role she'd wanted as one of the good fairies. This wasn't the kind of wife she was. She didn't sneak around and spy on her husband. Even by accident.

And besides, she knew better than to assume anything. What was the old saying? That it just made an ass out of U and me. There could be any number of reasons that he was so angry on that call and he would probably tell her about it as soon as he got the chance.

Which was now.

Libby walked over to the fridge and took out an open bottle of wine before plucking a glass from the shelf and joining him out in the garden. His brows tightened in surprise and he immediately turned off the match on his phone.

'I didn't hear your car.'

'I had a glass of wine after work and didn't want to risk driving home. But I was upstairs finishing off some work when you walked in.' She sat down in the other chair and studied his face. His blue eyes were dark, the colour of a winter storm, and his mouth was tight. 'How was your day? You look tired.'

'I'm fine. Just busy.' He rubbed a hand across his eyes, as if trying to erase whatever she was seeing. Her stomach dropped and the terrible sense of discombobulation continued. It was like she was playing a new role. One she wasn't familiar with. He reached for the bottle and filled her glass. Then held his beer, waiting for her to do the same.

She did and the clink of the crystal against the bottle sang out in the night. She put down her glass without taking a sip and studied him. This man she'd been married to for so long. The man who'd chosen her to be the mother of his precious children.

Please. Tell me about the creditors. About the person who went to the office. And why you sounded so angry.

'Did I hear you on the phone when you came in? I had my headphones on so everything was muffled. It almost sounded like an argument.'

'Argument? What?' The tiny lines between his brows tightened and he lifted his bottle to his lips and drained it before finally letting out a short bark of laughter. 'You must have heard me talking to Mick. He was trying to wind me up about next week's darts final. You know how much he likes talking shit.'

'Oh.' Libby managed to mouth the words as the world began to rock. Why had he lied to her? She picked up her glass, more to hide her shock, but Nathan didn't seem to notice as he got to his feet and pocketed his phone.

'And I hate to leave you out here alone but I have to finish the speech for tomorrow night.'

'The fundraiser for the surfing club?' she said, as much to jog her memory as anything. It was an annual event and despite being black tie, it usually descended into a drunken mess. She'd stopped going several years ago. Looking at him, she tried to hold his gaze. 'It could be a good chance to look for other investors. How's that going? Did Tom give you an answer yet?'

'No, and if he doesn't hurry up, he'll miss the chance. I've got another meeting tomorrow, and it's with Grant Hancock, who we've worked with for years. Don't worry, your weekly Pilates class is safe.'

'You know I hate that class, right?' The words ripped at her throat, jagged and sharp, as he pecked her on the cheek and disappeared inside.

Ice spread through her limbs, rendering her powerless to move. She didn't often push him on work, assuming he needed to switch off from it the same way she did. But up until now, she hadn't known he was hiding anything from her. But *what*? Was the business doing worse than he'd let on? Except why wouldn't he tell her? She didn't care about money.

Well... that wasn't entirely true. She loved their life, and their house. But they had enough for what they needed. Nathan owned the house outright thanks to Julia's life insurance and their combined incomes made them comfortable.

She shivered as a tiny thought nudged at the back of her mind. Reminding her that Nathan wasn't the only one lying. Libby hadn't told him anything about Hayley. And why was that? Because she didn't want him to think she was failing in her role as Sam's stepmother. After all, it was one of the reasons he'd wanted to get married.

To make sure that his children didn't grow up with only him for guidance.

But she'd failed spectacularly with both Sam and Sienna. And now Nathan was pulling away from her. Pain shattered through her as the tiny thought expanded and grew, refusing to let her ignore it any longer.

He thinks I'm a bad mother.

* * *

Libby rubbed her eyes. She hadn't fallen asleep until after two in the morning, and by the time she had woken up, Nathan had already left for the day.

And so had Sam, if the trail of toast crumbs and three packets of cereal boxes sitting on the counter were anything to go by. She poured in a splash of milk and stirred her tea. It sloshed over the sides, which only added to the mess. Of course it did. She took a sip and looked at her phone.

There was another message from Dalton Towers Care Home

asking if she could call them. Libby gritted her teeth and made a note in her calendar to do it later in the day. It was probably just about her mother's upcoming birthday. It was the one day of the year that she forced herself to speak with Angela. Or to be more precise, with the husk of a shell that her mother had become. She'd once confessed to Denise that they didn't get on and that even with the dementia, it was difficult to speak with her.

Her friend hadn't been able to understand it. After all, if Angela couldn't remember anything, wasn't that better? Didn't it give them both a chance to form a new relationship? Except for Libby, it didn't work like that. Because if she tried to think of Angela in a different way, it might seem like she'd forgiven her for Todd. Or worse, let Todd think she'd forgotten him and what he'd gone through at their mother's hands.

So, no. There would be no forgetting, and while she would plaster on a smile and take the call with Angela and whatever carer had been stuck on duty with her, she wouldn't enjoy it.

Libby took a long sip of tea to try and push away the darkness that always came with thinking about her mother. Then she waited until it had passed and rolled her shoulders, feeling her equilibrium return.

Once she was more settled, her fingers brushed along the screen of her phone until she found the bank app. She usually left the finances to Nathan but after he'd lied about his phone call, she suddenly realised how little she knew.

They had a joint account that her pay went into and that Nathan would put money into every few months. He'd explained it once, saying that the accountant had recommended it, and Libby had never thought to question it.

She scrolled back through, looking for deposits, but all she could see were her monthly wages. Libby frowned. That didn't make sense. She went back further, until she finally came to a deposit from TLC. But it was from almost eight months ago.

Eight months.

She took a sip of her tea, which was now cold, and went through their other accounts, but there was no sign of any money coming in from Nathan's company. How had she not known? Suddenly, she felt stupid. Like one of those women who never knew their husbands were cheating on them.

And now here she was.

But why wouldn't he have told her? Was he protecting her from something? Or hiding it? She hated that he didn't trust her. Didn't think she was on his team. Because she was. Always. She pushed away the sting of rejection and went over what she'd heard.

If someone managed to get Mo talking, there's no telling what she might have said.

Libby sat up. She'd met the surly cleaner several times over the years and while Nathan found her frustrating because of her loyalty to Adrian Fuller, Libby had a soft spot for her. Then again, she'd seen Mo at her worst: when her husband had suffered a heart attack in the middle of the night and then had to watch as Libby and Jonathan tried to revive him. They had managed to get him stabilised and into hospital, but he'd had a second attack a few weeks later and had passed away, leaving Mo to manage a large mortgage on her own.

It was because of that Libby had suggested Eloise get her in to clean the house a few years ago when her regular cleaner had gone to visit her daughter in America. And while Eloise hadn't found fault with her work, she'd complained a few times about Mo's lack of respect.

Libby shut the banking app and booked another Uber. She didn't know Mo's phone number, but she knew where she lived, and she quickly booked a car before racing upstairs to finish getting ready.

Ten minutes later, her phone beeped to let her know her ride was outside. Libby slung her handbag over her shoulder as she hurried out of the gate. There was a green Fiesta outside the house, with a blonde-haired woman gripping the steering wheel. Libby gave her a vague nod and walked over, her mind full of what she was going to say to Mo.

The muffled roar of a car engine and the squeal of tyres broke her thoughts and she let out an involuntary shout as the car suddenly sped past her and disappeared down the usually quiet street.

Her heart pounded as a white Fiat drove up to her. A middle-aged man gave her a wave and her phone beeped again. It was the car she'd ordered. Which meant that the green Fiesta belonged to someone else entirely. Her skin prickled. Fiona had told her that a woman had gone to the lock-up where Hayley had been held and was asking questions. Blonde and in her mid-thirties.

Was this the same person?

Except why would she be outside her house?

Libby's stomach tightened and her jaw ached from being clenched. She could only think of one reason. That they knew something they shouldn't.

13

Gemma drummed her fingers on the steering wheel and glanced at the cup of coffee sitting on the dashboard. She wanted to drink it, but had no idea how long it would be before she could make a toilet stop. Across the road, a large truck pulled out of the TLC factory. There were two men in the cab and the flat deck was stacked high with scaffolding that had been strapped on.

She'd been parked up outside the factory for the last hour, waiting for Nathan Curtis to leave so she could confront him. Her heart pounded at the thought of even standing near him, let alone talking to him. But there was nothing else for it.

Between the repulsive sales rep who'd caught her talking with Mo last night, and the mess she'd made this morning, it was only a matter of time before Nathan realised that someone was watching him.

It was all her fault. She should never have gone back to the house. But she had, and then Libby Curtis suddenly appeared from nowhere and walked directly towards the car, even giving her a vague wave.

The whole thing had caught Gemma by surprise and she'd

sat there like a stunned idiot, unable to turn the key and start the engine. And then when she finally did get it going, the roar and squeal of tyres would have made any boy racer proud.

Thinking about it caused the heat to travel up her neck to her cheeks. There was no way Libby hadn't noticed her. And, as Gemma had driven away, she finally understood why Stephen had been so worried about her coming down in the first place.

Because when it came to Colin Wallace, Gemma lost all reasoning.

Doesn't mean she saw me.

But of course, she had. Everyone in a three-mile radius must have seen her, or at least heard her. Which meant Gemma could no longer stay in the shadows. It was only a matter of time before Libby told her husband about the blonde woman in a green car, and who knew what would happen then.

The police? Or... worse? And while she could make it easier by taking the car back early and getting another one, her limited resources made that impossible. So, here she was, forced to play her hand, all because of her own stupid mistake.

A second truck emerged an hour later and Gemma leaned back in the seat, the late-morning sun warm on her cheeks. Her eyes began to flutter shut before the sound of a car engine jolted her awake. She shook away the grogginess as a black Audi pulled out of the dirt driveway and out onto the road.

Her hands shook as she turned on the engine. This had to work. She let another car go past her before pulling out and joining the traffic heading towards the coastline. Gemma didn't know Bournemouth very well, which meant if she lost him, she'd be in trouble.

'So, I won't lose you,' she told herself as the car in front of her suddenly turned off, allowing Gemma to close the distance.

Large trees dotted the avenues and the houses sped by until

Nathan suddenly made a sharp left hand turn. Gemma hit the brakes to slow down enough to follow him and her tyres squealed as she found herself on a narrow lane that came to an abrupt halt with a river at the end.

Nathan's indicator flicked on and he turned into the rowing club. Gemma slowed down, but a truck was blocking the entrance to the hotel on the other side of the street, which meant she had no choice but to follow him into the car park.

She grimaced as she slowed down even more. Her palms were sweaty as she gripped at the steering wheel. Following people always looked so easy on the television shows but real life was proving otherwise.

Her heart pounded against her rib cage as Nathan pulled the car into an empty bay and climbed out. There was another empty space, and she carefully reversed into it, knowing that it would be better if she wanted to leave in a hurry.

She fished a cap out of her handbag and crammed it over her blonde ponytail before sliding out of the car. Nathan didn't turn around as he walked past the building and over to where several long boats had been pulled onto the grass.

Next to them a tall boy was doing push-ups, his arms lean but muscular in a white workout top. When Nathan got closer, the boy rolled onto his back and flipped up to his feet. He untied the black hoodie from around his waist and shrugged it on.

She recognised him immediately both from her research and from sitting outside his house for the last two mornings. It was his son, Sam. The rower, with a promise of a bright future. At least that's what she gathered from the online articles she'd read about him. There had been numerous local write ups of him over the years, holding medals and trophies. The most recent ones had even talked about his prospects of getting a scholarship to a prestigious American college for rowing.

Gemma pressed herself back into the shadow of the building as Sam folded his arms.

Seeing them side by side, it was easy to see the connection. They both had tanned skin and a wide mouth. But while Nathan was rugged with short hair, Sam was tall and lean. And neither of them looked like Colin Wallace, who'd been a lot broader, with a thick neck and black hair.

But then her own father had also been large, with wide-set eyes and wild hair that was nothing like her own which was straight. It didn't mean anything.

Sam didn't look happy. His mouth was downturned and his lower lip was protruding in a way that reminded Gemma of a four-year-old about to have a tantrum. He seemed to mumble something but she was too far away to hear. Whatever it was must have annoyed Nathan because judging by the veins in his neck it appeared as if he was trying very hard to hold something back.

Anger. Gemma shivered as Sam gave an indifferent shrug and headed towards a trailer that was stacked high with rowing boats. His father followed him, fists clenched. There seemed to be a heated conversation about something, but it didn't last very long, and she got the distinct impression it was all one sided, with Sam just adding the occasional grunt.

Then Nathan picked up a drink can and threw it to the ground.

The lid split as it hit the concrete and carbonated soda shot up into the air in a fountain. Gemma jumped back, shock reverberating through her as Mo's words came back to her.

His wife feared him.

But Sam hardly flinched. Was it because he was used to his father's explosive temper? If only she knew what they were fighting about. She strained to hear what they were saying, but couldn't because of the wind and the sound of a nearby lorry.

And then Sam snatched up a sports bag from behind the wheel of the boat trailer and sprinted down the path that ran alongside the river. It all happened quickly after that, one minute Nathan was staring at his son's retreating back and the next he had spun around and was marching back to his car. Right past where she was standing.

Gemma didn't have time to look away and his cool gaze swept over her, the anger still there, flickering away in his dark irises.

This was it. Her one chance to confront him. To demand the truth about who he really was and what he knew about his father's secrets. Her heartbeat thundered in her ears with a thump, thump, thump. But her throat was dry and her mouth was filled with cotton wool, making it impossible for the words to come out.

And then he was gone, storming towards his car, the moment gone forever.

No. This wasn't how it was meant to be.

She wanted to cry, but like her silent words, her body wasn't even capable of doing that. Instead, she just stood there, frozen as she watched him go. Shame and disgust hummed through her veins. She'd let everyone down. Her parents, herself, and all the other families caught in the terrible melancholy of unknowing. A vortex that only let them live a half life.

And she couldn't do the one thing they needed her to do.

No. Gemma squeezed her eyes shut and dragged the blurry image of Lucas into her mind. It was from an old photograph that she'd memorised as best she could. Because that was all she had. Anger swelled in her chest, acting as fuel, and life returned to her body. She ran across the car park and scrambled into the hire car.

By the time her shaking hands had turned on the engine,

Nathan's car had roared off, as if he was impatient to be somewhere. Gemma pressed down on the accelerator and followed him, faster than she felt comfortable with, only just managing to keep up as he erratically wove his way through the traffic, not bothering to indicate as he went.

Her brow was covered in sweat by the time he pulled into a long suburban street with matching pebble-dashed, semi-detached houses. Cars were parked on either side and young kids raced up and down on the pavement. Finally, he slowed down before stopping outside one of the houses.

There were no more spaces, so she was forced to keep driving, until she finally pulled into a spot further up the road. She awkwardly twisted around. Nathan was still in his car, staring at a house. His gaze was dark, like a gathering storm.

The hairs on her arms prickled in response to the intensity of his gaze. What was going on? Was he waiting for someone to come out? And more importantly, what had they done to cause such a reaction from him?

Her hand tightened around the door handle. Should she get out to see what he was doing? The question was answered when a large transit van drove past and came to a halt just outside the same house. Curiosity won out and Gemma climbed out of the car as a second van arrived. She increased her pace until she reached a group of neighbours who were huddled on the pavement.

'What's going on?'

'No idea. Must be more reporters, hoping to get a story. They've been turning up on and off since the poor doll got out of hospital yesterday.'

Gemma stiffened. 'W-who got out of hospital?' But even before the woman answered, she knew exactly who was inside the house.

Hayley Terrace.

The girl who'd been kidnapped and held in a lock-up in a very similar style to what Colin Wallace had used.

Gemma let out a shaky breath and almost wanted to laugh with exhilaration. This whole trip hadn't been a wild goose chase, or a random coincidence. She'd been right all along. There was a connection. And every day, she was finding more about it. Not just that Nathan had a temper but that he was now sitting outside the victim's house. Was it like some kind of sick trophy? Or was he planning to try again?

Whatever it was, he *was* involved, and it was getting easier and easier to believe that he was also related to Colin Wallace. Which meant there was no way she was leaving Bournemouth until she had the answers she wanted.

One way or another, Nathan's father would pay for what he had done.

14

Sienna gripped the handlebars of her bike as she came to a stop at the entrance of the Christchurch Rowing Club. It was an ugly, two-storey, box-like building with red brick around the bottom and a veranda on the top. Sienna had always figured the architect hadn't bothered with aesthetics since people would be busy looking out to the River Stour. Still, would it have killed them to have added a few softening features?

The car park was half full and down by the water a bunch of junior girls were doing burpees, all bare legs and tied-back hair as they shouted encouragement to each other. Sienna's muscles burned in sympathy. She'd hardly done any exercise since quitting and couldn't say she missed it.

She rode down to the path, but it was far too busy to navigate all the walkers, so she climbed off her bike and unstrapped her helmet. The black dye had made her hair stiff and brittle and she tried her best to soften it up with her fingers. She probably looked a mess. Which was how she felt. It had been a week since the bonfire and her bones ached with exhaustion.

She shuddered, hating how quickly her life seemed to be

spiralling out of control. And there was only one thing that gave her any kind of peace. But until she could talk to Hayley, that wouldn't happen.

There wasn't much breeze, and the dark water was flat, while the moored boats floated serenely on the surface. She'd grown up on the water thanks to her dad, who'd taught them how to swim, surf and row before Sienna could even remember, and it still felt weird to be back here as an observer, not a participant. Then again, everything felt weird right now.

There was a loud squeal from the nearby playground and Sienna winced. It was full of small kids screaming and running around while their parents were dotted along the edges, talking.

She increased her pace, eager to be away from the noise. Further along the path was a green park, punctuated by wooden seats and the long, sweeping branches from the weeping willows that dotted the riverbank. It was a serene image.

If only that could be her.

What she wouldn't give to simply forget about all the crap going on at school and home right now. All thanks to Tate.

The guy who'd stepped between her and Hayley and blown up their lives.

Sienna's stomach twisted with the irony that she'd managed to let her brother's nemesis get under her own skin so completely. And it had all been for nothing. Worse than nothing. First Sam had stopped speaking to her, and then Hayley, leaving Sienna alone with only her dark thoughts for company.

But that was nothing compared to the guilt that kept jabbing at her temples, refusing to leave her alone. No wonder she was so tired.

She sighed and scanned ahead until spotting a figure casually stretched out on the grass, half concealed under the low hanging canopy of one of the willows. His head was resting against an upturned school bag as if he didn't have a care in the world.

Her idiot twin.

He'd called her midway through her last class and when she hadn't answered, he'd kept calling until she finally had. He was drunk. Very drunk and needed her to drive him and the car home. Part of her had longed to say no. After all, she did have a life of her own and it wasn't like he could just pick and choose to let her use his car when it suited him.

But since her only other plans consisted of cycling to Hayley's house and being told by her mother, yet again, that it was too soon for visitors, Sienna had begrudgingly agreed. Plus, if he was as drunk as he sounded, maybe she'd find out why Hayley had sent him a text message from hospital.

We need to talk.

The words kept pushing through Sienna's skull, sharp and unrelenting. What did Hayley want to talk to him about? Was it about her? And what happened?

Dread coiled in her stomach. She had to find out what Sam knew. And if he was going to tell anyone.

'Hey,' she called out once she was close enough. She rested her bike against the wooden bench.

'Eh! My favourite sister.' Sam raised a hand in the air at her before unsteadily sitting up. His hair was sticking out erratically, while his eyes were glazed over. Had he taken something? Her throat tightened with panic. Libby had told them enough stories about teenagers who mixed alcohol and drugs together and they never ended well. Maybe she should've called her dad.

Except Sam would never forgive her, let alone tell her what was going on. Besides, he was going to some fundraising thing and Libby was doing some saintly thing for their grandmother and pretending that she enjoyed it, rather than just wanting to prove she was good enough. So pathetic.

'Why weren't you at school?' she asked as he lurched to his feet. He stumbled to one side and Sienna had to use all her strength to prop him up.

'I was training. But then realised that was a stupid idea.' He gave a careless wave of his arm, as if the last ten years of his life spent rowing was nothing. 'This is more fun.'

'Getting wasted on your own?' She glanced at his school bag that was still in the grass. Would he fall over if she bent down to collect it? In the end, she decided to use her foot to hook the straps and lift it up.

'Neat trick.' He burped, not making any attempt to take the bag from her. 'Hey, we should go somewhere. You want to hang out?'

Sienna raised an eyebrow as he once again leaned against her, this time almost sending them both crashing to the ground. She had to use both hands to push him back up. 'Think I'll pass. Aren't you meant to be training? Not sure drinking lager should be on your weekly plan.'

'Why? You jacked in rowing and went all emo. Maybe I should wear eyeliner?'

Sienna glared at him. 'It's not the same. I never loved it like you did. And what the hell are you going to tell Dad?'

'As if he'd care. Besides, it's not like he's ever done anything with rowing. He does all his sports for the fun of it. So why should I bust a gut trying to be a professional athlete because he wants me to?' he said indifferently, though it did start to explain why he was so drunk. Since regardless of what Sam said, their dad would care a lot. Which would mean more arguments. What a mess. Suddenly, her brow started to throb with the start of a headache.

'Where's the car?'

'Mayors Mead.' He nodded his head in the direction of the river.

'We need to get you home in case Libby decides to come home early.' She hooked his bag over her shoulder and nudged him in the general direction of her bike. The five-minute walk seemed to take forever but finally they managed to reach the car after navigating their way around all the boat trailers. Letting out a groan, she managed to load him into the passenger side of the car. It took longer to get his seatbelt on than put her bike into the back.... for the second time in as many days.

She climbed into the driver's seat and checked her mirrors before turning on the engine. Metallica blasted out from the speakers and her teeth rattled, along with the entire car. She quickly turned the music off.

'What did you do that for?'

'To save my ear drums,' she retorted before carefully reversing, her hands gripping the steering wheel at ten and two, like she'd been taught. She checked both ways and waited until there was enough of a break in the traffic before turning out onto Wick Lane. By the time she'd reached the lights, Sam was asleep.

Ten minutes later, she pulled into the driveway. The only car there was the beat-up old Toyota that Jonathan insisted on keeping. It seemed weird that a grown man would have a car that most students would turn their nose up at.

But Jonathan was cool. More to the point, if he did know Sam was drunk, she doubted he'd say anything. She carefully parked the car and nudged her brother.

'Wake up. We're home.'

He blinked several times before blearily coming to.

'Thanks,' he slurred and fumbled with his seatbelt. 'I owe you one.'

Sienna twisted around in the seat until she was facing him. There were bags under his eyes and his skin was splotchy and red, making him look about twenty-five. This was her chance.

'Sam, do you know what happened to Hayley?'

At the mention of Hayley's name, his hand dropped down to his lap and his whole demeanour changed. 'You wouldn't understand.'

Oh, no. She *had* said something. The world stopped and Sienna gripped at the steering wheel despite the fact they weren't moving.

'Understand what? You need to tell me what you know. What happened to her?'

He refused to look at her, as if she was contaminated. Guilty. Evil. She was all of those things, and more. But she was also tired and just needed it to be over. She needed the truth. Still her brother wouldn't look at her.

She wanted to shake him. Command him to tell her, just like he used to do when they were younger.

'It's all fucked up.' He yanked open the door and bolted for the house. Sienna watched him disappear inside while the terrible numbness that had been with her since last weekend crept up her neck and wrapped itself around her windpipe. Her throat ached. She couldn't breathe. Couldn't think.

'Everything okay between you two?' Jonathan appeared. He had sawdust in his hair and was carrying a toolbox with him. It was the ongoing joke of the family that her dad ran a manufacturing business but couldn't even bang a nail in straight, which is why he paid Jonathan to do any small jobs around the house. Still, he was more like an uncle than a random friend of her parents. 'Not still fighting about Tate, are you?'

'No, it's all cool.' Sienna swallowed. When Tate had first started flirting with Hayley, Sam had been quick to make his opinions known to anyone who would listen, not seeming to care how embarrassing it was for her. And while she didn't mind Jonathan mentioning it, having to deal with the 'talks' from her parents about safe sex and love triangles had been the worst experience of her life.

As if reading her mind, Jonathan gave her an encouraging smile, his brown eyes catching hers. 'I'm pleased to hear it. By the way, don't suppose you know where Libby is? I was going to take her out for a drink but she's not answering her phone.'

Sienna shrugged. 'Gone around to Grandma's. Something about dry cleaning. And if you want my advice, find yourself a better drinking partner.'

Surprise rippled across Jonathan's features but then he gave her a reluctant smile. 'I don't know what's going on between you two, but you're still family. And that means you need to look out for each other.'

Sienna swallowed. Would he still think that if he knew the truth about what had happened to Hayley? About what she'd done?

But she was saved from answering when Jonathan's phone buzzed. She hurried to her room and lay down on her bed hoping she could close her eyes and never wake up.

15

The house that Nathan had grown up in was a large, picture-book cottage in Talbot Woods. The gravelled driveway was flanked by manicured trees that ran down the boundary line while rose bushes and lavender were spread out around the two-storey, white cottage.

Libby parked in front of the garage that was no longer used and gathered up the dry cleaning she'd brought with her. Her mother-in-law had grown up with money and Libby hadn't been able to get her out of the habit of having all her clothes dry cleaned. Nathan had been amused at her attempts over the years, and not at all surprised that she'd failed. He'd laughingly told her that his mother had a way of always getting what she wanted.

And it was true. But not in the way he made it sound. Unlike Libby's own mother, who'd been manipulative and domineering, for the most part Eloise was sweet and charming, even if she did get overly protective of Nathan and the kids from time to time. Still, Libby could respect that, and at least it showed she cared.

She swung the plastic covered collection of tweeds, woollens and silk over her arm and plastered on a smile to suggest she was being a caring daughter-in-law. And she was since this was one of the many errands she happily did for Eloise. But this afternoon, she could have happily gone straight home for a long bath and a glass of wine.

And, if she'd managed to speak to Mo and find out who the woman was that she'd been speaking to, that's exactly what she would have done.

But the usually chatty cleaner hadn't been at home when Libby had gone to her house earlier in the day and the old man who lived next door said he hadn't seen her since Thursday. Said it wasn't like her to leave her cat for so long. On cue, an old ginger tom had wandered over and rubbed her leg, hoping for food.

Libby had given him a pat and then written Mo a quick note and slipped it through the letterbox, asking her to call as soon as she could. Then she'd asked the old man for Mo's number. He didn't have it but had been happy to take the five pound note she'd given him to buy cat food.

She still hadn't heard from Mo by late afternoon and since Nathan wasn't answering his phone, she'd called the office and spoken to Rita, who'd taken great delight in telling Libby that Mo hadn't come in for work and that no she couldn't hand out personal information without breaching the privacy act.

It had left her at a bit of a standstill until she remembered Eloise would have it.

Usually Libby would have just called, but her mother-in-law had a shrewdness to her and Libby didn't want to appear too desperate. The thought almost made her laugh since instead, she'd called up the dry cleaners and paid an extra fifty pounds for them to finish the order early. *Not desperate at all.*

Taking a deep breath, Libby went up to the door and grimaced to see it was open despite the fact it was almost six at night. Eloise refused to believe that anyone would take advantage of her.

'It's me.' Libby stepped into the mudroom and hung the dry cleaning on one of the hooks before heading further into the house. The lounge was painted white with a gold velvet sofa and two wingback chairs flanking one of the many Turkish rugs that her mother-in-law had collected over the years, while the walls were filled with a selection of artwork. But apart from the photos on the dresser, and the collection of rugs, there was none of the usual light debris of a life that made a place feel like a home.

It was as if the house itself wouldn't let Eloise relax and be herself. Nathan once said she'd hoped to have a large family but after his father died, she never even considered dating, which left the two of them to rattle around in the large house designed for more.

It was why he was so keen for Eloise to move into somewhere smaller, maybe a retirement village. But despite the practicalities of it, Eloise wouldn't entertain the idea and seemed to content to live her Miss Havisham type existence, only without the wedding dress and rotting food.

Her mother-in-law was sitting on the sofa, immaculately dressed in a blue navy skirt and a crisp white blouse. Her grey hair was pulled back to show her long neck and stunning cheekbones. Her eyes were the same ocean blue as Nathan's but her skin was porcelain compared to his sun-weathered complexion. There weren't many photos of Eloise when she was younger but Libby knew she must have been a knockout.

'My dear, so lovely to see you.' She put her book down on a side table.

'You too, but you shouldn't leave the door unlocked. It's not safe. And I have a key, so I can let myself in,' Libby reminded her, though she knew it wouldn't do any good.

'I know, but it seems so silly to be scared in my own home.' Eloise looked up, her gaze sweeping past Libby and out into the hallway, as if waiting for more people to walk in. Nathan. Sienna and Sam. But there was only silence that followed Libby into the room.

Eloise's mouth flattened into a frown, clearly disappointed that the rest of the family wasn't there. When she'd called earlier to say she was popping round, she hadn't accounted for the fact Eloise would want to see her son and grandchildren.

'Sorry, it's just me tonight. I got a call from the dry cleaners and your order was ready early and I know you're going to the opera on Tuesday and would want your coat back,' Libby said, trying not to react to Eloise's crestfallen face. 'Nathan's at a fundraiser and the kids are studying. I hope you're not disappointed.'

'Don't be silly. I don't expect them to visit me all the time. They have their own lives. But tell me, how are they doing? Is Sam...' She tailed off, and though her voice was polite, there was a hint of steel in it. As if all of Sam's actions could somehow be blamed on Libby. Now it was her turn to be disappointed. She had hoped that they'd moved past this conversation.

Libby swallowed, trying to remind herself that was just Eloise's way. And besides, Libby couldn't fault her, since didn't they both want the same thing for Sam? For him to thrive and be happy?

'I've got him a tutor. Sam wasn't happy about it, but Danny's great and I think they'll get on well,' Libby reassured her.

'I see,' Eloise said, though her expression was still troubled. 'You know I don't like to interfere but break ups can be *tricky*. Especially when it comes to men. It's important that they aren't given too much rope. They need guidance to stop them from being their own worst enemy.'

Libby leaned forward as the twin spikes of curiosity and jealousy battled it out.

It was an unspoken rule that they didn't talk about Nathan's first wife much. And while Eloise occasionally mentioned her, she'd never told Libby about what Nathan had been like in those months after Julia's death.

Curiosity won.

'Is that what happened to Nathan after she died?'

Eloise blinked and then let out a soft laugh. 'Oh, no. He didn't destroy any gardens or try and drown his sorrows like Sam did...' She broke off and the smile faded. 'He just went in on himself. I wasn't sure he'd ever be happy again. And then you came along.'

Libby let out a slow breath as Eloise's words washed over her, helping her reset the picture in her mind that had always been there. The four of them happy together in their wonderful life, with Eloise close by. And that's what it would be. As soon as this whole thing with Hayley was put to bed.

'Thank you. Oh, and before I forget, I've been so busy lately that I haven't had a chance to give the house a good spring clean. I was thinking of asking Mo... but I don't have her number. Would you mind if I get it from you?'

Eloise's smile flattened in a tight line as she studied Libby. 'You know, I could speak to Rosetta. She might have room in her schedule and is very thorough.'

'Usually, I would take you up on that, but I bumped into Mo a few weeks ago and all but promised the job to her. So stupid that I didn't think to grab her number. Of course, I could just ring Rita at TLC on Monday, but I was hoping to get it all sorted tomorrow.'

Eloise closed her eyes as if weighing it up and Libby had to resist the urge to just go to the old-fashioned address book that was sitting on the stripped pine writing desk by the window.

Especially since it wasn't like she was asking for something huge. Just a phone number.

Except it was huge. Because the sooner she called Mo, the sooner she could find out just who the woman asking questions was, and what she wanted. And then she could turn her attention to Nathan and why he had lied to her.

After what seemed like eternity, Eloise opened her eyes and nodded to the address book in question. 'It should be in there, but if you do use her, make sure to check under the beds in case she hasn't done it properly.'

'Thank you, I will,' Libby promised as she stood up and flipped through the book until she found Mo's number. She took a photograph of it with her phone, pleased that the rapid thumping of her heart had settled back to its normal rhythm. 'Now, let me go make a pot of tea. And don't worry, I know where the good biscuits are.'

'You are sweet,' Eloise said as Libby headed out to the hallway and through to the next room. The kitchen had been remodelled several years ago but still had its old-world charm with a huge, ceramic butcher's sink, a collection of copper pots and an Aga.

A tea tray had already been set out, including three more cups, as well as a plate of Nathan's favourite Bakewell tarts, scones with jam and cream and the delicate club sandwiches Eloise insisted on buying at great expense from the local delicatessen. Another stab of guilt coursed through her. Eloise had expected them all.

Next time, she would insist that they all came with her. Libby filled the kettle and quickly transferred Mo's number into her address book and called it. But there was no answer. Libby left a brief message and then followed it up with a text.

Once that was done, she walked over to the oak dresser. It was the one part of the house that Eloise allowed a little junk to collect, and Libby always gravitated there, mainly because of the baby photos of Nathan.

They were propped up between a collection of porcelain cups and saucers. And she went to her favourite one, taken when he was about four. She picked it up, like she always did, and studied it. He was standing next to a red brick archway, tiny hands grasping at the bricks and one foot raised, already determined to climb it. His mouth was set in a line of concentration and his eyes gleamed as if trying to work out how high he could get.

He was still the same, turning everything into a challenge, from his training schedule through to how he attacked the garden.

The shrill sound of the kettle boiling broke her thoughts and she put the photo back, her hand brushing against a letter sitting on the lower shelf of the dresser, with the familiar green logo of Nuffield Health in the corner. It was a private hospital in Bournemouth and before she could stop herself, Libby picked up the letter and scanned it. It was to confirm the date for Eloise's hip replacement surgery.

What hip replacement?

Her fingers tightened on the paper and it creased down one side. This made no sense. She'd been encouraging Eloise to get a consultation about her hip, which had been getting increasingly bad since a fall several years ago. So why didn't she know about it?

Was it yet another thing that had slipped through the net?

There was a cough from out in the other room, which Libby suspected was Eloise's polite way of telling her she'd been in there too long. She quickly poured the hot water into the teapot carried it all in, including the letter.

'You're having your hip done?' Libby said without preamble. 'Why didn't you tell me?'

'I got the appointment a few months ago and you had your hands full with both of the...' Eloise trailed off and Libby's shoulders tightened once again at the unspoken words.

The children.

Eloise thought Libby couldn't cope. Or didn't approve of *how* she was coping. Libby swallowed.

'Does Nathan know?'

Eloise shook her head. 'I know you're both busy. By the way, you haven't told me how your own mother is? Have you had an update lately?'

The heat returned to Libby's cheeks as if she'd been slapped. And while she doubted Eloise meant to do it intentionally, it still stung. She knew Nathan and Eloise didn't really understand her own complicated relationship with Angela. Or the torment her mother had put her and Todd through. And maybe she should have trusted them, but talking about it had never been easy, because it was paramount to admitting her failures as a daughter and a sister.

She dug her nails into the flesh of her arm and mustered a smile. 'I spoke to the nurse. She's not doing so well. But they're hoping the new medication might calm her down a bit. Now, stop changing the subject. We need to talk about your operation. You'll have to stay with us while you recover.'

'Nonsense. You and Nathan have your own lives. You don't want to be running around after an old woman,' Eloise protested. 'I was going to ask if you could recommend anyone to come and help me for a few weeks.'

'I'm sure I can,' Libby said, knowing Eloise was extremely well off, and could afford to hire a carer. 'But all of your bedrooms are on the first floor, whereas our own guest room is on the ground level.'

'That's very kind of you, Libby,' Eloise said before her voice began to shake. 'But I don't want... I don't want it to look like I can't cope.'

'You don't want Nathan to use it as a reason for you to sell the house,' Libby finished. It was something he'd mentioned several times, but she'd never given it much thought up until now, just assuming it was because he was worried about her.

But was there another reason? After all, he was Eloise's only son and the house was worth a great deal of money. But then, if he really did need money, why didn't he just ask his mother? Libby knew she had an extensive portfolio.

Unless he had asked.

Nathan was reserved with most people but he and Eloise were close. Had he already mentioned his worries to her? Did she know something that Libby didn't?

'Now I sound like a silly old lady.' Eloise choked, her eyes bright with tears. Libby went over to her and dropped down into a crouch, so she was eye level, then took Eloise's hand in hers.

'Never. And I swear that Nathan won't think that. He's just been... a little stressed,' she said, heart pounding as she tried to sound casual. 'With his expansion plans. Did he mention them to you?'

Eloise's tears evaporated and she withdrew her hand. 'Yes, and I told him it was a terrible idea. If he wants to build a second site, then do it somewhere down here. The North is a dreadful place.' Her face went tight as she casually dismissed half of the United Kingdom in one judgemental swoop.

'Oh.' Libby swallowed back her questions, knowing that once her mother-in-law had made her mind up about something, she didn't tend to change it. Instead, she poured the tea and spent the next half hour talking about the upcoming opera, next door's dog who refused to stop barking and the poor quality of bananas, before Libby slipped upstairs to put away the dry cleaning and give the bedroom a bit of a straighten. Eloise was waiting for her in the kitchen when Libby returned.

She'd packed the Bakewell tarts and scones into an old wicker basket and held it out.

'You'd better take these or they'll go stale.' Her face was set in a stoic, upbeat mask that made Libby determined that next week, all four of them would visit. 'And I've put a little something in to go towards Sam's tuition. Now, before you say anything, I know Nathan doesn't like it when I help. But it seems silly not to be able to give you something for my grandson and I have more than enough money.'

Libby pressed her lips together, knowing that 'a little something' would be a pile of well-cared for fifty-pound notes tucked into an envelope. While she loved Nathan's refusal to lean on his mother, she also understood Eloise's need to show her support. And, of course, the fact that mother and son were both as stubborn as each other made her heart full.

'Okay, but no more.' She picked up the hamper and they both walked to the front door, Eloise leaning slightly on her stick. The night sky was bright with the moon and stars adding light to the shadowy garden. Libby put the basket into the back seat and transferred the slim envelope of cash into her handbag.

A gust of wind swirled up, almost pushing her towards the car. Laughing at the unexpectedness of it, Libby pushed the hair out of her eyes, just as an engine accelerated. Her head snapped around, half expecting to see the green Fiesta again, but instead it was an oversized motorbike.

She had to stop being so jumpy. Then she frowned. If the same woman had turned up at Nathan's work and then their house, was it a stretch to think she'd been to Eloise's house as well? Her skin prickled and she turned back to her mother-in-law.

'Have you seen a green car?'

'Green car?' Eloise paused and titled her head before frowning. 'Not that I can recall. Why? Is there a reason I should have?'

Libby forced herself to give a casual shrug. 'No. I just remembered that the last time I was here, I saw a car blocking the driveway across the road. I wanted to make sure no one had done the same to you,' she said, slightly in awe of how easily the lies came to her. 'Let me know if it does happen.'

Eloise gave her a thoughtful glance, before nodding. 'Of course. Now off you go and don't worry about me.'

Libby started the engine and reversed out of the driveway, stopping to try Mo's number again. But it went straight through to voicemail, which meant Libby was still none the wiser about who the woman was. Or what she wanted.

16

Gemma tried to ignore the black smudges under her eyes as she stared at herself in the steamed mirror on Friday night. Then again, it wasn't like she'd come to Bournemouth for a spa week. She was here to get answers. She finished drying herself off and slipped into her favourite tracksuit bottoms and an old T-shirt that she'd stolen from an ex-boyfriend. Once that was done, she wrapped her hair in a second towel, promising herself to style it later. Not that she would, but it felt better to pretend.

She picked up the half-empty wine bottle and poured herself another glass before sitting down at the square table that was pushed up against the wall of the hotel. It had become her makeshift desk and was covered in notes and articles that she'd downloaded from the Internet, as well as every newspaper that had covered Hayley's case.

After the exhilaration of witnessing Nathan Curtis's rage and then the dark fury in his eyes as he'd sat outside Hayley Terrace's house, she'd been left feeling wrung out and exhausted. And totally unsure of what she was meant to do next.

Part of her had wanted to call Stephen. To thank him for the videos he'd sent of Thelma and Louise going about their daily guinea pig lives. And to ask for his advice. But she already knew what his answer would be. Come home. Stay out of it.

But it was much too late for that.

Which left her stuck, trying to decide on her own. A slight headache had formed at the back of her skull, which she'd tried to shake off with a shower. But it was still there, hence the wine. It had to be worth a shot.

Gemma swallowed another mouthful. She needed to think. It wasn't enough to just believe that Nathan was really Colin Wallace's son. She needed proof. And then she needed to force him and his mother into telling her what they knew. That's where it all got a bit blurry.

Her phone was on the table, and she picked up, hoping for a text message from Mo Quigley. It hadn't been hard to find the outspoken cleaner's full name. It was just a quick internet search through the old TLC advertisements and there she was. Definitely skinnier, but the same defiant eyes that had kept her in the job for so long. It had been just as easy to get her number as well, from a well-meaning woman who had once worked with Mo.

When this was all over, Gemma wondered if she should start a consultancy to help people be a bit more aware of what information they give away. After all, while she knew her own intentions were good, that wasn't the same for everyone.

Why hadn't she returned her message?

Gemma closed her eyes. Another option was to confront Nathan's mother, Eloise. To make her admit that she was really Marion Wallace. And while she didn't doubt she could do it – after all, the woman was old and lived on her own – she was worried she'd have the same body breakdown as she'd experienced with Nathan.

She'd already messed things up twice, first with Mo and then when she'd been spotted by Libby Curtis. She couldn't afford another mistake. She toyed with the stem of her wine glass. Damn Libby for coming out when she did and forcing her hand. That's what had put her in this position, and—

A thought hit her as she sat up.

Maybe Libby Curtis was the way in. After all, wasn't this how the whole thing had started? Not only did she attend Hayley at the scene, but she was an outsider. Were there things she'd noticed about Nathan and Eloise? Anything to suggest that they had been living a lie?

She pushed her glass away. Did that mean Libby might believe her? Might even be an ally? After all, Gemma had witnessed Nathan's temper first-hand. And Mo had told her that his first wife had feared him and wanted to leave the marriage.

Did Libby feel the same? It was possible, and hope flared through her. Spurred on by the people behind her, whose need for answers and longing for it to be over matched her own.

Gemma got to her feet and searched for her coat. She should go there now and talk to her. After all, she'd followed Nathan home and then watched as he'd been picked up in an Uber and dropped off at a fancy motel for a fundraiser. Libby might be in the house on her own.

Then she caught sight of herself in the mirror. Her hair was wrapped in a towel, her eyes were red from fatigue and wine and she was wearing a tracksuit. Probably not the best look. And more importantly, this wasn't just something she could wing. She'd learnt that the hard way with her encounter with Nathan. This time she needed to be prepared.

Which would mean research. After reading the initial article that Fiona Watkins had written for the *Bournemouth Globe*, Gemma hadn't bothered to investigate Libby further. Instead, she'd purely seen her as a possible link to Marion and Ian Wallace. She could see now that it had been a mistake.

Wine forgotten, Gemma dragged her laptop over and got to work.

She hit a couple of walls, but she'd spent too many hours working in a call centre and learning how to get behind their internet firewalls, along with online shopping and games, to pass the time, and she knew a trick or two.

She flicked on one of the VPNs she subscribed to and changed browser and ten minutes later she'd found a copy of Libby's birth certificate. Gemma chewed her lip as she went over it. She was born in North London and her parents were Angela Hislop and Ethan Wright. She kept on searching until she came up with a third name. A brother. Todd Hislop, who'd died at fifteen.

Her whole body went stiff as she searched for the cause of death. Excessive blood loss caused by cuts to his wrists. Gemma's head started to pound. Hell. Libby Curtis's brother had committed suicide. It was a terrible thought. Sucking in a breath, she continued to search. There wasn't much but she did find a brief notice in a local paper in 1997 about an upcoming court appearance for Angela Hislop with regards to an outstanding debt.

Interesting. Gemma clipped the article and dragged it into the folder she'd created. She then found a more recent photo of an arts and crafts show from a retirement home in Hull, that named the residents, including Angela Hislop. A place called Dalton Towers Care Home. The event was held a couple of years ago, but it was worth investigating to see if Angela was still there. After all, just because Gemma's own relationship with her parents had been non-existent didn't mean that everyone else was like that. Libby and Angela could be close. Maybe Todd's death had brought them together? And if they were, then talking to Angela could be well worth Gemma's time. She could find out if Libby had mentioned anything about Nathan. She clicked on the contact form and started to type.

Because when it came to the truth, Gemma refused to leave any stone unturned.

17

Libby stepped into Tesco and walked straight to the stack of baskets, ignoring the trolleys altogether. It had been a long day and the last thing she felt like doing on a Sunday night was standing in the kitchen. Which meant pre-packaged lasagne it was. Besides, if she added parmesan cheese and a homemade salad, it might be almost considered home cooked.

She dropped the family-sized meal into her basket and headed for the alcohol section to pick up Nathan's favourite Australian cabernet. Then she picked up a bottle of chardonnay as well, hating herself for having to resort to food and alcohol to help her have a conversation with her husband.

But it wasn't something she could ignore.

On her way to work that morning, she'd swung by Mo's house but there was still no sign of her. The ginger tom had been napping on the step; she opened the tin of Harriet's food that she'd brought with her and fed him before posting another note through the cleaner's front door.

She still hadn't had a chance to talk to Nathan either. It was sometime after one in the morning that he'd stumbled in from the fundraiser and he'd been gone again before she'd woken up. That wasn't a surprise, since his favourite hangover cure was surfing, and she'd become enough of a surf widow to know when the wind was good.

At least he'd be in a good mood.

It would help. Bile churned in her stomach at what was to come. Not because she feared him but because she hated that he hadn't trusted her. They were meant to be a team. That was more important to her than anything. And after years of being dragged around by her mother, without being given a say in what school she went to, or what city they lived in, Libby wanted to belong. She *did* belong. And she wasn't a kid any more. Once, she might not have been able to stand up to her mother, but now she had a voice and she would use it to remind Nathan that he didn't need to keep secrets from her.

'You going to stand there all night, love?' a voice said from behind her, and Libby blinked, realising she was still standing in front of the same wine display.

'Sorry,' she mumbled and hurried to the front of the store. It didn't take her long to go through the self-checkout and out into the early-evening gloom. The wind had picked up and Libby used her spare hand to stop her hair from flying in all directions.

Still, walking against the wind was practically a full workout. She was panting by the time she reached the car and her arm ached from the two bottles of wine and lasagne in her shopping bag. She put it down on the ground and pushed a strand of dark hair out of her eyes as she fumbled for her car keys.

A sharp light glinted in the corner of her eye, and she glanced across the roof of her own car to a late-model Fiesta.

A bright-green, late-model Fiesta.

It was the same car that had been parked outside her house yesterday morning. Something visceral swept down her spine, turning it to ice as she watched a woman in her mid-thirties climb out. She had familiar blonde hair and a pair of fitted jeans that hugged her slim legs.

Libby just stared at her, unable to move or speak.

Her. The one who'd visited the lock-up. More than likely the one who'd been speaking to Mo on Thursday night. The one who knew something about Libby and her family that she shouldn't know.

The woman stared back at her, unspeaking as a swirl of energy shifted between them like invisible threads binding them together, while pushing away the outside world. Libby narrowed her eyes and studied her. She was young. Maybe early to mid-thirties with brown eyes and blonde hair that had been cut into a shoulder-length bob, more for convenience than fashion. In return, the woman seemed to be conducting her own examination and Libby let out an irritated growl. Enough.

'Who are you?' she used the same sharp tone she sometimes did with patients who were drunk or on narcotics. A shock tactic that could sometimes help break through the fugue state. The woman flinched.

'My name's Gemma Harrington. We need to talk.'

'Whatever it is, I can't help. Now, if you'll excuse me, I'm already running late.' She tightened her grip around the car keys in her hand. She'd done several self-defence courses over the years, to help with the more dangerous elements of her job, but she'd never had to use any of them in her daily life. But she would if she had to.

It was bad enough that Fiona had questioned her about what happened, but she couldn't risk it again. Her name couldn't keep being linked to what happened to Hayley Terrace. Her *family* couldn't be linked to it.

The ice in her spine splintered and sent shards of pain throughout her entire body.

It had to stop. She couldn't bear the idea of her world falling apart. It had happened once before when her brother had killed himself and she'd barely managed to pick up the pieces. She couldn't do it again.

'Please, Libby. I saw the article in the newspaper last week and there are lots of things you don't know about it.' The woman – Gemma – held up her hands as if to show she came in peace. It didn't work and Libby took a step back towards her own car.

All her instincts had been right. Somehow, this stranger knew what had happened. About Sam. About—

She cut herself off. It didn't matter what she did or didn't know or think. She wasn't the police. Just a person trying to harass her in a car park.

'I have nothing to say. One newspaper story was enough.'

'I'm not a journalist.' Gemma gave a sharp shake of her head, blonde hair catching in the wind that was circling them. Then she stepped forward, her hand outstretched, as if to grab Libby's arm. 'I'm sorry. I didn't mean to scare you.' She stepped back, colour rising in her cheeks.

'Then stop stalking me,' Libby snapped, the emotions of the week finally spilling over. Why was this happening? This constant onslaught. Was it a test? Karma? Someone's idea of a cruel joke? All Libby knew was that she couldn't keep going like this.

'You're right.' Gemma's body stiffened as if she'd been hit. 'I'm sorry. I didn't mean to... well... it's hard to explain. If you could give me five minutes.' There was a pleading tone in her voice and

Libby, who'd spent her entire career trying to help people feel better, let out a low growl.

'You have three.'

Three minutes for Libby to find out what she knew. And how it would affect her family.

Gemma nodded as two red dots formed on her cheeks. 'I-I run a blog on a man called Colin Wallace. He was convicted of kidnapping a young boy over forty years ago, and while the boy escaped, it's still believed Colin was responsible for the deaths of at least twelve other boys, who all went missing in the same part of Yorkshire over a four-year period. But Wallace died without ever confessing to his crimes.'

Wait, what? Her jaw slackened in confusion. Had Gemma purposely used Libby's own shock tactic to try and throw her? But as she studied the other woman's face, there was no hint of misdirection. Whatever she was talking about, she believed it.

But who was Colin Wallace? And how did he fit into what happened to Hayley? Especially if he was dead. Then she remembered Fiona talking about all the influencers and true-crime bloggers that had been turning up to report on Hayley's attack.

Was that why she was here? To try and pin the crime to others that had happened?

'You've got the wrong person.'

'No, I haven't.' Gemma's eyes glistened and her hands began to shake. Ah. Now she understood. Libby had seen enough trauma reactions to know one. Something about Hayley's kidnapping had triggered Gemma and sent her spiralling. Despite herself, Libby shivered in solidarity. She knew it because the same thing had happened to her. But she wasn't the one to help this woman.

She had enough real problems of her own without getting

dragged into a crazy conspiracy theory. And the three minutes was up.

'I have to go.'

'Wait. Let me finish.' Gemma's voice shifted and the uncertainty was gone. Replaced by a firmness that stopped Libby from moving. 'The details of Hayley's kidnapping have several similarities to what Colin did to his victims, and there's growing research that certain genes can increase erratic, violent behaviour.'

'What are you saying?' Her arms fell back down by her sides and a lump formed in her throat.

'I'm almost certain that Colin Wallace's son is your husband, Nathan.'

The world stopped and silence bled out around them. It blocked out the swirling wind and engine noises from the nearby road until there was only one thing that Libby could hear.

I'm almost certain that Colin Wallace's son is your husband, Nathan.

The words stabbed in her mind like a tattooist needle. She wanted to swipe at the air around her, to drag them away, but her limbs were like lead and all she could do was stare at the other woman.

It had to be a joke.

It *was* a joke. Gemma was obviously delusional, and for some reason, had decided to fixate on Libby and her family. Was that why she'd been outside the house? And why she was seeming to imply not only that Nathan's father was a killer, but that somehow, it had affected Nathan. Tarring him with the same brush.

Except there was no brush. It was all a lie. Nathan's father, Keith, had been a good man. A loving father and husband.

There's growing research that certain genes can increase erratic, violent behaviour.

The terrible thought formed before she could stop it and she shook her head, trying to dislodge it. But it was too late.

All she could think of was Sam's aggressive attack on Andi's front lawn. Nathan's short fuse that appeared from time to time. Even Sienna's temper flare ups.

No. It didn't mean anything. Except why did everything keep going back to Hayley Terrace? It was like Libby was being taunted with it. Would things have been different if she hadn't agreed to the shift? If she'd simply gone home and heard about the attempted kidnapping on the news, like everyone else? Would she have spent Saturday night having a glass of wine with Nathan and waking up on Sunday, slightly hungover, before spending the day relaxing around the house?

And would the rest of the week have followed the same trajectory? Unfolding the same way it always did. A comfortable blur of work, family and laughter. The kind of days and weeks and months that Libby had used to weave herself a family.

It must have shown in her face and Gemma gave her pleading glance.

'I know it's a lot to take in.' Her voice was almost apologetic. As if she'd just told a child that Santa Claus and the Easter Bunny weren't real. As if it was a necessary evil that gave her no pleasure. 'But Colin Wallace was a monster. He kidnapped a ten-year-old boy and held him for forty-one days in a lock-up in the middle of the woods. He was only caught because Colin's wife followed him one day and found the boy.'

Her throat ached and she began to sway.

The compounding thoughts and worries she'd been having were nothing compared to this. It was like moving from black and white to colour. A whole new universe that was trying to impose itself in her mind. But to let it in meant she'd have to let something else out. And she couldn't do that.

She'd fought for this life. This wonderful life. After everything her own mother had dragged her through. The pain of losing Todd. Of almost losing herself in the aftermath. But she'd fought back and now had everything she wanted. She wasn't going to give it up on the whim of a stranger.

'Why are you telling me this?'

'Because no one has seen or heard from Colin Wallace's widow and son in almost forty years. They moved to Spain not long after the trial and seemed to disappear. And then I read about what happened to Hayley Terrace. The kidnapping and the escape from the lock-up. But what really made me come down here is your husband's last name. Curtis. Before she was married, Marion Wallace's maiden name was Curtis.'

'That's it? You've gone to all this trouble over a last name which isn't even uncommon?' The steadily rising panic that had been creeping up her chest, squeezing in on her lungs, disappeared as if someone had thrown cold water over it.

Gemma flinched. Obviously not the only one to get a reality check. 'No, of course not. But the ages do add up, and the block of lock-ups where Hayley had been taken to all had brand-new, identical doors that came from your husband's company, TLC Manufacturing.'

'TLC has been a Bournemouth institution for forty years. It would be hard *not* to find a garage door made by them,' she retorted. Gemma's cheeks reddened and she was once again clutching her hands.

'Please, I know it sounds far-fetched but there's a connection. I spoke to a woman there, Mo. And she told me some things. We could go and talk to her together—'

At the mention of Mo's name, Libby stiffened. She'd been surprised that she still hadn't heard back from the cleaner, but it hadn't occurred to her she might have met with foul play. But the fact that no one seemed to have seen her since Thursday night, when Gemma had spoken to her, caused her skin to prickle.

'If you did anything to hurt her...'

'Hurt her?' It was Gemma's turn to stiffen. 'Why would I do that? She was helping me. And she told me things about Nathan —'

'Stop.' Libby held up a hand.

She'd heard enough. Even if Gemma didn't have anything to do with Mo's disappearance, she was clearly unhinged.

Nathan's father had never been in prison. He was from Devon and had owned a successful real-estate agency before dying when Nathan was ten years old. He'd been a good man.

She had no idea who Gemma really was but she obviously had some kind of vendetta against Nathan. Had she worked at TLC Manufacturing and been fired? Or had something else happened to send her spiralling? It was impossible to say but the fact she was using Hayley's kidnapping to further her own cause was just cruel.

Libby picked up her bags of shopping and stepped past her, forcing Gemma to move further away.

'Shit. I've messed this up. But I swear I'm not crazy.' Gemma fumbled for a card and pressed it into Libby's coat pocket. 'Please. At least look up Colin Wallace, or better yet, ask your husband. Ask him about driving to Hayley Terrace's house. About fighting with your son. I'm begging you. Your husband isn't who he says he is. You need to find out the truth. Open your eyes and stop protecting them.'

Libby began to sway.

How dare this woman talk to her like this.

Talk about her *family* like this.

The only ones she needed to protect them from was Gemma.

Libby's boiling-hot anger was replaced with cool rage and she straightened her back; her resolve fixed.

'If I see you near any of us, I'll be calling the police.'

Libby plucked the card from her pocket and thrust it back at the woman before climbing into her car and starting up the engine. And she would call the police. She would do whatever it took to keep her family safe.

18

Libby stared at the computer screen in the small office that she and Nathan shared, too late realising her mistake. Last week, her search history had involved losing weight and looking at bikinis for women over forty, and it never even occurred to her that she might not want anyone to see what she was doing. But in the hour since she'd returned from the supermarket, she'd gone straight to the computer and started researching. And that was despite spending the whole car ride home refusing to even give Gemma's wild accusations the time of day.

But they were like an ear worm going around and around in her head.

Since then, she'd discovered that Gemma Harrington did indeed run a very small blog dedicated to Colin Wallace, accusing him of murdering a number of young boys who'd gone missing in the Yorkshire area in the nineteen eighties. There was also a book that she'd self-published. Libby had skimmed through it and from there, it had been a quick descent into the myriad of questions that kept queuing in her mind.

Who is Colin Wallace?

Is it possible to inherit a murder gene?

What happened to Marion Wallace née Curtis?

Nothing had been conclusive and it wasn't until she'd come across an article about the difficulties of hiding your online research that she realised her mistake. What if Nathan somehow decided to look at her history? Did he even know how to do that? And why would he want to? But none of it changed the fact that if he did see what she'd been doing, he'd be horrified.

And yet she was still there. Stuck on the computer, almost too scared to leave. Like the time she'd been so terrified when reading *The Shining* that she couldn't put it down in case even greater horrors took hold in her mind.

Open your eyes and stop protecting them.

That had been Gemma's desperate plea.

Libby stared at the screen. A hazy photograph of Colin Wallace stared back at her, his arm around his wife, Marion. The shot was black and white, and Marion's face had been shaded by a wide hat, but the slant of the mouth and straight nose bore a passing resemblance to Eloise.

All these tiny things she kept finding were so small and insignificant on their own, yet together, they took on a whole new meaning. *Only if I let them.* She shook her head. These were her thoughts and she could control them. If she stopped all the separate parts from spilling over and touching each other, it would be fine.

But that's not what they wanted to do. They kept trying to draw together, like cells merging to create life. To create something that hadn't existed before. If only she knew what that thing was.

Ding.

The timer on her phone made her start and she quickly cleared her browsing history and then closed the laptop, pleased to finally stop looking at the stark images of the man who had died in prison without confessing to any of his other crimes. And he could be her father-in-law.

Stop it.

Wasn't she always telling the kids not to believe everything they read on the Internet? Yet here she was, letting a stranger take up space in her mind. She stood up abruptly, making sure to hide the laptop under a mountain of paperwork for good measure, before heading downstairs to the kitchen to check on the lasagne.

In the end, she hadn't even bothered to add parmesan cheese or make a salad, which meant the meal was ready. Not that Nathan had come home.

Where was he? Didn't he know she needed him here? So she could see the man she'd spent the last eleven years loving. Let his presence push away the thought he might have been lying to her the whole time.

Your husband isn't who he says he is.

Turning off the oven, she walked through to the formal sitting room on the other side of the hallway. It had been dubbed the gold room because of the large gold velvet sofa that ran along one wall. Like his mother, Nathan didn't display many family photos but he did keep a scant collection in an ornate wooden box on the shelf. Libby lifted it down and flicked through the dog-eared snaps until she found what she was looking for.

Keith Curtis.

Nathan's father had a slim build with blue eyes and a square chin, giving him a Paul-Newman vibe as he stood in front of the Eiffel Tower, arms stretched out wide. He looked like a typical English tourist. And more importantly, nothing like the man Gemma had told her about. Colin Wallace had been dark and brooding, with a heavy-set brow and a blue shadow around his chin which suggested he had to shave a lot.

Out of respect for Nathan and Eloise, Libby had never asked about Keith since his memory was so painful to them both. The man who died before his son was fully grown, and who had kept Eloise stuck in her house, the memory of him too strong to tempt her to start a new life.

But as she stared at the photograph, her curiosity grew. She reached for her phone and clicked on the app she often used to identify plants and flowers in the garden. She'd occasionally used it on a photograph and figured that it might not hurt.

She held it above the photograph of Keith and clicked. It scanned for several minutes but there were no links for Keith himself, just for the Eiffel Tower.

It wasn't really a surprise since Nathan's father had died almost thirty-five years ago and while he'd been successful, he'd hardly been newsworthy. And it wasn't like social media was around then, which meant he didn't have any kind of internet presence.

Headlights flashed through the window as the Audi headed up the drive and Libby's heart pounded. Nathan was home. She slipped the photo into the box and replaced everything before stepping into the hallway just as the door pushed open.

Nathan was leaning heavily against the door frame, his jaw tight with pain. He stiffened at the sight of her, clearly not expecting her to be there.

'H-hey,' he said, a forced brightness to his words. 'You should see the other guy.'

Libby rushed forward. He was wearing beach shorts and one of his favourite old T-shirts. Salt crystals gleamed from his lashes and skin. Surfing. She scanned him for bruises or cuts, which were the usual culprits but then she saw he was favouring his left foot. Most likely a sprain.

'I bet he looks a sight,' she tried her best to match his tone as she slid an arm under his shoulder and guided him through to the sitting room where she'd just been. 'What happened? Did you come off?'

He shook his head, teeth gritted. 'Nothing so dramatic. I landed hard during a floater.'

Libby grimaced. She'd watched him surf enough times to know he was referring to when he turned up onto the broken foam of the wave and rode along the top before dropping back to the open face of it.

She eased him into a sitting position on the sofa and knelt on the floor in front of him. At least he'd opted not to put his shoes back on when he'd left the beach and was still wearing his flipflops. She carefully inspected his ankle. There was definite swelling but she knew better than to suggest they go to A&E. Nathan hated hospitals.

'Okay, this might hurt.' She gently slipped her hand under his foot, which was still warm, and pushed up before slightly twisting it.

'Might?' His leg stiffened in response.

'Sorry,' she said, her hands moving up to his tibia and fibula. He winced as she gently put his foot down. 'Looks like a high ankle sprain.'

'Hell.' His face paled at the implication. Considering his age and how active he was, Nathan didn't get many injuries, which was probably good, because he hated being side-lined. 'So much for the holiday. What a bloody disaster. It wasn't even a great wave.'

'There are other things to do in Spain besides surf.' Libby tried not to think about the stunning resort they'd chosen because it was on the side of a cliff that led down to a private beach, by way of hundreds of stairs. Still. That was a problem for later. 'I'm going to get my gear and some ice. Don't move.'

'Hahaha.' Nathan managed to flash her smile as he swung his leg onto the sofa, well used to having his muscles iced. 'And Lib, sorry. I was so short with you the other night. I wasn't at my best. I had planned to make it up to you tonight but I've screwed that up. Forgive me?'

She stopped at the door, looking back at him. His face was open and despite the pain clouding his eyes, there was worry and regret there. This was her Nathan. The beautiful man who'd been part of her life for so long. Who'd given her the chance to become a mother to his children.

The indecision and confusion that had been trying to jab their way into her mind dissolved. And she swallowed back all the questions she might have had. Whatever money problems there were, they could sort them out together. And as for everything else... well... she'd make sure that didn't come to anything.

'Always,' she told him, voice hoarse.

'Thanks, Lib. For all of it.' His voice was full of tenderness and her heart swelled. It was all okay.

'Don't be daft.' She slipped out of the room to collect the first-aid kit, along with an ice pack. Twenty minutes later, she'd wrapped his ankle and made sure it was elevated while he polished off two plates of lasagne.

Sienna was out and Sam had refused to eat with them, so they'd had their meal on their laps. But all her questions about his phone call and the true state of his business had been washed away by her run in with Gemma Harrington. And there was no way she wanted to discuss that with him. Even without his injury.

She didn't plan on talking about it to anyone until she'd done more research and then made up her mind. In the meantime, she and Nathan were together and happy, and so she'd pushed it all aside and talked to him about the minutiae of the day, as well as giving him an update on Eloise. At the mention of the operation, his face had gone even paler, and Libby had quickly changed the subject.

She stacked the dishwasher and was waiting for the kettle to boil when Jonathan appeared at the wide glass doors. There were three bottles of beer from a local brewery poking out of his rucksack and he gave her a broad smile.

'This is a surprise.' She waved him inside.

'I take it you've forgotten.' Jonathan raised an eyebrow as he joined her at the counter and lifted out the beers. Libby wrinkled her nose. Forgotten what? Then she groaned.

'You finished doing the storage units for Nathan and you're here to collect your home-cooked dinner and night of company,' she said, quoting the price he always gave Nathan, regardless of the job.

'That had been the plan,' he agreed, concern filling his eyes as he studied her. 'It's not like you to forget. You really do need this holiday.'

She rubbed her neck. 'Preaching to the choir. But at least I bought enough food to feed an army and I promise I'm going to catch up on sleep this weekend.'

'Good.' He nodded and Libby dished him up a big plate, grateful that his appetite would at least make a dent in the meal. She opened the fridge and took out a jar of parmesan. He'd eaten with them so often, she knew his habits almost as well as the kids. 'Sienna mentioned you were around at Eloise's last night? Any drunken escapades I should know about?'

Despite herself, Libby mustered a smile. The previous Christmas, Eloise had managed to get Jonathan more than a little tipsy on her sherry, much to everyone's amusement.

'We stuck to tea,' Libby assured him. 'Though I did find out she needs a hip operation in a couple of months.'

'Either that's short notice or she was trying to hide it from you.' Jonathan's smile faded, replaced with concern.

Libby sighed. 'You know what she's like. Didn't want us to worry, which of course makes us worry more. Still, I insisted that she move in with us until she recovers.'

'Always good to make use of a paramedic in the family,' he said, though he still looked worried. She didn't blame him. He'd spent enough time with them to know that despite her need to be independent, Eloise was getting older.

'I might be good in an emergency but I'm not the best nurse,' Libby admitted and then picked up the tea tray and nodded for him to follow her. 'Let's go through. We're sitting in the gold room.'

'On a Sunday night? That is fancy.' He followed but stopped at the threshold, his gaze landing on Nathan, who was lying down, leg up on the sofa. He let out a groan and turned back to her. 'How bad is it?'

'It's nothing,' Nathan called out but Libby ignored him.

'High ankle strain. See if you can talk him into getting an X-ray.'

'Who needs a hospital when I've got you two,' Nathan sang out again.

'He's worse than old Mitch,' Jonathan said, referring to a regular patient who they ferried to and from his home for his hospital appointments, all the while being accused of trying to implant a chip in his arm. Libby repressed a smile as they walked in. At the sight of the beer, Nathan's eyes lit up but Jonathan shook his head. 'Sorry, buddy. I'm guessing she's dosed you with painkillers. This is all for me and Lib.'

'You're on your own.' Libby, who longed for a beer, shook her head. This morning's headache had come back with intensity. Jonathan shrugged and picked up a single glass from the small bar Nathan kept on an antique dresser and then settled down on the other sofa.

'So, I did think we could talk strategy for next week's darts final but I'm starting to think we should discuss the pair of you. Between his ankle and the bags under your eyes, I'm a little worried.'

'You see a lot worse than this every day,' Libby reminded him.

'Yes, but this is different. You're my favourite family, and even when it feels like the world is turning to shit, at least I know there's some good out there.'

'You sure this is your first beer?' Nathan's brow furrowed together.

'Relax. I'm not getting soppy.' Jonathan put down the beer and retrieved a notebook from his rucksack. 'Now, let's talk darts...'

Libby quickly got to her feet, grateful for the opportunity to slip away. She'd sat through enough of Jonathan and Nathan's strategy sessions to know that it would be hours before they finished. And she needed to be alone so she could think. To work out a way to shift all the broken pieces and tiny parts into a cohesive narrative that made sense. That could sit perfectly with the life she had.

'I'm going to leave you two to battle it out while I deal with some bills. Plus, I need to send Sienna another text to find out when she's going to be home.'

'Thanks, Lib.' Nathan blew her a kiss and Jonathan wiped his brow in a dramatic fashion, as if his faith in people was restored.

If only it were that easy.

Her temples pounded and she pressed out a couple of headache tablets and swallowed them. Her phone was on the kitchen bench and she picked it up only to see that the screen was still full of photographs of the Eiffel Tower. Shit. Shit. Shit. How could she have just left it there with a photo of Nathan's father clearly visible for anyone to see?

Heat rushed up her cheeks at her own stupidity.

What would Nathan have said if he hadn't been stuck on the couch? But she already knew. He would have gone icy still and then retreated to the garage to use the gym equipment or gone for a long run until he'd managed to get himself under control. And she couldn't even have blamed him. She tried to think how she'd react if he suddenly had a photograph of Angela up on his phone.

It would be like a knife to the heart. A blood-soaked betrayal.

And it would prove that she believed Gemma instead of her own husband and his mother, who'd been nothing but good to her. It was the wake up call she needed and Libby tapped the screen to delete the search.

But before she could, her eyes focused in on Keith's familiar face, but instead of the Eiffel Tower, he was standing in the middle of a paddock wearing a bulky, argyle knit jumper, looking every inch the gentleman farmer.

Libby pressed on the image, expecting it to go back to a newspaper article or some kind of local history site that might tell her more about Keith Curtis. But instead, it took her to a database of stock images for sale. She frowned and went back to the original search and found yet another photograph of him.

This time, he was at some kind of party, surrounded by a group of twenty-something women, all gorgeous, despite the big eighties hair and heavy make-up. This time it linked to an old newspaper article from the late seventies about a new night club in Chelsea.

She scanned the article looking for names, but the only

caption was 'fresh from Paris catwalks, a group of models relax and have fun.' Okay. That was weird.

Yes, she could clearly see that Keith had been gorgeous looking but no one had ever mentioned he'd done modelling. She got out of that screen and went back to the search page where there were more photos. She clicked on another one, which this time did lead to an article.

Local farmer, Gareth Ward, has traded in the wellingtons for brogues, becoming London's next big thing in the fashion world...

Libby, who was still standing by the kitchen bench, looked up, almost expecting to see someone laughing at her. Having a joke at her expense. But no one was there.

How could Gareth Ward be Keith Curtis?

The tightness in her temples was now like a vice, clamping her brow together. She winced in pain as she clicked on the name, Gareth Ward. The page filled with links to his modelling biography, and many photoshoots, including the same Eiffel Tower shot that Nathan had in the wooden box.

She ignored them and went to Wikipedia where there was a photo of an older Gareth and a stunningly beautiful older woman. They were both in their sixties and were standing together in front of a group of school children.

After leaving the modelling world in the late eighties, Gareth and Luisa wanted to make a difference in the world and set up their own school in Luisa's hometown in Argentina. Determined to help those in need, the couple...

Libby's vision blurred and she dropped down onto the

nearest chair. What did it mean? But it wasn't really a question. Because as far as she could tell, it only meant one thing.

For whatever reason, Eloise and Nathan had pretended that the man in the photo was Keith Curtis. The loving father who'd lived with them until long after Gareth Ward moved to Argentina with his wife.

Gemma's words flashed into her mind.

I'm almost certain that Colin Wallace's son is your husband, Nathan.

And that's why she'd gone looking for Nathan's father. To prove that Gemma was wrong. But instead, she'd found the opposite. Whoever Nathan's father really was, it wasn't the man under the Eiffel Tower.

Which begged the real question. What if Gemma was right?

19

'I'm sorry Nathan couldn't make it.' Libby walked Danny out of the house on Monday afternoon. As usual, Sam's car was parked at an erratic angle, half on the grass, with all the swagger of someone who actually paid rent.

She made a mental note to move it before Nathan got home. He'd been due an hour ago but there had been no call and he wasn't picking up. Usually something like that wouldn't bother her since they both had such busy jobs. But it had been Nathan's idea to meet Danny, which made his absence more noticeable. Plus, it was hard enough keeping him off his ankle when he was around the house. She hated to think how much pressure he'd been putting on it.

'These things happen. And at least Sam showed up, which is promising.'

Libby wasn't so sure. When she'd made the introductions, Sam had been uncommunicative, almost to the point of being mute. But after a five-minute silent standoff, Danny had asked if he could see what modules he was up to, and Sam had grunted something and disappeared upstairs, leaving Danny to follow him. She had no idea what they'd talked about, or if they'd talked at all. But Sam hadn't climbed out of the window and Danny hadn't run screaming from the house. She was going to take it as a win.

'I guess the big question is, are you happy to take him on?' Libby fiddled with her wedding ring. Danny was silent, as if considering his words carefully. She tried to swallow but her throat was dry.

Finally, he spoke. 'It's clear he's smart. He's let me take home some of his old tests and workbooks, which will give me a better idea of where he's struggling. And if I can get him to re-engage with his studies, I will. But I don't want to waste your time or mine, so let's book in for four sessions and then we'll reassess. How does next Monday sound?'

The lump in her throat lessened as relief seeped through her. The concerns she'd had about Sam had compounded, making it almost impossible to think or sleep.

Did he? Didn't he?
Did he? Didn't he?

And yet it had been impossible to confide in any of her friends. Especially about Hayley. After all, what kind of mother would even think something like that? And so the thoughts had just been festering. Twisting every word and action into something dark and sinister. Especially now he was potentially related to a man who might have killed a dozen young boys over the course of his life.

But having Danny somehow felt like an ally. Someone to share the load with, even if it was in only a small way.

'Thank you.'

He gave her a friendly shrug, as if waving it away and then climbed into his car. She waited until he'd backed out of the drive before retrieving Sam's keys from the hallway so she could move the car. She turned on the ignition and leaned back in the driver's seat, her mind still oscillating between the family that lived such a perfect life in her mind and the actual family in her house.

She took a deep breath and then stiffened. The dank stench of stale fast food, body odour and damp towels was gone, replaced with a blanket of chemically scented air freshener. She twisted around to look at the back seat. The litter that had been there had been removed, along with the football boots, surfboard wax and the other debris that had collected there.

Had Sam cleaned the car himself?

The same boy who needed a map to show him where the dishwasher was rather than the bench above it, where he tended to leave his dirty plates. Usually, she would have been delighted at such a spontaneous transformation. Except it was too easy to guess why he'd done it.

Because he was looking for something.

A grey hoodie.

Libby's head began to spin and she leaned back in the car seat again.

And maybe she'd be able to forget it existed.

Except now she couldn't. Because no matter how many times she kept trying to take Sam off her list, things kept moving him back up there. It had to stop. She turned off the engine and stalked back into the house. They needed to talk.

She took the stairs two at a time until she was standing outside his bedroom. As usual, the door was shut. She knocked two times.

'Sam? Can we talk?' The silence was almost comical. She knocked again.

More seconds ticked by and still no answer. Irritation prickled her skin. Did he think she had nothing else to do with her time? Hysterical laughter built low in her belly. There were so many things clawing for her attention that her thoughts had started to resemble a hurricane, trying to drag everything into a unifying circle of perfect destruction.

She knocked harder.

'You know he can't hear you, right?' Sienna's voice floated out from behind her. Libby turned around. As usual, she was all in black, though the flowing Victorian skirts had made way for a pair of black jeans. Silver rings glistened from her fingers and her nails were painted the same chewing gum pink as Hayley's.

Was it intentional?

'Well, he'd better start.' Libby knew she was sounding petulant as she continued to stare at Sienna's fingers. The nails weren't acrylic. It was just a similar coloured nail polish. But why had she chosen it?

'You're the ones that forked out for the noise cancelling headphones.' Sienna's mouth settled into an aggrieved pout. A reminder of the running tally she kept in her head about how much more Sam received than she did. Libby didn't have the energy to go down that rabbit hole.

'Has he said anything to you?'

'About what?'

About what happened to his car the Friday before last. About his connection to Hayley. About why he couldn't even look her in the eye. Libby once again rolled her neck to push back the rising tension.

'About what's bothering him. H-has something happened?' Libby asked.

'How should I know?' Sienna shifted from foot to foot before finally meeting Libby's gaze. But her eyes were filled with uncertainty. Clearly, she knew something and wasn't sure whether to confide in her.

'Please. Sienna, I'm worried. Talk to me.'

Sienna's slim shoulders sagged. 'Sam and Dad had a fight on Friday afternoon.'

Libby stiffened, trying to cast her mind back. Friday was the day she'd seen Gemma Harrington outside the house and tried to talk with Mo, before ending up at Eloise's house after work. And Nathan had gone straight from work to the fundraiser, so she hadn't seen him until Saturday night when he limped in.

He certainly hadn't mentioned anything about a fight.

Another thing he'd lied about.

And another thing that Gemma Harrington had told her that turned out to be true. Somehow, she knew Sam and Nathan had fought. Her stomach tightened and nausea burned up her throat. Please don't let her be sick. No. No. No. She took a deep breath. She had to calm down.

'What was it about? Where did it happen?'

'I have no idea. He wouldn't tell me anything but there was something going on and when I p—' she broke off but her eyes had a guilty flush that was matched by the tell-tale creep of red going up her neck.

'When you *what*?' Libby's voice was firm. The kind she used when her patients were getting lost in a tangle of pain and trauma. Sienna winced, as if knowing she'd been caught out.

'Sam called me at school and asked me to meet him at the park by the rowing club. He was drunk and wanted me to drive him home.'

'He let you drive the car?' Libby's eyebrows furrowed, before realising her first question should have been, why was he drunk in the park at three o'clock on a Friday afternoon?

'Why didn't you say something sooner?'

'I didn't want him to get in trouble.' The colour in her cheeks deepened, turning them almost purple against the dull afternoon light.

'Why were they arguing?'

Sienna returned her attention to her Doc Martin clad feet for several moments. 'Something about training and being pissed off at how hard Dad pushes him. Especially when it's not like Dad ever competed at a top level.'

Libby swallowed. She'd always thought Sam loved sports as much as Nathan did. She couldn't remember a time when he hadn't been kicking a ball or demanding to go to the beach or the swimming pool. Was it really because Nathan had been pushing him? And Sienna? Hell...

'Is that how you felt about rowing? Is that why you dropped out?'

'What?' Sienna's whole body seemed to snap in on itself like a Venus Flytrap closing around an insect. 'No. I couldn't give a shit about that. And clearly neither did Dad. He didn't even try and stop me. But then I'm not the golden child. Maybe I should get drunk and then he'd care?'

'That's not true,' Libby said, then stopped herself. Did she have a point? They'd both been concerned when she'd announced she would no longer be wasting her life doing a stupid sport that she hated but Nathan seemed to have taken it all in his stride. Yet, his face when she'd mentioned the idea of Sam not pursuing rowing was completely different.

As if his life depended on it.

But why would it matter so much?

And what did Sam mean about Nathan not competing at a top level? He ran marathons all the time and was forever surfing and kayaking. Then she frowned, thinking back to the lack of photos in Eloise's house. She couldn't remember him ever talking about school sports or going to national competitions. She'd assumed it was because he wasn't competitive with anyone but himself.

And yet, he'd been at nearly all of Sam's matches, running up and down the side-line, sometimes more than the players themselves.

'Stop kidding yourself, Libby. And stop trying to act like we're some perfectly happy family. The sooner you admit that we're just as fucked up as everyone else, the better off you'll be.'

The words were like a slap and Libby clenched her jaw to stop herself from replying. But she wanted to. She wanted to tell both Sam and Sienna that they had no idea how lucky they were. A beautiful house with enough money to buy them whatever they wanted and parents who loved them. But if they did want to know what a fucked-up life looked like, she could tell them about hers. About what *he* did to her. About finding her brother in the bathroom, too late to stop the belt from crushing his windpipe and sucking the life out of his fifteen-year-old body. And the mother who didn't once stop to ask if Libby was okay.

But of course, she couldn't say any of that. What right did she have to argue with whatever it was the kids were going through? No matter how painful it was to be pushed aside.

Sienna gave her one last dismissive glare before stomping her way down the stairs. Moments later, the front door slammed shut. Libby didn't even have the energy to chase after her and ask when she'd be back. Instead, she walked down to the kitchen and poured a glass of wine, hoping it would help corral her thoughts.

Why hadn't Nathan told her about the fight?

More importantly, what had made him lose his temper in the first place? It wasn't like him. Her skin prickled as the face of Colin Wallace loomed in her mind. But she shook it away. Even if Nathan was his son, that didn't make him a monster. And yet...

Libby closed her eyes as the tiny pieces she'd been trying to avoid thrust their way into her mind. The Friday night that Hayley was kidnapped, Sam insisted that he was playing

Dungeons and Dragons, Sienna was at home and Nathan had been at his mother's house.

But that wasn't true.

Eloise had told her that Nathan cancelled. Which meant Libby had no idea where her husband had been last Friday night. Or why he'd been washing towels and some clothing on Sunday morning before she was out of bed. And the call she'd overheard that he'd quickly dismissed. As well the fight that he hadn't told her about.

It seemed like there were lies upon lies upon lies upon lies.

But why? A white-hot, burning pain swept through her body. What was her husband hiding from her?

20

Sienna was panting by the time she climbed off her bike. Her calves ached and she could hardly feel her cheeks thanks to an unexpected offshore wind that had turned the sky into a swirl of orange and red. Was it a reminder that it was a bad idea?

Then again, right now, every idea she had seemed to be a bad one.

It was the first time she'd been to Steamer Point since Hayley had been found and there was no sign of any police tape. Just a few bunches of dead flowers tied to a picnic bench. Fury flared up in her and she stalked towards them. Hayley hadn't died. It was probably done by people like Zoe, hoping it would get her some extra Insta followers.

What a fucking cow.

She yanked the first bunch out, the stems already brittle and dead. There was a note attached, the writing smeared from rain, that said;

*Stay **Strong**. You Got This.*

Sienna scrunched it up and dropped it to the ground before using her heel to stamp it down. What was it with people? All people.

She'd been stupid to think she could talk to Libby. To explain how worried she was about Sam. And about—

'Nice show, Curtis,' someone drawled from behind her. It was a voice she recognised all too well. Tate Raymond. Her irritation morphed into confusion as she turned to face him.

He was sprawled on a nearby bench that overlooked the English Channel. His usual pile of blond hair was gone, replaced by a buzz cut that emphasised his wide cheekbones and strong jaw. Both hands were wrapped around a bottle of vodka. Which probably explained the dark smudges under his eyes.

'You look like shit,' she retorted, peering around to see if Zoe or any of his other friends were around. If they were, there was no sign of them. Sienna narrowed her eyes. 'What the hell are you doing here?'

'Admiring the view and getting extremely drunk. You?'

Trying to get away from family so that I can have some space to think.

'None of your business,' she said instead.

He shrugged, not seeming to be bothered by her rudeness. She chewed her lip. Speaking to Tate was the last thing she felt like doing but the idea of climbing back on her bike and riding home wasn't much more appealing. She settled on glaring at him.

He held her gaze while lifting the bottle to his mouth and taking a gulp. His face puckered. Then he waved it at her.

'Want some?'

'No thanks,' she said, and then, unsure what else to do, she stalked over to the bench and sat down next to him. 'You shouldn't be drinking.'

'Why not?'

'Because you've only got a limited number of brain cells and you might need them one day,' she retorted before taking the bottle out of his hands. It was half empty. Why was she even surprised? 'You and Sam are both stupidly alike. Actually, you're both just stupid. Full stop.'

'I'm nothing like your prick of a brother.' Tate stretched for the bottle but she held it out of his grasp.

'Please. The pair of you have had it so bloody easy your entire life. All you do is squabble over who's the best, without noticing that you're both the best at everything. At sports and at school. And then there are all the girls throwing themselves at you. But all you both do is moan, drink and screw it all up.'

Tate glared at her, his green eyes glimmering in the fading light. Then he lunged and snatched the bottle from her hands. His breath stank of alcohol and a waft of body odour suggested he hadn't showered in a couple of days.

He held it up in the air like a podium winner and then took another long drink.

The silence was broken by the waves below them and for the first time since Hayley had been found, Sienna felt like she could breathe. It was over too soon and Tate shifted slightly and leaned back against the bench so that he was staring up at the darkening sky.

'My life isn't quite as charmed as you think. They almost arrested me because of Hayley. Her parents stared at me like I was some kind of monster. And now Zoe's dumped me—'

'What?' Sienna's spine stiffened and she twisted to face him. 'Since when?'

'Shit. Forget I said that. It's nothing. I'm drunk.'

'Yes, you are,' she agreed before taking the bottle off him once again. 'Now, back to Zoe. Was it the buzz cut?'

He glared at her. 'She decided that it was too embarrassing to be seen with me. What if people thought I *did* do something? And then there was the whole thing about her being painted in a bad light because Hayley was meant to be her bestie before we hooked up together.'

'When did this happen?' Sienna leaned forward, unable to hide her curiosity. She might not be in Zoe's gang, or friends with the most popular girls, but this kind of gossip usually travelled fast.

He resumed his stargazing and shrugged. 'It's not official yet. Zoe wants to wait until things have settled down in case anyone thinks she's being a "heartless bitch".' He waved his arms around attempting to do air quotes.

'Personally, I think it's past time that people found out what she's really like,' Sienna retorted before wrinkling her nose. 'If she's dumped you, what the hell do you care what she thinks?'

'I don't care what she thinks. I care what she'll say.'

Ah. Now that sounded more like Zoe. 'She's got something on you. What is it?'

'Like I'm going to tell you,' he retorted, then turned to her, clearly lacking any impulse control at all. 'About what happened on Friday night when Hayley—' he broke off and made a choking noise. Was he crying?

Her stomach churned and she tightened her grip on the bottle. This was about the party?

'What happened?' she wanted the words to come out like a demand. A force of energy that he'd be compelled to answer. Instead, they were hardly above a whisper, dragging along her throat like razor blades. Something bad had happened to Hayley and Tate knew what it was.

He closed his eyes, long, dark lashes like soot against his pale skin. It hadn't been that long ago that she'd fantasised about the lashes and the smooth line of his jaw. But now there was nothing but faint irritation.

He let out a bitter laugh. 'I drank too much and couldn't get it up.'

Sienna couldn't move. Her whole body had been poised for a sucker punch that didn't come. He wasn't talking about Hayley at all. It was about him and bloody Zoe. Then the absurdity of it hit her and she let out a bark of laughter.

'*That's* why she broke up with you?'

'Are you finding it funny?' he snapped.

'Very.' She nodded as she held up the bottle. 'And a word to the wise. Don't try and fix a problem with the same thing that caused it.'

He let out a soft sigh. 'Yeah, yeah. You made your point. And the reason she broke up with me is because I told the police about it. It was my alibi. But it also meant it was her alibi too, and she felt like I'd cast her in a bad light. Can you fucking believe it? I suppose you're going to tell everyone now.'

'In case you haven't noticed, I don't exactly have many people to tell.'

'Thanks, Curtis,' he begrudgingly said before they fell into more companionable silence. As the night blanketed them, Sienna tried to move the puzzle pieces around in her mind. If Tate and Zoe had been together, it meant they weren't involved in what happened to Hayley. Which led back around to the problem she'd been grappling with all week. What happened that Friday night and why was Hayley sending Sam text messages?

We need to talk.

She swallowed hard and turned back to him. 'Tate. Was my brother at the bonfire?'

His face scrunched up. 'I don't think so.'

'Are you sure?' she demanded. Her pulse hammered.

'Yes, I'm sure. Your prick of a brother is an obnoxious twat with a voice like a foghorn. If he'd been there, I would have bloody heard him. Anyway, why are you asking me? You were there too.'

Sienna's heart stopped beating as she stared at him. 'No, I wasn't.'

He blinked, tilted his head to one side and studied her. 'Yeah, you were. I saw you.'

'Please, you were drunk. You couldn't see shit.' Sienna scrambled to her feet.

'Hey. Where are you going? I thought we were hanging out?' He called after her, but Sienna didn't stop as she ran back to her bike, trying not to trip on the uneven ground.

She should never have come here. Back to where it had all happened. It was too soon. It would *always* be too soon.

And now someone knew about it.

21

The wine had been a mistake and Libby's head was pounding. She put down the magazine she'd been reading. She'd only picked it up to try and stop her mind from overthinking. But it hadn't worked, hence the headache. She checked the time. It was almost eight at night and there was still no sign of Nathan.

Which was probably for the best because Sienna hadn't reappeared from wherever she'd stomped off to and Sam was still up in his room refusing to even acknowledge her. Parenting. It wasn't for the faint hearted. Not that she was really a parent. A bitter voice in her mind mocked at her. And it was true. These days, Sam and Sienna looked at her like she was an outsider. An inadequate substitute that was somewhere just below a political dictator or kitten stealer.

Her phone rang and she picked it up, her limbs heavy with exhaustion. It was Nathan. Libby closed her eyes. There was a time when her heart would surge with love just from seeing his name flash up, but now there were so many emotions, all clambering to take up space on the stage in her mind. The latest was about the fight with Sam. Why hadn't he told her about it? At least Sam had an excuse. He was a teenage boy who was pissed off at the world. But what excuse did Nathan have?

Still unsure, Libby accepted the call.

'Hey. I was beginning to think you weren't going to answer.'

Libby swallowed and tightened her grip on the phone. 'Sorry. Was just in the other room. Where are you? I thought you were coming home to meet with Danny.'

'Shit.' Nathan let out a long groan. 'I totally forgot. I swung by Mum's house on the way home to talk about the operation... and well... it took a bit longer than I expected. Did Sam do a runner?'

She listened to the genuine concern in his voice, so at odds with everything she'd been learning about him. The secrets, the lies, the fight. And yet still she couldn't say anything, knowing that if she did, it might create a chasm that they couldn't come back from. And that's not what she wanted.

'No, turns out you were the only flight risk,' she said, trying to force a lightness into her voice that she didn't feel. 'Danny's starting next Monday and we'll assess it in four weeks.'

Nathan was silent and Libby almost thought he was going to tell her the truth. *Please. Just let me in.* But then it was gone and he let out a bitter chuckle.

'It sounds like it went better than the conversation I had with my mother. She said I'm trying to ride roughshod over her wishes. All because I think she should move out of the bloody house,' he said.

Libby pinched the bridge of her nose, hoping to push back the throbbing tempo of the headache just enough to allow her to think. 'I know it makes sense to us for her to get into something smaller but we just need to wait until she figures it out for herself. She's scared, that's all.'

There was more silence. 'You're right. Anyway, I'm still here. Said I'd go through the paperwork with her but half of it is buried away in the safe. And Lib, sorry about missing the tutor.'

Libby swallowed but before she could answer, there was a knock at the door. 'Hey, I've got to go. Text me when you're leaving.'

She finished the call and stood up. Her jeans were crumpled and there was a curry stain on her shirt. Still, it hardly mattered. She walked out to the hallway and peered through the peephole to where Adele Terrace was standing.

Libby straightened and opened the door. Adele looked terrible. Her eyes were bloodshot and dark roots were sneaking through the previously bright-blonde hair, while her lips were chapped and dry. Libby tugged at the collar of her shirt, trying to ease her guilt. She'd meant to get back in touch and check in on her but hadn't got around to it.

Which was a lie.

The real reason was because she had chosen to put the safety of her son ahead of Hayley's own wellbeing.

'Libby, I'm sorry to turn up unannounced.' Adele hugged her arms around her waist as if trying to hold herself together.

'It's fine. How are things going?'

It was a terrible question and Libby hated herself for asking it. Because unless she'd invented a time machine that had stopped her daughter from going through such a traumatic experience, there was no good answer. But it had slipped out of her mouth before she could stop it.

'Apart from drowning down the rage and stopping myself from screaming at all the journalists and bloody self-proclaimed internet detectives that keep turning up on our doorstep, I'm doing... shit.' She let out a tinny laugh and then gave Libby a reluctant smile. 'No, don't look like that. I know you didn't mean to ask. Problem is, we're not taught how to behave when our life goes to pieces.'

Libby could second that.

'All the same, I'm sorry. Do you want to come in?'

Adele shook her head a little bit too quickly. 'I can't stay long. But there's something I wanted to talk to you about.'

'Oh. Um, okay. What is it?'

'This is awkward, and I hope you don't take this the wrong way, because we love Sienna.' Adele paused and chewed on her lower lip. Something crossed her face, and she leaned closer, as if worried someone might overhear. 'Hayley's still not ready to see anyone and, well... she's finding it all a bit intense.'

Intense?

Libby blinked. She knew that Sienna had been worried about her ex-friend, but from what she could tell, the entire school had been, along with the rowing club. But it still didn't explain the wary expression that had filled Adele's eyes.

'I'm not sure I follow. Has something else happened?'

'No.' Adele gave a quick shake of her head. 'Not exactly. Sienna came around to speak to Hayley a couple of days ago and I explained she didn't want to see anyone but there have been quite a few text messages and she's taken to standing behind the tree across the street staring at the house. I-I'm sure she's worried, but right now, the best thing she can do is give Hayley some space. I'm sure you understand.'

Libby's spine stiffened. It was all too easy to picture the new version of Sienna hidden behind a tree like a black shadow as she watched Hayley's house. And the mood swings and anger. The refusal to even talk to them any more.

She tried to swallow but her mouth was dry.

'Oh. I see. I'll talk to her.' She finally managed to squeeze out the words. 'And I'm sorry. Like you said, I'm sure it's because she's worried. But I'll make sure it doesn't happen again. Tell Hayley I'm sorry.'

'I appreciate that, Libby.'

'Of course.' She plastered on a bright smile, as if it was no big deal that her stepdaughter had developed a fondness for hiding behind trees and staring into other people's houses.

Adele's phone broke the jagged tension that had built up between them and she studied the screen.

'Sorry, I've got to run. And thanks for being so understanding about the whole Sienna thing.'

'Of course.' Once Adele had left, Libby went back inside and leaned against the closed door.

So now there was a 'whole Sienna thing'. She wanted to burst out laughing. Or crying. Or both. What was happening to her family? And why was she the only one to see it? It was like she was trying to hold onto a picture that had fallen into the water and was dissolving into nothing, right in front of her eyes.

22

Libby stared at herself in the mirror the following morning.

Putting on concealer had seemed like a good idea, until she realised that she'd somehow picked up Sienna's foundation instead. It had been made for much lighter skin, which meant Libby didn't just look tired, she also looked like a ghoul.

Still, it was the least of her problems. She resisted the urge do any more repair work and walked into the bedroom to grab her coat. Nathan had slept in the spare bedroom, worried he might disturb her sleep because of his ankle. She could have told him it wasn't his ankle that was the problem but he'd been gone before she'd woken up. And by the time she'd headed downstairs for breakfast, Sam and Sienna had also disappeared, leaving only a pile of dirty dishes in their wake.

Who knew that the real secret to get her family out of the house on time every morning was to make sure she needed to corner each one of them for a serious conversation? Maybe it was for the best?

Libby wasn't a morning person, and everything was compounding so quickly that the three people she lived with were turning into strangers. Or maybe she was the stranger? After all, the three of them had been a unit before she'd been brought in as a late addition. An outsider.

Was that why she felt so powerless? Frustration caught in her throat. She hated that she couldn't fix things any more. Because what was she if she couldn't do that? Her conversations with Nathan had skirted around the many questions she wanted to ask him and instead had landed on everyday domestic details that stopped her from reaching the truth.

Or was it because she was too scared to ask?

And what about the kids? She'd been trying to talk to Sam since Sienna had told her about the fight but she'd only managed to see his back as he disappeared out of the door this morning. And then there was Sienna, who had apparently been stalking Hayley.

It was like one of those dreadful 'hold my beer' memes where everyone was trying to outdo each other. All while Libby stood by, helpless to stop it from happening. She'd tried to wait up to talk to Sienna last night but her stepdaughter had stomped into the house a minute before her curfew and had headed straight to her room before Libby could even untangle herself from her seat on the couch.

Out of habit, she loaded the washing machine and fed Harriet before fishing her car keys from her bag and stepping outside. She didn't have to leave for another half hour but the idea of sitting in the house made her skin itch. Maybe she'd drive down to the water and clear her head.

The electric motor from the garage door buzzed as it opened, and Sienna appeared, pushing her bike out. Her face was set in a scowl that only increased when she caught sight of Libby. Clearly, she'd been counting on that extra half an hour to make her escape.

Libby swallowed, trying not to be offended. Besides, she'd long ago realised that when it came to parenting, it wasn't about being popular.

Sienna turned away and quickened her pace but Libby was a good head taller than her and caught up in five long strides.

'Hey, how about I give you a ride to school?'

'No, thanks.' Sienna tried to keep pushing the bike but Libby held onto the handles. The last week and a half had been like a rollercoaster ride that Libby had no control over. A passenger who could only scream and hang on tightly at each dip and bend. But when it came to sullen teenagers... it wasn't her first time.

'Let me rephrase that.' Her voice was firm and she held Sienna's gaze. 'I'm going to give you a ride to school, and before you ask about getting home, we can put your bike in the back of the car.'

Sienna shut her eyes, as if calculating her chances of escape. She gave an exaggerated sigh and let go of the bike, letting Libby take its full weight. Then she marched over to the car and climbed in, leaving Libby to load the bike. It took five minutes of manoeuvring to make it fit and she managed to get bike oil on her jeans. Libby gritted her teeth as she finally settled into the driver's seat and shut the door.

Next to her, Sienna had her Doc Marten boots up on the dashboard and her earbuds were plugged in. Libby started the engine and reversed out of the driveway, but once she was on the road, she peered over at Sienna.

'Can you please take them out. I want to talk to you. About Hayley.'

Sienna's eyes darkened but she took out the earbuds, still staring straight ahead. Libby knew from experience that this was as good as it was going to get.

'Adele Terrace came by last night. She said that you've been going around there a lot... and that it was making Hayley a little... uncomfortable.'

Sienna was silent but there was a tiny flicker at the corner of her mouth, as if she was holding herself back.

'I know that you must be finding it hard but if you ever want to talk about what happened between you and Hayley. Or about Tate. I'm here for you. Believe it or not, I do understand—'

'Please do *not* finish that sentence.' Sienna still didn't turn to her, though her cheeks turned crimson. 'Or I will vomit. And you can tell Adele Terrace that just because I went around there a couple of times, I'm not the weirdo here. The real question she should be asking is why Hayley's other friends like Zoe *haven't* been around there.'

Libby came to a red light and turned to her, brow furrowed. 'What do you mean?'

But whatever had prompted Sienna's outburst had gone and she was once again staring moodily out of the windscreen. 'Nothing. Now, if we're done with the third degree, can I please go back to my audiobook? It's for an English assignment. Not that you'd care.'

The last part was a sharp barb, no doubt at the fact that Sienna's grades were still excellent despite Sam getting all the attention. Libby opened her mouth but shut it again. It was too early in the morning to get caught up in yet another argument about Sienna's perceived unfair treatment compared to that of her older brother.

'Fine.' The light turned green and they made the rest of the trip in silence. Libby's grip tightened on the steering wheel as she tried to push down her growing frustration. Why couldn't she make her family see that she was on their side? That she wanted to help? All they had to do was ask.

23

The vastness of the ocean made Gemma's eyes ache as she tried to take it all in, watching as the swirls of water rippled their way into the shore before retreating again. Had Lucas ever seen it? She couldn't remember her parents ever talking about trips to the seaside. Pain tore at her chest, the familiar guilt always there. Everything she did was because her brother hadn't done it. It was the very point of her existence. Well, that and to finally end this thing.

Which was why she was sitting on the beach, trying to pretend that she was the kind of person who loved the way the sand caked her wet feet. It was a lie, of course. She didn't even like going barefoot around her apartment. But all the same, she lifted her head to the faint sun as if she was in paradise. How could people bear this?

It must have worked because no one looked at her strangely as she sat there. She was just another tourist enjoying the beach after visiting Bournemouth pier. All around her, children darted past while seagulls marshalled around a group of holiday makers eating fish and chips. And there... only twenty metres away from her was Sam Curtis.

He was tall and muscular and his wet hair clung to his face in clumps as he walked out of the water and over to where he'd dumped a towel. He'd been here for an hour, playing football in the sand with a group of friends, but they'd all peeled off, leaving Sam alone.

And so Gemma had stayed where she was, trying to convince herself that what she was about to do was a good idea. It was proving a difficult task. She could almost hear Stephen's voice in her mind.

You're crossing a line, Gem. You need to stop this and come home.

He was right, of course. Gemma had approached Libby and it had backfired spectacularly.

But it was too late to turn back. Even if Libby Curtis didn't believe her – and it was obvious that she *didn't* – Gemma was committed. She'd pressed the proverbial doorbell and announced her presence. If Nathan didn't know about her yet, he would soon enough. And she still didn't have the proof she needed.

Not from lack of trying. After her failed conversation with Libby on Sunday afternoon, she'd decided to focus her attention on Eloise and had parked outside her house yesterday, determined to go inside. But her plans had been foiled by a taxi that turned up at 9 a.m. and had taken her to a hospital appointment, followed by a trip to the hairdressers and then a nail bar. And then Nathan had arrived to visit her later in the afternoon, limping heavily. And Gemma, who was tired and hungry after a day of fruitlessly following an elderly woman around town, had admitted defeat and gone back to the hotel.

And now here she was. Her last chance, because tomorrow, she'd be on a train back to Manchester. It had been Stephen who'd finally convinced her that it would be madness to throw in her job and risk losing her flat. Not to mention keeping her guinea pigs in the lifestyle to which they'd become accustomed. But that didn't mean she wouldn't try and find out as much as she could.

She'd hoped to talk to Libby again. That's why she'd sent her an email before breakfast which was part apology and part plea for help. But so far there had been no reply and Gemma didn't have the luxury of time.

So now she was following Sam.

What had he and his father been arguing about? And why had it ended in Nathan driving to Hayley Terrace's house? It had to be connected.

In the distance, Sam wrapped the towel around his waist and dragged a T-shirt over his head. He was still half wet and it clung to him in damp patches. Gemma shuddered at his casual tolerance.

Once he was done, Sam hung the towel over one shoulder and scooped up his trainers before heading towards the road. He was leaving. Gemma scrambled to her feet, kicking sand up in all directions as she did. Her legs were stiff from sitting for too long and seemed to move with agonising slowness as her feet sank into the soft sand. Her muscles screamed in protest and she made a mental promise to start going to the gym as soon as she got back to Manchester. Wouldn't Stephen be—

'Hey, you were there the other day at the rowing club.'

Her heart slammed into her chest as she looked up to face Sam Curtis. The gentle slope of the beach made him seem even taller and Gemma froze, realising too late that she hadn't been quite as inconspicuous as she'd thought.

Shit. Shit. Shit.

Her attempts to talk to Nathan had backfired, she'd totally

stuffed it up with Libby and if she made a mess of her conversation with Sam, then she might as well pack her bags and go home early. She swallowed, though her mouth was dry. This was her shot. For Lucas and her parents, and for all the victims and their families. For the lives that had been ripped apart forever because of what one man had done. For the need to know the truth, no matter what the cost.

'You're right,' she agreed, impressed with how calm her voice sounded. 'I-I wanted to talk to you. About your dad.'

'My dad's a fucking arsehole,' Sam's green eyes narrowed and his whole body went rigid. Gemma sucked in a breath. His anger was palpable.

That was a good place to start.

'There's some things about him that I thought you should know.'

'Like what?'

'Probably best if we go somewhere and have a drink.'

Sam rubbed his chin, as if weighing something up. Then he shrugged. 'I have to be somewhere at five.'

Gemma's heart thumped in her chest, so loud, it almost drowned out the crash of the waves. He'd agreed. Now she was finally getting somewhere.

'That's plenty of time.'

24

Libby rubbed her eyes. It was late afternoon, and her shift had finished on time, but lack of sleep was making her brain feel foggy. Or maybe that was the way her brain was going to be from now on. Across the car pack, Jonathan was talking to one of their colleagues but on seeing her, he held up his hand to signal her to wait.

She tapped her foot as he jogged across the tarmac to her. He'd changed out of his uniform into a garish blue shirt with bright-yellow flames on it. Of course. It was the darts final. She'd half-heartedly tried to convince Nathan not to go because of his ankle but she'd known it was a losing battle. Which meant it would be her and the kids in the house.

Only two potential explosions instead of three.

'Hey, I'm glad I caught you,' he said, coming to a halt, not at all out of breath. 'I just had a very weird conversation with a woman called Mo. She wanted me to give you a message.'

'Mo?' Libby's mouth went dry. It seemed like a lifetime ago that she'd gone to see the cleaner. Back when she thought she wanted to know what Nathan had been hiding from her. But since her conversation with Gemma, Libby had been like a pendulum, swinging between the need to know, and the need to very much *not* know. 'How do you even know her?'

'I don't.' He shook his head, sending his fading blond hair spiking out around his face. 'Well, I vaguely recognise her from that TLC anniversary party you and Nathan dragged me to. But she was my last job and for some reason, she recognised me. I have a bad feeling I probably got drunk at the party and started singing karaoke.'

More like he'd instigated a game of strip poker but Libby wasn't in the mood to be distracted. 'I'm still not sure I follow. What do you mean she was your last job?'

'We had to collect a patient from Fordingbridge and bring her back here. And it was Mo. She'd been visiting her sister and was mugged. Bloody arseholes. What kind of pond scum would do that? Anyway, she said you'd left her a couple of messages but she'd run out of phone credit and with all the drama, hadn't had a chance to top up. But she will call you in the next day or so.'

'Oh, my goodness,' Libby managed to croak as a terrible knot formed in her stomach. Mugged. Was it just a coincidence or was there a reason for it? She closed her eyes and thought of the sharp tone of Nathan's voice when she'd heard him on the phone. That was back when he thought the outspoken cleaner had been talking to a creditor. But it wasn't that at all. She'd been speaking to Gemma: the woman who was convinced Nathan wasn't just the only son of Colin Wallace, but that he'd also inherited something dark from his father.

'I know you keep telling me that everything is fine... but Libby... it doesn't seem fine. I really think you need to consider booking a week off work.'

Libby opened her mouth to reply but nothing came out. She really had no idea. In the end, she just nodded her head and squeezed his hand. 'I'll think about it. In the meantime, you had better go. I don't want me getting blamed if your team is forced to forfeit the match because you're late.'

His jaw tightened with indecision and then he nodded. 'Okay, but I mean it about work. I think you should consider it.'

'I will.' She promised and waited until he disappeared back to his car before climbing into her own. She turned on the engine and cranked up the radio, letting Nirvana drown out her thoughts. Because really, that was the whole problem. If she didn't think about anything, then there would be nothing to worry about. It was a simple solution, if only someone would remind her mind of that.

At least the afternoon traffic was obliging and fifteen minutes later, she pulled into the driveway. Her phone pinged as it signed onto the household Wi-Fi network and out of habit, Libby picked it up and studied the new messages.

There were a couple of bills and a newsletter she followed but her eyes drifted over them to the one from Gemma Harrington. Anger burned like acid in her throat. She hated that this woman seemed to know more about Libby's husband and his family than she did. It didn't matter that she'd been right about Keith Curtis not being Nathan's real father.

Not even a real person.

But that didn't lessen the rage. It had the opposite effect. It had taken something from Libby. Ripped it from her, leaving behind jagged ends so that nothing could be put back together again. And now she'd sent an email.

Her finger hovered over the screen. She had to delete it. No matter what Libby did next, or what she discovered, it would happen on her own. She didn't want Gemma's voice in her head any more. It was Libby's life. She had the right to decide what to do.

And yet, she pressed down and opened it.

Libby,

I'm sorry about Sunday and can only imagine how upset you must be. What right does a stranger have to come up and make such terrible allegations about your family? I know it was wrong of me... and yet there was no other way. Trust me, I tried to find one. But I've long learnt the cost of staying silent and it's not something I can do any more.

Which means I need to tell you something that only one other living person knows. One of those missing boys, Lucas Richmond, was my brother.

He was a living, breathing person for ten years. There was a scar on his knee where he tripped on my mother's slipper and fell onto this miniature train track. The diecast metal pressed into his flesh, forever scarring it. Of course, I've never seen it because this all happened before I was born. Before my parents changed our last name. But he was alive and existed and his heartbeat was the joy of my parents' world.

He mattered then and he matters now.

And I know you understand because of your brother's death.

I won't ask what happened, or, how you coped. But I can only guess the thoughts that must have lived with you.

And I'm sorry for bringing it all up. For stepping over lines that I have no right to step over. But I need your help. If you know anything about Colin Wallace. About his past crimes. Or about what his scions might do then please, please get in touch.

I'm staying in room twenty-three at the Cambridge Court Hotel until Wednesday morning, and my phone number's below. I know this is hard, and that I'm being a bitch, but for the sake of my brother, don't protect the wrong people. Let us have some peace.

Gemma

Libby's vision blurred and she dropped her phone into her lap. How did Gemma know about Todd? It wasn't something she discussed with anyone. Not even Nathan. Had she found it all on the Internet? The tiny, shredded ghosts of her past all floating in unconnected pieces of binary code until a stranger had come along and pieced them together.

The words looked so harmless written down like that. *Your brother's death.* And for someone else, they might be harmless. Just words, with no meaning attached. They might not even see the sharp needles that each letter dragged along her skin as they pierced into her heart, digging into the deepest parts of her.

But to Libby, they were poison. Pumping thoughts and memories through her veins that could only eat her from the inside out. Of the years that Angela had dragged them from one terrible flat to another one. Bringing in a new boyfriend or fiancé every few months, and then when it ended, Angela's darkness would appear, blaming them for everything that was wrong in her life. Then she met *him* and it got even worse. The beginning of the end. He almost took Libby's virginity and then when Todd punished him, Angelia's rage had done the rest. Six months later, Todd was dead.

Pain ricocheted through her body. Sweeping her back in time, pushing the emotions through her, forcing her to revisit it over and over.

Stop. She held her hands up to her ears, trying to block out the sound of her brother's voice. The pitch of his laugh, the scent of his skin when he was still so young. The last time she'd seen him.

The images blurred together, moving into her house and settling down in all the cracks as Nathan, Sam and Sienna continued with their daily lives. No. She didn't want this. It was wrong. Her new life wasn't meant to be like this. The memories needed to stay back where she'd left them.

Todd was dead because of her.

It was the single thought that had almost brought her to her knees, which is why they couldn't be here. Todd had to stay in the dark place so that Libby could live in the light. But now it was here, tearing through her mind like a burst water pipe. And then she started to laugh as Gemma's words blinked back at her.

Let us have some peace.

But Libby knew it was a lie. There was no peace. No let up. Only a hope of doing better next time. And that's what she was doing with her life. Making sure she was not the kind of mother who hung her kids out to dry. Who put herself before her family. And with that, she deleted the email.

Gemma Harrington would not destroy her life.

25

'You *what*?' Stephen all but yelled.

Gemma held her phone away from her ear. It was to be expected, and in retrospect, she probably shouldn't have mentioned it while her body was pumped full of dopamine from her conversation with Sam. But Stephen had called and she'd found herself relaying the entire conversation.

'I swear it's not as bad as it sounds.'

'You told a teenage boy that his grandfather might be a serial killer and that you're worried Nathan was the one who attacked Hayley. *Who*, from what you told me, was a friend of his sister.'

'Apparently, the two girls had a falling out six months ago over Tate Raymond. The same boy the police interviewed,' she said, barely pausing for breath in case Stephen tried to interject. 'Which means Nathan could have easily met Hayley on several occasions. Not to mention both his children were in the same rowing club as Hayley.'

'Gemma. You know as well as I do that it doesn't mean anything. There's no evidence to suggest Nathan Curtis is anything more than what it says on the packet: a family man with two kids and a business.'

'So why does his son hate him so much?' Gemma reminded him. After their initial conversation at the beach, Sam had made it perfectly clear what he thought of his father, telling her several stories about how Nathan tried to shame Sam when he didn't get top marks at school. 'And the argument I saw them having was because Sam wanted to quit the rowing team and Nathan wouldn't let him. He's clearly trying to dominate him.'

Stephen was silent for a long time, obviously considering his next words. 'How did you leave it? Do you think Sam will tell Nathan about the conversation?'

'Definitely not.'

'I still don't understand what you were hoping to achieve?'

Some of her excitement faded. Her original hope had been that Sam might have proof Nathan had done something to Hayley. But while he'd disclaimed any knowledge, he'd been determined to go home to see what he could find out.

'I just need the next step. And if we can get proof of who Nathan really is, then it's one step closer to finding out what happened to Colin Wallace's victims. And to possibly stop history from repeating itself.'

'Except you're due back tomorrow,' he reminded her.

Gemma sighed as she reached the car park. A wind had picked up and the heavy cloud cover gave the place a gloomy feel. She scanned the grounds, searching for her car. But it wasn't where she thought it was.

Crap. She spun back in the other direction and narrowed her eyes. How hard was it to find a bright-green car?

'Don't worry. I sent my boss a text and will be back in work on Thursday, selling the most shit computer software known to man. But I'll come back down for a long weekend once I hear from Sam.'

'Okay. Call me when you get back to Manchester. I'll pick you up from the station.'

Gemma was about to tell him not to be silly but she bit down on her tongue. It would be nice to see him again. They could possibly go to the pub so she could talk through her theories. 'Thanks, Stephen. I'll see you tomorrow.'

She finished the call and walked back the way she'd come. Ah. There it was, hidden by the shadows of the exposed red brick wall of a block of shops. No wonder she hadn't been able to find it. She wove through the parked vehicles and thrust her hand into the large bag on her shoulder. It was filled with notebooks, headphones and the extra jumper that she'd brought along, just in case. Note to self: she really needed to travel more lightly.

Once she reached the car, she rested her bag on the bonnet to look for her keys. They were tucked right at the bottom and her fingers clasped around them. She—

A hand clamped across her mouth, pushing a wad of fabric between her teeth, as an overpowering scent of nail polish remover raced up her nose. Gemma dry retched and tried to lean forward to clear the thing in her mouth, but the iron-like grip held her upright, forcing her to keep breathing in the almost-sweet odour.

Help.

She tried to shout but her words were muffled and she gagged again.

'Oh no, you don't.' A low voice flittered across her ear like a stone skimming across a lake. Then a hand slipped around her waist as her knees buckled. Her vision swam and her body began to float away.

No. Not like this, she wanted to say. *Please. Not like this.*

But it was too hard and her limbs were no longer hers. Then the darkness dragged her forward and the words were gone.

26

This was a mistake.

Libby's breath was ragged and she tried to slow down her pounding heart. She wasn't a bad person but the last week and a half seemed to be pulling back her skin layer by layer, leaving her exposed and vulnerable.

And bloody angry.

It was all too much. It was like she was trying to keep shutting the lid of a suitcase, but everyone kept putting in extra clothes, making it impossible to close. And Gemma's words kept pounding in her ears.

I know you understand because you had a brother once, too.

To think it was the slicing pain of those words that had finally pushed aside the bone aching weight of inertia that had prevented her from action. It was the reminder that she couldn't stand by and watch the people she loved get destroyed. But she couldn't help them without knowing the truth. Which is why she was here.

Libby sucked in some deep breaths to calm down and

stepped back into the shadows as a taxi pulled out of the driveway.

Eloise was in the back seat, her newly blow-dried hair perched on her head in an elegant bun. Libby couldn't see the outfit underneath the Burberry coat and Dior scarf that she'd brought back from the dry cleaners last week but she knew it would be either the burgundy cross-over dress with the full skirt, or the Jaeger silk skirt and blouse with the lace jacket. And regardless of the outfit, she'd be wearing the lustrous pearl necklace and earrings that she'd owned for as long as Libby had known her.

The opera was the only thing that could lure Eloise out in the evening, and since Nathan would be at the pub for at least another two hours, it meant that Libby could find proof that Colin Wallace wasn't Nathan's father.

She waited until the taxi disappeared down the road. Her lips were dry and she licked them, knowing it would only make it worse. A brittle laugh caught in her throat. Oh, to go back to a world where having cracked lips was the worst thing that had happened to her.

There was also a good chance she was losing her mind.

Which was why she was here. She had to find out for herself what the truth was. If Colin Wallace was really Nathan's father, and if it meant Nathan or one of her kids had somehow inherited the darkness from him. Her skin prickled with the idea of it. *Please let it be wrong. Please let it all be one big fat lie.*

It would all be okay. She'd only done it to keep her family safe. Regardless of what she found, she wouldn't hurt them, not like she'd done to Todd. She would always protect them. Always.

On cue, her phone beeped. It was a text message from Sienna.

Where are you? Why isn't there any food to eat?

Libby pressed her lips together. After receiving Gemma's email, Libby hadn't even got out of the car. Instead, she'd reversed out of the driveway, her mind swirling with too many things. It was like her past and her present were trying to merge in some kind of hideous montage that didn't belong together. Magnetic opposites that should never be combined. It had taken all her strength to push it back down. To try and win back control.

And she almost had.

But it wasn't enough. She couldn't keep ignoring the growing concern about her family. Nathan's lies, Sam's guilt, Sienna's secrets. It was all happening at once and Libby needed to know why. Was it something she'd done? Was she a bad person? Or had it come from somewhere else? *Someone* else? And then she remembered that Eloise was going out for the evening, which meant Libby could look for herself.

And more to the point, there was plenty of food in the cupboards if Sienna looked. None of which she had the energy to explain.

Order something in and use my card.

There was no reply and Libby put her phone away before walking up the driveway. Her shoes sounded like drums on the gravel, playing in time to the mounting guilt that was building in her chest.

She pushed it aside. She wasn't doing anything wrong.

And it was true... in a way. Eloise had given Libby a key years ago and she often popped in to drop off shopping or dry cleaning, or to give the place a quick dust and polish if she was on an afternoon shift. It was almost dark by the time she reached the door but the automatic lights that Nathan had insisted on installing last year flicked on. Libby unlocked the door and stepped inside.

During the day, the light walls and lack of clutter gave the house an airy feel but at night, it had the reverse effect, and the long, empty hallway was cold and uninviting. Nathan had never admitted that he didn't like the house he'd grown up in, but she'd always sensed it, and for the first time she understood why. It felt like a mausoleum.

Goosebumps prickled Libby's skin and she rubbed her arms as she fumbled for the torch app on her phone. Despite telling herself it was perfectly fine for her to be there; she didn't turn on the lights.

The torch beam bounced off the marble floors and her trainers squeaked as she walked, as if eager to announce her presence to someone. *Stop being stupid.* She increased her pace and reached the living room at the end of the house. While she'd never seen the safe herself, Nathan had told her about it several times, so she walked directly to the large oil painting that hung over the fireplace.

The curtains were drawn but the room still felt cold, which suggested Eloise hadn't put on the fire while she'd been in there. The realisation distracted her. She hated that her mother-in-law was part of the growing population who fretted about using their heating because of the rising cost of living.

After this whole thing was over, Libby would need to have another talk with her about it. Or, better yet, get her to sell the place and move into something that was smaller and easier to heat. Then she caught herself. If Nathan was somehow involved with what happened to Hayley, would there even be an *after*?

She put her phone down on the mantlepiece and lifted the

painting off the wall. The plaster frame was heavier than she'd expected and she staggered back, trying to balance the weight. Her muscles tensed as she regained control. That was way too close. Sweat beaded at her brow as she leaned it against the fireplace and then straightened up.

The safe was there. Like Nathan had said.

It was almost identical to the old one they'd had before replacing it last year, which meant she knew how to open it.

Boom. Boom. Boom. Libby's heart pounded and a buzzing sound rang in her ears, her body on high alert. Immediately, she closed her eyes and focused on the beat, allowing it to slow down to a more rhythmic pace, just like she did at work. Once she was calm, she opened her eyes and raised a hand to the dial. Eloise used the same password for absolutely everything. 1982. The year Nathan was born.

Her fingers keyed in the number followed by the hash key and the door swung open. She'd done it.

The sweat on her brow had increased and was now dripping down her face despite the temperature of the room. Libby ignored it and reached for her phone so she could shine the light in. There were several document folders as well as a collection of velvet jewellery boxes. She took several photos of how they were placed before carrying them over to the table so she could methodically work through them.

One of the folders contained a birth certificate and passport along with a collection of old insurance policies, all made out to Eloise Curtis. There was also a death certificate for Keith Curtis and a single gold wedding band that looked like it belonged to a man.

The second folder was filled with Nathan's school work and report cards and she paused to scan through a couple. The comments were surprisingly like the ones Sam had been receiving lately. The final folder contained the house documents and numerous share options and bank statements, but even after carefully studying them, there was nothing that linked her to another life.

The jewellery boxes contained several pairs of diamond earrings and a necklace that Libby had seen many times over the years. And there was also an empty box which no doubt housed the pearl necklace and earrings Eloise was currently wearing.

There had to be something else. Some photographs of the wedding or Nathan as a baby. She walked back to the safe and held the torch up, but there was nothing.

Disappointment coiled in her chest as she collected the folders and carefully put them back the way she'd found them. Then she scooped up the jewellery boxes and carried them over. The toe of her shoe caught on the edge of the fireplace and one of the boxes fell to the floor. It landed with a dull thud and bounced behind a chair. Libby winced and put the rest of the boxes back before getting onto her knees to retrieve it.

A trail of dust now coated it and she made a mental note to have a talk to the cleaner. She brushed it off, then frowned as her fingers brushed the velvet. What she'd thought was dust was the start of what looked like the letter M. She held it closer to her torch and once again ran her finger across the top. A faint outline of a name was embossed on the box. It had been dulled with age but when she held it at an angle, she could make it out.

Marion.

The box once again fell to the ground and Libby's hand began to shake. Marion. It was the name of the woman who'd been married to Colin Wallace. The one who had taken her son to Spain and never been heard of again.

Beep. Beep. Beep.

Libby froze, adrenaline roaring in her ears before remem-

bering the alarm she'd set on her phone. The one to remind her
not to take too long in case Eloise decided to leave the opera
during the interval, something she was prone to do if she didn't
like the performance.

Her chest was tight and she had to swallow back the rising
nausea as she carefully arranged the jewellery boxes according to
the photo she'd taken. It didn't take long for her to lock the safe
and put the painting back on the wall.

Her breath was coming in shallow gasps and she swallowed
hard as she hurried for the door. She needed to get outside into
the fresh air. This wasn't meant to happen. She'd come looking
for proof but it wasn't really what she'd wanted. There was meant
to be nothing. It was all meant to be a lie.

But it wasn't. Because if Eloise really was Marion Wallace,
then that meant Nathan was Colin Wallace's son. *Wait.* She tried
to slow down her whirling mind. Just because Nathan and Eloise
lied about their past didn't mean that what happened to Hayley
was connected. It could be a terrible coincidence. Not all children inherited their parents' traits. Or their grandparents'.

None of this was helping her decide what to do. It was ironic
that when it came to her work, she was always so calm and in
control. When others crumpled, she could always think clearly.
But now it was like her mind was trying to trudge through a
swamp and she kept sinking into it.

Her shirt was too tight around her neck and her chest felt like
an iron band had been wrapped around it. She needed to get
away from the house. Tugging at her collar, Libby hurried down
the path and onto the street.

The cool night air nipped at her cheeks as she sucked in the
fresh air. Her throat burned but it did help ease the constriction.
She jogged down the road and turned into the slip lane where
she'd parked her car. By the time she climbed in, her hands were

shaking as she fumbled to put the key in the ignition. She was a mess.

Her phone rang and Jonathan's number flashed up on the screen.

She didn't want to speak to anyone but Jonathan was almost like one of her kids and she couldn't bring herself to ignore one of his calls in case it was something important.

'Hey, is everything okay?' she asked.

'I was going to ask you the same thing,' he replied.

'What do you mean?' Her breath caught in her throat.

'I'm at your place. Thought I'd come by to see if everything was okay since Nathan was a no-show. Is he with you? I figured you'd convinced him to see a doctor about his ankle.'

Libby stiffened. She hadn't banked on anyone even knowing she'd left the house. Not that Jonathan would think much of it but she would have preferred it if he hadn't turned up and discovered her absence.

'I don't understand?'

'Nathan didn't turn up for our match. He sent a text to say he was on his way and that was the last I heard from him. He's not answering his phone and bloody Clive is such a stickler for the rules that at seven thirty-one, he declared victory. Smug little prick. Is he with you?'

'No.' Libby's stomach tightened. Was she going to be sick?

She hadn't spoken to Nathan since breakfast, and even then, he'd been short. Jonathan made a clicking noise with his tongue and Libby winced. It was obvious he was worried but she had no idea what to tell him.

She had no idea what to tell herself any more.

'Lib... where are you? Your voice sounds faint.'

She swallowed. 'I'm fine. I had to go to the supermarket.

Nathan probably got held up at the office. You know he's working on a new deal.'

'Well, when he gets this deal across the finish line, it will be his turn to buy the round,' Jonathan said, though there wasn't any malice in his voice. 'I might as well head home since he might stay at work for hours and your kids are both upstairs ignoring each other. But the cat was pleased to see me. I fed her, by the way.'

'Thanks. I'll see you at work tomorrow.'

Libby finished the call and checked her messages.

She hadn't heard from Nathan since eight thirty in the morning and it was now almost nine at night. It wasn't like him to miss anything. In fact, he was a stickler for being on time.

Unless something had happened.

No. It was too awful to contemplate. Just because Nathan and Eloise had lied about who his real father was, didn't mean that Nathan was following in his father's footsteps.

Or that Sam and Sienna had inherited their grandfather's darkness.

Her mind went back to her conversation with Fiona.

Hayley hadn't broken out of the lock-up where she'd been taken; the door was unlocked. Someone had let her out. Like Marion Wallace had done all those years ago. She'd found out what her husband had done and freed the young boy. Saved his life but condemned her husband.

Had she done it again for Nathan or her grandchildren? Except Eloise – no, Marion – wasn't in the best of health, which meant that while it wasn't impossible, it would have taken a great deal of effort. And why do that instead of calling the police? But Libby already knew the answer. Eloise loved her family and would do anything for them.

She'd already proven it once.

Am I any better?

Libby thought of the pink false nail she'd found in Sam's car. The one Hayley Terrace had lost that night. And what had Libby done? Destroyed it, to keep her son safe. And the hoodie that was hidden away in the laundry cupboard, like a time bomb waiting to go off.

The hoodie wasn't the only time bomb.

If Nathan and his children really did share the same blood as Wallace, did that mean they had something inside them that was ticking? Ice spread through her limbs, weighing them down like anchors, as she realised she could no longer ignore the elephant in the room that was Colin Wallace.

She needed to confront her husband.

Except she had no idea where he was. *Or what he was doing.*

Which only made everything that much worse.

Because as far as Libby could tell, there was only one reason why Nathan had disappeared. Because he had something terrible to hide. What she hated most was that he didn't trust her enough to keep those secrets. She'd done it before and she would do it again. If only he gave her the chance.

27

Gemma's head pounded and her throat was raw, like she'd swallowed glass. Bloody hell. How much had she drunk last night? But her mind refused to answer. It must have been a lot. She reached for the water bottle that was always by her bed. Pain radiated out along her shoulder and her stomach churned. Was she going to be sick? Sweat gathered on her brow and she forced herself to lie still until the nausea subsided.

She tried to prise her eyes open but another blast of pain jabbed through her, this time at the back of her skull. The metallic aftertaste of medicine coated her mouth. Was that it? Had she taken a sleeping pill? She never slept well, though tried to limit her use of the drugs, hating the way they left her groggy and disorientated. She licked her lips, trying to get some moisture into her aching throat and this time, managed to keep her eyes open.

The room was dark, though there was a faint glow of light from the far corner. Her brows pressed together in confusion. She never left a light on in her bedroom and her laptop was in the lounge. Something wasn't right but her mind seemed to be full of cotton wool.

Gemma closed her eyes again and tried to push down the rising panic.

Where was she?

Her vision swam as she tried to probe her memories, pushing through the barrier of fog. She needed to think. It wasn't her bedroom because there was no hum from the fridge or the familiar click, click, click of the Japanese waving cat that sat on the shelf. Sluggishly, it came to her. She was in Bournemouth. That's right. She'd caught the train down on Wednesday and was staying at the Cambridge Court Hotel to research Colin Wallace, and—

The car park. Jagged flashes splintered her mind and the memories quickened. Looking for her keys. The hand across her mouth. The unknown voice in her ear, and—

No.

Gemma tried to scream but her throat was raw and dry as ice travelled through her body, holding her captive. Her heart slammed against her ribs, at odds with the numbness travelling through her limbs. Someone had done something to her. Knocked her out and brought her... somewhere.

All the things Stephen had told her might happen were now a reality. She was the victim. The one on the page. The photograph in the paper. The dead one that the family gathered around to mourn. Her brother's fate was now her own.

Stop it.

She slammed away her panic. It wasn't the time. She'd done enough research and spoken to enough people to know that time was vital because the longer she stayed where she was, the harder it would be to fight the inertia. Like the story of the elephant who'd been chained up since it was small, so that by the time it reached its full size, it didn't even think of escaping. And yet it could have done so at any time. The chain that was holding it wasn't connected to anything and the only thing trapping it there was a thought.

Gemma wouldn't be the elephant held hostage by nothing more than a memory of a past experience.

She had to think. What day was it? What time? But her mind was all sludgy and the thoughts kept drifting away like clouds. *Come back*, she wanted to shout but her throat still ached. Swallowing hard, she opened her eyes again and waited until they had adjusted to the gloom.

The glow in the corner was coming from an old-fashioned standard lamp that cast dull shadows onto the brown floral carpet and clashing wallpaper. To one side was an orange sofa and next to it was a record player. A single record sleeve was leaning against it. She was too far away to see the name of it, but she already knew.

Verdi's Requiem, 'Dies Irae'.

Her head began to spin as she dared look down at her hands. Her wrists were circled in iron manacles that ran back to the wall. More chains went down to her feet. Gemma began to rock backwards and forwards, no longer finding any comfort in the story of the elephant. Her chains weren't a thought or a fear. They were real.

Then she turned to the wall, already knowing what she'd find. A single line carved into the wood.

Day one.

28

Libby rolled over and pain ricocheted through her shoulders. Her eyes were gritty from lack of sleep and her body ached from her night spent on the gold velvet sofa. There was still the faint scent of Nathan's aftershave from when he'd been there the other night, when she'd treated his ankle.

The night before everything had changed.

She fumbled for her phone which had fallen to the floor during the night. It was almost eight in the morning, and sometime in the night, the temperature had dropped, leaving the room cold. She tugged at the blanket she'd wrapped around herself, and Harriet, who'd been curled up near her feet, let out an irritated meow and jumped down.

Her shift started in an hour but there was no way she could go. Like she'd told Jonathan, it was part of the job to be fit and healthy. And she most definitely wasn't.

She brought up Denise's number on her phone and sent her a text message saying she wouldn't be in. Then she groggily got to her feet and stumbled to the window. The spot where Nathan's black Audi usually sat was empty.

He hadn't come home.

Pain lanced at her heart, tearing away the tiny slither of hope that he'd returned and could explain everything. That somehow, she'd managed to get things twisted around in her head. But his absence told her more than any words.

He was guilty.

She turned back to the room, which was when she saw the piece of paper. It was jagged down one side, as if it had been ripped from a notebook. And next to it was a stack of neatly folded newspaper clippings.

They hadn't been there last night, and for a moment, she stared at it. When the kids were smaller, they'd sometimes leave her little notes to say how much they loved her. It was usually followed by a request for ice cream or being allowed to watch an extra movie. And she'd always said yes because apparently she had a deep need for people to like her. Love her, even.

But as she picked it up, Nathan's neat, cursive writing burned into her retinas.

He'd left her a note.

Which meant he *had* come home. Somehow, that made it worse. He had walked into their home and looked at her while she slept. And then he'd walked away again. She stared at the note, eyes gritty from lack of sleep.

Dear Libby,

I'm sorry that I didn't wake you last night. I wanted to, but I couldn't muster up the courage to admit the truth, once again proving that you deserve a better husband than the monster you got. There are so many things I should have told you... and I have a feeling that you've found out some of them on your own.

There's a woman in town. Gemma Harrington. I've known

*about her for some time. She writes a blog, all about... well...
my father. But I suppose you know that by now since I'm sure
she's told you. She was the one who went to the factory and
was speaking to Mo and then I saw her again on Friday when I
went to the rowing club. And finally, when I was on my way to
the darts final, there she was, talking to Sam. To our son.*

*I'm afraid to say I didn't handle it well. You know me, Lib.
When it gets like that, I need to move. To do. Anything to stop
the darkness. But of course, I can't do anything of those
things, so I had to just go and wait it out, until the anger faded.*

*That's why I stayed away. I didn't want you to see me like
that. Like my father.*

*There. I've said it. And if Gemma hasn't told you about
him, I've enclosed enough information to get you up to speed.
I found them last week in a safe upstairs. In the pink bedroom.
I didn't even know it was there until I went searching for her
health records for the hospital.*

*I'm sorry I didn't tell you sooner. I always promised my
mother I wouldn't share our secrets with anyone. And I've tried
to keep my word, but when Julia became pregnant, I felt I
needed to be honest with her.*

*What a terrible mistake. From the moment she knew, it
changed us in a way that couldn't be fixed. Sometimes, I
wonder if that's why she died in the hospital. Because she
couldn't bear to know that our children carried my father's
blood.*

I didn't want that to happen with you.

*But now it's happened anyway and I want you to know I'm
sorry. You are the mother that my kids need, and the wife I
love. Please, even if you never want to speak to me again.
Don't take it out on them. You're all they've got.*

Hell. Now I'm sounding ominous, and I don't mean to

scare you, my love. But there are things I need to do. Things that... I've ignored for too long. I know it's not right and that what I do might have consequences. But I have to finish what I've started.

It's the only way for our family to have a chance. Which is probably the real reason I didn't wake you up. So that you couldn't talk me out of it. I hope to return in two days. I've sent the kids a text and told them I'm in Birmingham looking for locations for a factory. But if you decide to tell them more... well... I'll leave that decision up to you.

Please forgive me.

Nathan (and no, I can't use that other name. Even if it's the truth of who I am, it's not who I want to be.)

She closed her eyes and the letter fell into her lap.

All the excuses she'd being trying to muster up. All the explanations were finally gone. The letter was a full stop. A confession.

You deserve a better husband than the monster you got.

She wanted to cry. Wanted tears to stream down her face to signify this betrayal, but they wouldn't come. Instead, there was a hollowness inside her. He'd told Julia the truth and she'd turned on him. If he had told Libby, would the same thing have happened? Some people might have. But not her. A spouse shouldn't be judged on the actions of his father and she'd already shown herself that when it came to her family, she put them first.

Did Nathan know that?

Was he scared that her acceptance might bring out the monster even more? A numbness crept into her veins as the terrible truth slid through her. Nathan had been right. Libby had lived with her monster of a mother and watched her destroy everything. But now Nathan was almost commanding her to not do that again.

You are the mother my kids need.

She forced her frozen limbs to move and got to her feet. Upstairs, she could hear Sam shuffling around, his zombie-like movements suggesting he'd gone to sleep even later than her. A moment later, the shower started.

Libby shut her eyes. She should wait until he came downstairs and talk to him, along with his sister. But what could she say? How could she answer the questions they might have when she wasn't sure of anything herself? But she knew someone who could help her. She hoped she hadn't left it too late.

The Cambridge Court Hotel was several blocks back from the Pier but had a general area of neglect. The Victorian bricks had been painted cream and several extensions had been added over the years, with no attempt to blend it all together, giving it a melancholy air of being trapped in the past.

There was a car park out the front, though there was no sign of the green Fiesta.

Libby swallowed down her disappointment and walked into the reception area. The walls were papered in a violent clash of burgundy stripes with a horizontal strip of flowers running across it. The reception counter was made of gleaming marble and the carpet was the kind of blue that airports favoured. She blinked, trying to ignore the assault of colours and textures as she reached the counter.

'Hi, can I help?' A man in his fifties appeared from behind a door.

'I do hope so. I'm meant to be meeting a friend for lunch and she hasn't shown up. Her name is Gemma Harrington and she's staying in room twenty-three.'

'Let me see if I can get hold of her.' He pressed a button on an old-fashioned phone system and held the handset up to his ear. After several moments, he shook his head. 'Sorry, she's not answering.'

Libby had already sent the woman an email and left two phone messages before deciding to try her room. She tried to soften her mouth and hide her tension as she smiled at the man.

'Have you seen her today?'

He frowned, as if rewinding a tape in his mind, then shook his head. 'No. I don't think so. Would you like to leave a message?'

No. Libby wanted to scream. She didn't have time for messages. But she managed to hold it in. 'Thank you.' She took the piece of paper and pen and quickly wrote down her name and number and asked Gemma to call her as soon as possible. In the meantime, her mind continued to whirl. Where was Nathan, and what had he done?

29

Gemma was so thirsty. It was all she could think about. That and the fact a second line had been carved into the strip of wood by the bed. It must be Friday. She was meant to check out of her hotel at ten and be on the train by eleven thirty.

She had no idea of the time. Or if anyone at the Cambridge Court would report her missing. And what about Stephen? What would he think when the train pulled in and she wasn't on it. Would he be worried? Or just pissed off, assuming she'd decided to stay longer and damn the consequences?

Painfully, she twisted around to the bench beside the bed. A bottle of water was sitting there, along with an apple and a brown-bread sandwich. Also, a bucket had appeared at the foot of the bed. It had been the same yesterday.

How had that happened without her knowing?

Her head swam as she leaned forward to reach for the bottle, then winced as her raw skin chaffed beneath the cold steel of the manacle. She could feel one of the cuts start to bleed as she fumbled for the bottle before finally managing to grasp it. Her hands shook as she unscrewed the lid and the faint metallic tang of tablets caught in her nose.

Some kind of drug.

Was that why she hadn't heard anyone come in? Because they'd laced the water with something? Or was it in the food?

Her throat ached as she stared at the water bottle, hating the cruelness of it. Were they watching her now? Laughing at the terrible dilemma they'd given her? Drink and succumb to the drugs or don't drink and die of dehydration. She slumped back against the wall, still clutching at the bottle. Her limbs were drained of energy and it took all her strength just to stay upright.

It made a mockery of her plan to escape. And to think how much she'd laughed at the stupid girls in horror movies who gave up without even trying. But now she was one of them. A stupid girl about to die.

Stop it, a voice deep inside her hissed. Her body might be weak but she still had her mind. And she had to figure out who was behind it. Sam? Had he secretly resented what she'd told him? He was strong enough to have done it. Or... was it Nathan?

Her skin prickled. He seemed the more likely. She'd seen him yell at his son and then sit outside Hayley Terrace's house. Had Libby told him about their conversation? More than likely. She was such a fool to have even come down here. And for what? Stephen had been right.

You're chasing ghosts, and sometimes that can be worse.

Why hadn't she listened?

All the times he'd tried to bring her back into the light and away from the hyper fixation that had become her family inheritance. Family trauma. Suddenly, another life flashed before her. One of her and Stephen together. Not just having the occasional hook up and friendly banter as they supported each other through their careers. But something deeper. Shared. A life that didn't just revolve around work and Colin Wallace.

Tears jabbed in the corner of her eyes for the life she hadn't been able to live.

He'd already taken enough from her and her family and now his son was going to continue the job. She blinked away the tears in her eyes as the door creaked open. The blackness was broken by a flash of dull light and then a figure appeared. They were wearing a mask on their face and their body was hidden beneath a huge coat.

A slim beam shone in her face and she recoiled from the glare. Her fingers tightened around the water bottle as the figure moved closer. There was a shuffle on the ground, as if the person had a limp, and Gemma began to shake.

'Please, let me go. I swear I won't tell anyone. You won't get in trouble. Just let me out.'

But there was no answer, just the scraping of a bucket against the floor. They were replacing her makeshift toilet. Then the light faded as the figure retraced their steps and headed back towards the door. Desperation spread through her limbs.

'No. Don't go. Don't leave me here.'

But it was too late. The door cracked open, and the figure stepped through it, before closing it behind them. The room once again returned to blackness and Gemma gave in to the tears.

30

Sienna pushed her bike through the archway that led to the cemetery and dismounted. There was a church to one side of her and next to it was small car park with a couple of gardeners unloading wheelbarrows. She ignored them and kept walking. At least it wasn't busy. Then again, she had no idea what constituted busy for a Friday morning. Luckily she hadn't been stopped by Libby this time. Her stepmother had been acting more than a little weird recently. Thankfully, she'd headed out in her car before Sienna had finished getting dressed.

There were two roads that split off to different parts of the cemetery but it felt weird to ride along them. Disrespectful. Though she knew it was stupid. Hearses did it all the time but it still felt wrong.

Trees were dotted between the headstones, casting finger-like shadows in the mid-morning sun. She used one hand to push her bike and the other to check her phone for messages. Okay. That was a lie. There was only one message she wanted to see. From one person. But there was nothing. She was so stupid to think they'd come. To think that they liked her. That they saw her as special.

Because she wasn't special at all.

I'm just the freak who goes to the cemetery to look at graves.

It was still better than sitting through another tedious day of lessons that she didn't care about. She slowed down to get her bearings. There was a square-shaped mausoleum to the left and she turned towards it.

The last time she'd been there was a year ago as part of the rowing club's annual 'Do Good Day'. Usually, it was bullshit. More like free child labour than anything as they were sent out to help at rest homes or to beaches to pick up litter.

But last year had been different. Her team had been sent to the cemetery with gardening gloves, buckets and instructions to tidy up the graves that no one cared for. Most of the girls were grossed out and had spent the day complaining about their nails.

But Sienna had loved it.

There was something so vast and otherworldly about pushing away the dirt and leaves from the flat concrete plinths so she could read the inscriptions. Those carved words and dates made all her stupid problems seem petty. Like why the hell would someone who died back in 1805 give a shit about whether Sienna Curtis had a slightly crooked smile that made her hate taking selfies?

It had been liberating.

Somehow, these people she didn't know had freed her. It was like they'd taken her to another world. No, another planet. One where she felt like she belonged. Then she'd heard it.

A sobbing noise.

It had come from somewhere behind her, and she'd turned, half expecting to see a ghost. Instead, there was Hayley Terrace. Impossibly gorgeous with her hair hanging half over her tear-streaked face as she stared at the solemn stone angel guarding the gravestone.

The angel's head was turned downwards, her expression laced with pain, as if somehow knowing that in the future vandals would break off her wings and age would turn her to a dull, mottled grey.

Sienna had been so shocked that she'd rushed to Hayley's side before she could stop herself.

'Hey, are you okay? Did you hurt yourself? There's quite a lot of broken glass around here.'

Hayley had turned to her then, tears still glistening on her impossibly black lashes. 'It's not that. It's just so bloody sad. Look. Kathryn Walsh was born in 1855 and died in 1870. She was fifteen. It makes everything else seem so, I don't even know what the word is—'

'Petty.' Sienna finished off, the words raw against her throat. It was stupid really. They'd known each other for ever but had hardly ever spoken. What was the point when Hayley was older, more popular, and totally into boys. But in that moment, something shifted and Hayley's eyes had widened, as if seeing Sienna for the first time.

It ripped through Sienna's body like electricity. Switching on things that she hadn't even known were there.

'Yes. Exactly. Petty. From now on, whenever I get caught up in my own shit, I'm going to think about Kathy W and remind myself it's not so bad.'

Sienna swallowed and pushed back the memories as she looked at her phone again. Still no message, but the two little blue ticks let her know that the person had read the text Sienna had sent. But was it even who she hoped it would be?

She flicked back to the photo that she'd posted last night. It was of the same stone angel that she'd photographed last year.

And she'd tagged it #gothcore. It was more to piss people off than anything. To remind her former friends to keep their distance. And it had worked. It hardly had any comments or even likes. Until one had suddenly appeared. It was a thumbs up from a name she hadn't seen before. Kathy W.

Kathryn Walsh.

Sienna had spent all night staring at it. Wondering. Hoping.

And then, she'd taken the risk. She'd sent Kathy W a message simply saying eleven o'clock in the morning. And so now she was here, to see if it was real. To see if it really had been Hayley and not just some stupid jerk trying to mess with her. Zoe or Tate. Or even Sam. She wouldn't put it past any of them.

Her heart pounded as she followed the curve of the road past the newer gravestones until she finally reached the one with the solemn angel. The weeds had grown back, and someone had tagged the statue, though it was now covered with some kind of paint to hide what had been sprayed.

Disappointment caught in her mouth but before she could turn, a faint scent of vanilla drifted towards her. Hope filled her but she didn't dare turn around.

'You know it's creepy, right? To ask someone to meet you at the cemetery,' a familiar voice said and Sienna's whole body reacted, sending trails of heat along her skin. It was her. She'd really come.

'Takes one to know one,' she retorted, before finally daring to look.

Hayley stepped out from behind one of the trees, half-hidden in the shadows. Her brown hair was pulled back and her dark eyes were rimmed with eyeliner, making her face paler than usual. Then again, she'd hardly been outside since it happened, so it might explain the pallor.

'Are you calling me a creep?' Hayley's movements were jerky

and uncertain, and her lower lip was dry, like she'd been chewing on it. But Sienna wanted to kiss it. And that had been the whole problem last time. The fact that she'd managed to have a crush on the straightest girl in school. Then Tate had come along, and Hayley had thrown herself at him, probably just to give Sienna the message more than anything.

Well, at least that's what she tried to tell herself.

'I've called you a lot worse.' Sienna shrugged and Hayley wrinkled her button-like nose.

'Nothing I didn't deserve. If it's any consolation, I am sorry, you know. About how things went with us. I didn't mean to cut you like that. I just got... freaked.'

Irritation skittered up the back of Sienna's neck. 'Yeah, well, for the record, I wasn't going to pounce on you or anything. You didn't need to ghost me.'

'I know. I guess I wasn't thinking straight.'

'Oh, you were thinking *very* straight,' Sienna retorted and then regretted it when Hayley's face drained of colour. 'Sorry. I'm being a dick. Forget I said that.'

'It's not that.' Hayley shook her head, though her eyes clouded over with pain. 'I'm feeling a bit... well... I haven't been out much lately. Mind if we sit down?'

Sienna swallowed and glanced at Kathryn Walsh's grave. Back where it all began.

'Sure.' She lowered her bike to the ground and waited until Hayley had perched herself on the edge of the base. Sienna sat down across from her. The concrete was warm from the sun. 'Thanks for coming. I didn't know if you were still avoiding me. According to your mum, I've been stalking you.'

Hayley rolled her eyes towards the sky and let out a snort. 'Yes, Adele has been on fine form. She's convinced that all my friends are guilty and won't let anyone into the house. Not that many have tried. And when it first happened it was too hard to even think about it, let alone talk. So maybe it was my fault as well. I just wanted to be on my own.'

'I get that. It must be shit not remembering anything.'

Hayley's lower lip trembled and her eyes glassed over, like she was on the verge of tears. 'But I do remember. That's why I'm here. I wanted to explain what really happened that night. The parts I can remember, anyway. Including the parts with you.'

Oh.

Icy dread swept through her, turning her to stone like the broken angel that hovered above Kathryn's grave.

This whole time, she figured that Hayley hadn't remembered. Isn't that what she'd told the police? And why she'd been ignoring Sienna's messages? Because she hadn't been able to remember the phone call in the middle of the night and the drunken plea for Sienna to collect her from the bonfire at High-cliffe. The bonfire that Sienna hadn't even been invited to.

And yet, Sienna had done it. She'd gone downstairs and realised she was the only one at home. Libby was working, her dad was doing something with their grandmother and Sam had gone to play Dungeons and Dragons. Except he hadn't taken his car.

So, she'd driven it out there and found Hayley totally off her face, standing by the side of the road. Sienna had lost it then. Anything could have happened to her. What the hell had she been thinking? Except it had ended in an argument and Hayley had told her to stop the car so she could puke, but instead, she'd climbed out and gone running off across the reserve.

'I hate you,' she'd screamed.

She'd been so fast, and Sienna had stumbled over a log, and by the time she'd righted herself, Hayley had disappeared. She'd kept searching but after an hour, she'd given up and returned to the car. Leaving Hayley to—

A sob caught in her throat and then it turned to a wail.

'I'm so sorry. I swear I tried to find you. I looked everywhere but you'd disappeared. I've been going out of my mind.' Sienna cried, the tears that she'd been holding back for the last two weeks trailing down her face.

'Wait. No, stop it. Sienna, it wasn't your fault.' Hayley's eyes were wide with horror. 'Is that what you thought?'

Sienna wrapped her arms around her torso to stop herself from falling apart completely. 'Of course it's my fault. You were off your face. I should never have let you get out of the car. Besides, Sam's such a pig, he probably wouldn't have even noticed if you had puked in there.'

Hayley gave a watery laugh, but it didn't last long. 'Stop blaming yourself. I'm the one who took the drugs. I'm such an idiot. When Zoe gave them to me, I should have chucked them away.'

Sienna sucked in a breath. 'Wait... Zoe gave you drugs? Are you sure?'

'Oh, yes. Not that she'd ever admit it, of course. She's been texting me all week asking what I remember. I think she's shitting herself that I'll tell the police.'

'Why don't you?' Sienna said, her voice a little above a whisper. 'Tell them what you remember.'

Hayley shook her head. 'I can't bear to go through everything again. And I know it's bad, because what if the sicko tries it again on someone else, and this time doesn't leave the door unlocked? But... I just want everything to go back to normal.'

Sienna had heard a rumour that the door had been left unlocked, which was how Hayley managed to escape, but it was the second part that caused her stomach to drop. She remembered the look of despair on Tate's face when she'd found him the other night. He clearly regretted breaking up with Hayley. Did that mean they'd be getting back together?

'Oh.' She got to her feet. This whole stupid thing has been a mistake. 'Well, I'd better get going and I hope you and Tate are—'

'Ew, Tate.' Hayley's whole face crinkled as if she'd sucked a lemon. 'No thanks. I've had enough of Tate to last a lifetime. In fact, I've had enough of boys,' she added as she got to her feet.

Sienna's mouth went dry and her heart thumped against her ribs as Hayley took a small step towards her. The shadow of the stone angel seemed to embrace them against the morning sun. Hayley's breath was warm against her check and Sienna's knees almost buckled.

Was this really happening?

'A-are you sure?' she managed to whisper.

'I've been sure for three hundred and eighty-one days, since you told me that being in the cemetery was like being in another world and it made everything else seem... petty. I got a little scared, that's all.'

Sienna was on fire as their eyes locked together. 'Next time you get scared, just say so. A lot less stressful than watching you date Tate.'

Hayley let out a watery laugh and then leaned forward.

Sienna's first kiss was everything she'd imagined. Right down to the gothic splendour of standing in a cemetery, and it wasn't until they pulled apart that she realised Hayley was holding her hand, their fingers entwined.

'Forgive me?' Hayley asked, a small smile on her lips.

'It could be a process,' Sienna said. 'Though it's a good start,' she added, which prompted Hayley to kiss her again.

'I can live with that.' Then she closed her eyes and a shadow once again passed across her face. 'I'm sorry I didn't tell you sooner. I really didn't think you'd blame yourself. If anything, I was worried you might have said something.'

'The advantage of having no friends, remember?' Sienna swallowed, as the other reason stampeded through her thoughts like a proverbial bull. Because she didn't know how her brother fitted into everything and she'd been terrified she might make things worse if she said anything. She was *still* terrified. Not that her meathead brother deserved it. But... she had to know. 'Why did you text Sam?'

'He didn't tell you?' Hayley chewed her lower lip, the colour draining from her face. Sienna went very still, like something dark and terrible was trying to drag her back down to the earth.

'Tell me what?'

'He was the one who sold Zoe the drugs.'

31

The last time I saw my son was on a Saturday morning. Alan was six years old and I'd kept him at home from school the day before because he had a temperature and was feeling poorly. But by Saturday, Alan was back to his usual self and was desperate to kick a ball around with the lads down the road. It was May but there was still a chill in the air, so I made him wrap up warm. Seems such a stupid thing to worry about now... after everything that's happened. But that's the way of it. You never know when your life is going to be destroyed. And that's what happened to us.

A year before Colin Wallace's lock-up of depravity was found and he was arrested, my only son went missing. We haven't heard from him since and his body was never found.

Had Alan been kept in the same lock-up? Or, in a different one somewhere else?

These are just some of the questions we might never have answers for, because Colin Wallace confessed to abducting and killing numerous boys, and then withdrew his statement, refusing to ever speak about it again. And in doing so, he has destroyed my family and taken away our peace. Colin Wallace lived as a monster and died as one as well.

Libby closed her laptop. She had to stop reading the interviews that Gemma Harrington had on her blog. And yet every time she tried, her eyes would drift back to the words. Like some kind of torture where she had to keep taking in all the pain and suffering that Colin Wallace's victims and their families had gone through.

Was it to try and goad her into action? To force her out of the inertia that kept preventing her from calling the police and telling them what she knew about Nathan? Except what did she really know? It was all still separate pieces of a puzzle that didn't fit together. And as far as she was aware, no other girls were missing.

Libby swallowed and tried to ignore the coil of dread in her stomach that was keeping her from deciding what to do. Would it be different when she heard back from Gemma? Or from Nathan? Did she need one of them to come in and convince her of the truth so that she could break the holding pattern she was in?

I have to finish what I started.

'There's no more milk.' Sam appeared in the doorway, holding the empty bottle towards her, as if she could somehow magically fill it. Libby frowned, not realising he was still in the house.

'Shouldn't you be at school?' She stood up and walked towards him. There were dark shadows under his eyes and his clothes were crumpled, like he'd slept in them.

'Shouldn't you be at work?' he countered. Libby raised an eyebrow and he held up his hands. 'Relax. I have a late start. Besides, it's only maths and now that I have someone to do it all for me, I should be fine.'

A week ago, Libby would've flinched at his needling, but now it had dropped so far down her list that she couldn't even muster up a scowl.

His face darkened, clearly irritated that she didn't take his bait, and he stalked out of the study and down the stairs, slamming the front door shut as he went. A moment later, the engine of his car fired up and the tyres squealed as he drove away. Libby sighed and followed his lead by heading downstairs.

She usually only allowed herself two cups of coffee a day but the way the morning had started, she wasn't sure she'd make it through to lunch without a third. Without Nathan there, the percolator was in the cupboard instead of sitting on the bench where he usually left it, and there were no freshly ground beans. Sighing, she dragged out the old-fashioned coffee grinder and had just finished turning the handle when Jonathan called.

'Hey.' She put him on speaker so she could finish her ritual. It was done and she turned on the hob before tucking her phone back under her ear.

'Everything okay? Denise said you were still sick.'

'I'm fine. Just got a temperature and that stomach bug that's been going around.' She hated lying, especially to a friend, but it was a hell of a lot easier than telling the truth.

'You poor thing. I hope Nathan's looking after you. Want me to bring something around for you?'

'That's very sweet, but I'm okay. I think I'm just going to sleep,' she said as the doorbell went. 'Hey, I've got to go, but thanks for checking in on me.'

'Of course. Hope you feel better soon,' he said and ended the call.

Libby turned off the coffee and hurried through to the hallway, Harriet threading her way between her ankles. 'Stop it,' she scolded the cat before half opening the door.

A man was standing there. He was in his mid to late thirties with pale blue eyes and brown hair that was sprinkled with grey. There was no sign of a clipboard or lanyard around his neck, which meant he probably wasn't selling anything. It almost made her trust him less.

She kept the door half open and put her foot firmly behind it. 'Can I help you?'

'I hope so. My name is Stephen Parker.' He had a northern accent, though not one she could place, and his voice was soft. 'You don't know me but I'm a friend of Gemma Harrington. I've just arrived from Manchester and I'm hoping you can help me.'

Gemma?

Libby's fingers tightened around the door frame and this time she made sure her shoulder was also behind it. However, he didn't seem interested in trying to force his way in. Instead, he took a slight step back, as if worried about being intimidating.

'What kind of help? I've only met her once and that was in a supermarket car park.'

'I know. She told me all about it.' He paused, as if weighing up his words. 'I'm here because she's missing. I've been trying to contact her since Wednesday night but I haven't had a reply. It's not like her, so I came down late last night. But she never came back to the hotel where she was staying.'

Missing.

Libby swallowed as images crashed into her mind, one after another. All the things she'd been reading about Colin Wallace. About the kind of man her father-in-law had been.

And the only saving grace about Nathan and Sam's strange behaviour was that no one else had been reported missing.

Until now.

'Are you sure she hasn't checked into another place? She had

a rental car; maybe she decided to go further around the coast. I-
it is beautiful this time of year.'

She was clutching at straws and Stephen's worried expression
confirmed it.

'She would never have left without paying the bill or taking
her luggage. Including her laptop. I paid the account and that's
when they gave me your details. The man on reception said
you'd been looking for her.'

Libby closed her eyes to avoid staring at the deep lines
carving their way into Stephen's face. Her decision to contact
Gemma was because she wanted some answers, and more information about Colin Wallace, but before she'd done that, she'd
researched her online to make sure she was telling the truth. Yet,
what did she know about Stephen?

'Can I see some ID please?'

'Of course.' He extracted his wallet and showed his driver's
licence. Libby quickly typed his name into her phone and found
him. A family lawyer at a community centre in Manchester.

Gemma's voice drifted into her mind.

Stop protecting them.

'Okay, what would you like to know?' she asked. He gave her a
solemn smile, his blue eyes meeting hers. As if to say thank you.
She brushed it aside, not wanting to dwell on the discomfort of
who she might be betraying.

'Why did you want to speak to her?'

'When she came up to me, she told me that someone called
Colin Wallace might be my husband, Nathan's real father. I didn't
want to listen but then she sent me another email, telling me
about her brother, Lucas.' Libby's voice shook as the reality
started to fully sink in. 'I couldn't stop thinking about it and then
I found... well... I wanted to get some more details from her. So, I

called her on Wednesday night and then went to the hotel yesterday.'

'What sort of details? Was it about what happened to Hayley Terrace?'

'Not really.' Libby rubbed her chin. 'It's all so confusing. I'd never even heard of Colin Wallace until I met Gemma, but...' she tailed off, hoping that he'd fill the silence. He didn't. She sighed. 'Some things weren't quite adding up at home, and the more I looked, the—' she broke off. It was terrible enough to think these things in her head but saying them out loud somehow made it all real. 'I wanted to ask her more questions. But I'm not sure how this can help you? She wasn't there and didn't return my call.'

'I understand. However, what I really need help with is talking to your son. I believe he was the last person to see her.'

What?

'Son?' Her throat still felt dry and the word burned.

He nodded. 'The last time I spoke to Gemma, she'd just had a coffee with Sam. I managed to find the café where they went and the manager confirmed it. He thought they'd left at about five-forty-five, which ties in with when she called me. It also potentially means that Sam was one of the last people to see her.'

He didn't say the word 'alive', but it hung in the air like a missile.

Her knees buckled and she leaned against the door frame, afraid she might faint.

And why hadn't Sam mentioned it?

She thought of his pale face and the dark shadows under his eyes. She'd put it down to too many late nights and not enough sleep. But had there been a different reason? Had he stayed up trying to research Colin Wallace, the same way she had?'

Or was it something else?

Stephen gave her an apologetic smile. 'I know this is hard but I need to speak to Sam. According to the manager, they were in the café for almost an hour.'

Libby swallowed. Her days of trying to pretend nothing was happening were over. If Gemma really was missing, then she couldn't keep covering it up... especially from herself. She nodded her head as if trying to give herself courage.

'Sam's at school. I-I suppose I could call him.'

'Thank you,' he said as she tapped the screen and then brought up Sam's number and called it.

She tried a second time but there was still no answer. That wasn't surprising, especially in the last six months when he'd only ever called or messaged when he needed food or money. Swearing, she brought up the school's number.

'Hi Beryl, this is Libby Curtis,' she said as soon as the school secretary answered. 'Something's come up and I'm trying to get hold of Sam. He's not answering his phone. Could you check if he's arrived at school? He left home about half an hour ago.'

'Hang on one moment. I'll see if he's on the attendance roll.' Beryl's voice was accompanied by a clatter of the keyboard. 'Hmmm. No, he hasn't showed up yet. But Libby, while I have you, did you know that Sam's been absent all week?'

'What? Are you sure?'

'Yes. I can see that we've sent out a text message to both you and your husband,' she said before rattling off two mobile numbers that Libby had never heard of before. She swore under her breath. The school records must have been updated. 'Is everything okay?'

No. Not remotely. Libby's throat burned and her skin prickled.

'I see... yes. It's fine. I'm at work and his father must have forgotten to tell me. Thank you.'

Libby ended the call but her hand was shaking as she turned

back to where Stephen was waiting. The muscles on his neck were tense and it was clear he'd understood the implications of her phone call.

'He's not at school.'

'Can you think of where he might be?' This time, he didn't hide the urgency in his voice.

Despite their recent fights, Sam was so much like Nathan that it hurt. And just like her husband, when things got too much, there was only one place Sam would go. Down to the water. She'd long ago installed a surfing app on her phone and made Nathan teach her how to read it so that she'd know where the swells were, depending on the wind. She tapped the screen and studied it.

Highcliffe Beach.

The same place where Hayley had first gone missing.

She shut her eyes. Part of her still screamed that this whole thing was a mistake. The idea that Sam or Nathan could hurt anyone was—

'Please, Libby. I know this is hard. But Gemma's missing and we need to find her as quickly as possible. And if Sam can help…'

'I know.' She reached for her car keys and bag. There was no sign of a car, so he must have come by Uber or taxi. 'We can go in my car. It's about fifteen minutes away.'

* * *

The car park was almost empty when Libby pulled in, making it easier to spot Sam's car. There was no sign of his surfboard but she didn't want to tell Stephen that. He'd already spent the entire trip tapping his long fingers against his leg, as if trying to shake off the unbearable tension.

She couldn't blame him. If the roles had been reversed, she would have been the same.

There were several people out on the waves but there was no sign of the distinctive longboard that Nathan had given Sam last year. Libby swallowed and scanned the beach before zooming in on it. The board was flat out on the sand and next to it was Sam. His head was slumped forward though his hands were moving, tossing something up into the air and catching it again.

'That's him.'

Stephen seemed to sense her tension and gave her an expectant look. 'Do you want me to come?'

Libby chewed her lower lip. Sam didn't always do well around strangers but there was no time to worry about that. If Gemma had been missing since Tuesday afternoon, they had to find out exactly what had happened and, for that, Stephen needed to be there. In case he needed to do what she couldn't. What kind of mother was she?

'Yes.'

'Okay.' At the end of the car park was a sloping zig-zag path leading down to the beach. They were silent as they descended and the wind nipped at their skin, sending Libby's thick dark hair flying across her face. She pushed it back as they made their way through the soft sand.

Sam continued to toss the ball up into the air before catching it, but his gaze was unfocused, as if he was looking at something out on the horizon.

It wasn't until Libby was almost next to him that he turned around. His eyes were red rimmed and his mouth was set in a distraught line.

She let out a small sob and was suddenly next to him. Holding him like she'd done so many times over the years. He was still hers, no matter what he'd done.

His body was stiff and unyielding before the fight seemed to drain out of him and his head pressed into her neck. They sat there for some time before he finally pulled away and looked at Stephen for the first time.

Libby slipped her hand into his. 'Sam, this is Stephen. Gemma Harrington's friend. And right now he's very worried about her. Is it true that you saw her on Wednesday?'

He rubbed his eyes, as if waking up from a long sleep, still groggy. But finally, he nodded.

'Yeah. She was at the beach and said she wanted to talk to me about Dad. We had coffee and she told me...'

Pain flashed across his face and he dropped his head again.

Something ripped at her heart. All she'd wanted to do was keep him safe. Make the world a good place for him. But she hadn't been able to do that. There had been something dark that had come for them both.

'She told me the same thing,' she whispered. He looked back up, eyes bleak.

'It's true, isn't it?'

'I... I think so,' Libby answered before looking up to Stephen and giving him a nod.

He knelt a few metres away, so that he was on eye level with them both. 'Sam, can you tell me what happened? What did you talk about and did Gemma mention that she was going anywhere else? Maybe to meet with someone?'

'No. When we were leaving, she asked if I could look for anything to prove Dad was really Ian Wallace. I said I'd think about it and then went to catch my bus. She wanted to give me a lift in her car, but I said no. I wanted to clear my head.'

'Did she say where she'd parked?'

He shook his head. 'No. All she kept talking about was that

she owed it to the families to find the bones. That's why she came down here. To talk to Dad and Grandma.'

'And you haven't heard from her since?' There was more urgency in Stephen's voice now. 'Did anyone in the café seem like they were watching you?'

'Sorry.' Sam shook his head, fatigue clear in his eyes. 'My head was all over the place. I can hardly even remember what she looks like, let alone if anyone else was there. Are you sure she's missing?'

'I'm sure,' Stephen said, his voice not as calm as it had been. Sam looked at the ball in his hands and then threw it as far away from them as he could, before turning to Libby.

'What's this about? Do you think that's why Dad's gone away?'

Stephen's whole body stiffened and his jaw went tight. 'What do you mean? Where's Nathan?'

Libby swallowed. She was so tired and her mind was all over the place. Like a juggler who couldn't catch all the balls. There were too many of them and they were falling all around her.

'I don't know.' She forced herself to return his gaze and saw the terror in his eyes. 'He came home at some stage on Tuesday night or Wednesday morning and left me a note but he hasn't been back since.'

Next to her, Sam thumped the sand with his hand and Libby shuddered as all the unanswered questions flooded her mind. About her son, about Nathan, about the blood they inherited. It needed to stop. She needed to find out the truth, no matter how much it hurt.

'Sam, do you know anything about the night that Hayley was taken?'

He went still, his exhausted eyes staring directly at her, but instead of the usual rage that followed, he simply nodded his head. 'Yes.'

Libby shut her eyes.

Here they were. Back at ground zero. The place where everything had started. It was all the things that she didn't want to know. Didn't want to believe were possible. But the bleakness in his voice told her that he was too tired to lie any longer. Which meant she had to listen.

'Tell me what happened?' she said softly.

'A few weeks ago, one of the guys that I sometimes... well... I get weed from him. Anyway, he said I could make a few extra quid if I wanted to sell some party gear. I only did it twice and then stopped. Not my scene at all. But then Zoe heard about it and kept asking. I should've said no... but in the end, I gave in.'

Libby's breath was sharp. 'That was the night of the bonfire?'

He let out a miserable sigh. 'If Hayley hadn't taken anything, she'd have been okay. And the prick who kidnapped her, wouldn't have had the chance.'

'T-that's it. You're sure?'

'Yes, I'm sure—' he broke off, eyes widening. 'You didn't think that I—'

'No,' she quickly said and then stopped herself. 'I don't know. I keep finding things that draw our family back to that night. And the fact you sold them ketamine, which is more than a party drug, by the way.'

He looked up, a bit of life finally showing in his eyes. 'No way. It wasn't ketamine. Wait, is that what the police are saying? I didn't know that.'

'I don't think it's been officially released.' Libby said, remembering that Fiona had told her in confidence. 'Are you sure that's not what the pills were?'

He shook his head. 'No way. Just E—' he cut off, catching Libby's sharp glance. 'I mean, not *just* E. Anyway, that means someone else must have given her the K.'

'But why didn't you tell someone? It could have made a difference.'

'I wanted to go to the police. I figured they should know but Dad wouldn't let me.'

'Nathan knew?' The words tore from Libby's throat. So many things kept compounding on top of each other. So many secrets. Then she remembered the fight Sienna had told her about. 'Is that what you two were arguing about?'

'He said there were things from the past that people might make a big deal of.' Sam looked away. His jaw clenched. 'I thought he was talking about how my real mum's dad died. The car accident. And that maybe he was just trying to protect me. But then Gemma told me about Colin Wallace and what he did to that boy.' He screwed up his eyes to stop the tears leaking out. 'Why is everything so fucked up?'

'I don't know.' She shook her head, but she wasn't sure she believed it.

You deserve a better husband than the monster you got.

Her husband thought he was a monster. That he was the same as his father. And that he had to finish what he started. She wrapped her arms around her chest to hide the hollow ache that was building up inside her. Her perfect life was a lie. It was empty. Barren. Gone.

Stephen abruptly stood up. 'I'm sorry, Libby, I need to go to the police. I'm not like Gemma. I'm not trying to chase ghosts and I'm not accusing your husband of anything, but the longer she's missing, the harder it will be to find her. And if he is involved—'

'It's okay. I understand.' Libby cut him off and helped Sam to his feet, her eyes fixed firmly in the distance, letting it fall out of focus so that it was just a blur.

Her heart ached at the destruction she'd caused. She'd saved

Sam the way she couldn't save Todd, but in doing so, she'd destroyed her husband. And the most terrible part was that she'd done exactly what her own mother had done. But in this case, instead of deserting her children, she'd deserted her husband. Still, it didn't make it better. It just meant she'd become the person she hated the most in the world.

32

'Do you want anything to eat?' Libby dumped her bag onto the kitchen counter three hours later, as Sam leaned against the door frame. His skin was still drawn, and fatigue had etched dark shadows under his eyes, but the terrible weight that had been pressing down on his shoulders when she'd found him at the beach had gone.

He shook his head. 'Nah. I'm wiped out. I'm going to crash.'

'Okay, but we do need to have a proper talk later. About the drugs... and about what Gemma told you.'

'I know.' He gave her a weary smile and left the room, scooping up the cat as he went. Harriet purred in approval. Giving in to her own fatigue, Libby walked across to the kettle. The coffee percolator was still sitting on the hob where she'd left it, but it was too late in the day for more caffeine.

The thought almost made her burst out laughing, since she doubted she'd be getting much sleep tonight, regardless of what she drank. All the same, she filled the kettle with water and reached for the loose-leaf peppermint tea. She then pulled out a second cup and glanced over at Stephen.

He was standing by the wide glass doors, staring out into the garden. They'd been in the police station for almost two hours as Stephen filed a missing person's report and then Sam spoke to a detective sergeant about selling the drugs to Zoe and Hayley. But because they hadn't shown up in Hayley's toxicology reports and Zoe hadn't reported it as a crime, the detective had sent them home with the comment that they would be following it up.

However, the outcome for Stephen hadn't been so positive, and while the police officer on the reception desk had promised to investigate it, she hadn't seemed in a hurry to do so. And then there was Nathan.

A fresh ache caught in her throat. Stephen had told the officer about Gemma's research and her belief that Nathan was Colin Wallace's son. And that he was missing. It hadn't elicited much interest from them, but Libby knew how quickly that could change if they found something.

She shut her eyes, hating how little control she had over everything. But it had to be that way. She couldn't keep trying to rewrite things to suit herself. She'd called her husband multiple times while they'd been at the police station, each time leaving him the same message.

Please talk to me before things get any worse.

But there had been no reply.

Which meant until she heard from him it was best not to think about where he was. Or what he was doing.

A wave of guilt rushed over her as she looked over to Stephen. The despair on his face when the police had all but dismissed him had been all too familiar and she'd found herself inviting him back to the house. Plenty of room on the road to despair.

'Would you like a hot drink?'

'No, thanks.' He stepped away from the glass doors. His movement was calm but the restless twitch of his hands and the fevered colour in his cheeks exposed his mounting concern. 'I have to do something.'

'I know.' Libby ignored the whistling kettle and gestured for him to sit down at the bench. He reluctantly looked at the stool before sliding onto it. She joined him. 'If I can help you, I will. What do you need?'

He raked a hand through his hair. 'While Colin Wallace was never charged, or confessed to any other murders, about five years after he went to prison, a private investigator who'd been hired by the families of the missing boys discovered eight lock-ups that had been rented by someone matching Colin's description.'

Libby sucked in a breath. 'D-did they find any evidence?'

He shook his head. 'No. Numerous tenants had used them since then, and there's also the suggestion that they'd been thoroughly cleaned before the keys had been returned. The lock-ups were all within a forty mile radius of Wallace's house. If Gemma has been taken by...' he paused, as if catching himself, 'a Wallace copycat, there's a chance they've done something similar.'

Understanding swept through her.

'You want to search all the lock-ups? There could be hundreds.'

'Eighty-four commercial ones that have been advertised in the last six months,' he corrected. 'I have a list of them.'

'That will take forever.'

'I know. But until the police take me seriously, I need to keep searching on my own. And since Ian... I mean Nathan... isn't here, it seems the most logical place to start.'

It was.

'We have a home office where Nathan keeps some files. I

could start going through them. See if I can find a rental agreement or an address.'

'Thank you, Libby. And please call me if you find anything. I'm going to book into a hotel. I'll call an Uber.' His eyes filled with gratitude as he pulled out his phone.

'I promise,' she said, trying to ignore the heavy weight of what she was saying.

Once Stephen had gone, she checked on Sam. His door was half open, no doubt to let the cat come and go as she pleased, and she peered in. He was sprawled out on his bed, his face soft with sleep, while Harriet was curled into the side of his chest.

I'm doing the right thing.

She quietly retreated and made her way to the office. Nathan's laptop was on his side of the long desk that they shared and she opened it up. They'd never been the kind of people to hide their passwords from each other and she tapped it in.

If there was something to find, then she'd find it.

* * *

By six o'clock, Libby was exhausted. She'd spent the early afternoon searching the office at home before driving over to TLC Manufacturing. The obnoxious Rita had almost refused to let her into his office until Libby said in a cool voice that she was part owner. Even then, the girl had given her a sullen look, refusing to even answer Libby's most basic question of when Nathan had last been there.

In the end, she'd closed his office door, leaving a disgruntled Rita on the other side. Then she'd opened his work computer, which had the same password as his laptop. But again, she hadn't been able to find anything except a large number of emails from creditors, as well as a profit and loss statement that made for alarming reading.

She didn't need Sam's math tutor to tell her that the business was in terrible shape.

Which also meant there was no way Nathan could afford to expand the business.

A quick look in his calendar confirmed it. Her throat went dry as she went back through his schedule. There was no mention of meeting with a rental agency or going to view a lock-up. But it hadn't been much consolation. On the way home, she'd stopped at Eloise's house, but her mother-in-law didn't answer.

Libby still had the keys but after her last search of Eloise's house, she hadn't felt up to going in there again. And so she'd arrived home and spent the last hour searching through all of Nathan's clothes, hoping to find something.

Instead, all she'd discovered was a bottle of her favourite Australian shiraz tucked at the back of the wardrobe along with a gorgeous gold necklace. For her birthday in two weeks. The one they were meant to be celebrating in Spain as a family.

'Sam, you piece of shit. Where are you?' Sienna's voice sounded out from downstairs, quickly followed by the stomp of Doc Martens and a door slamming shut. Libby scrambled to her feet and was halfway down the stairs as Sienna came charging up to her, closely followed by another girl with dark hair. Hayley?

'Libby, have you seen him? And don't try and protect him, because—'

'He's asleep,' Libby said in a low voice and herded them through to the kitchen. Sienna's lipstick was smudged and her dyed black hair was ruffled as if she'd been running. And... she and Hayley were holding hands.

Sienna seemed to follow her startled expression and let out a sharp snort. 'Please for the love of cats do not say anything. And why is Sam asleep? Do you have any idea what he's done?'

'Actually, I do. He told me this afternoon and we've been down the station so he could report it.'

Sienna's mouth dropped open and the bright colour in her cheeks faded. 'Are you sure?'

'I am.' Libby nodded and turned to Hayley. 'And he feels terribly guilty about it. He would like to apologise to you properly when you feel up to it.'

'You bet he bloody will.' Sienna tightened her grip on Hayley's hand, as if worried she was a helium balloon that might just float away. 'I still can't believe he was such a dick.'

'It's okay, Sina.' Hayley's voice was soft and her face was pale. 'He didn't mean it.'

'That doesn't make it right,' Sienna said, though the anger was gone, replaced by concern. Hayley gave her a shy smile but beads of sweat dotted her brow and her face had drained of colour. It looked like she was going to faint.

'Hayley, I'm going to slip my arm around you and help you lie down.' Libby gently guided her onto the floor and knelt beside her, checking her pulse. 'Is this your first day out of the house?'

She nodded, her face drawn and body trembling. Sienna's eyes filled with alarm.

'Is she okay? She seemed okay. But it was a bit windy when we doubled back on my bike. Is this my fault? I should never have dragged her back here. I was so mad at Sam. Hayley, I'm so sorry.'

'Sina, I'm okay, stoopid. I just feel a bit woozy.'

'It's okay, sweetheart,' Libby said as she instructed Sienna to bring her some cushions to prop up under Hayley's legs. She loosened the collar of her shirt and then put her hand on Sienna's arm to stop her leaning over too much. 'Let her have some air and when she's able to sit up, I'll make sure she's okay.'

'Th-thanks, Libby.' Sienna wiped away a tear, her eyes never leaving Hayley's face.

Half an hour later after a cup of sweet tea, Libby walked back to her car where Sienna was waiting, while Adele Terrace herded her daughter into the house.

Sienna was fiddling with her silver thumb ring when Libby climbed into the driver's seat but her eyes were glassy like she'd been crying. 'Is she really okay?'

'I think so. Though she's been through a lot and these things can take time. Why didn't you ever tell me that you liked...' she tailed off, not sure how to continue the conversation.

'Girls? Hayley? Why should I? It's not like heterosexuals have to announce their straightness. I don't want it to be a big deal,' Sienna retorted, sounding so much like her usual self that for the first time in days, Libby managed to smile.

'You're right. I'm sorry. Though I'm still not clear on what happened between you two. At one point, Adele thought you were stalking her daughter.'

'That's not what happened.' Sienna's eyes were bright. 'I was only there because I needed to make sure she was okay. After what happened—'

'What?' Libby stiffened.

Sienna wrinkled her nose. 'Okay, so don't freak out. But the night of the bonfire, Hayley rang me up. She sounded really drunk or something and wanted me to pick her up. But Sam and Dad were out, so... I borrowed Sam's car.'

'That was *you*?' Libby turned to her, thinking of the pink nail and the fact Denise's husband had seen the car at Harrington Beach that night.

'I know, it's bad and you're probably going to ground me for a hundred years, but trust me, I've already paid. We had a fight and Hayley got out of the car and ran off. I looked for her everywhere but couldn't find her. And yes, that makes me a hypocrite for getting mad at Sam when it's just as much my fault.'

Libby leaned back in the driver's seat. So, she hadn't been going mad. Both of her kids had been involved in what happened, though neither of them had been responsible. It should have made her feel better. But all it did was point the finger more firmly at her husband.

'I guess the important thing is that she's safe and back at home.' Libby started the engine and tried not to think of Gemma Harrington. Hayley had been able to walk out of her lock-up the following morning and physically was fine apart from exhaustion and the remnants of the ketamine. But if Stephen was right, then Gemma had been missing since Wednesday evening.

And the longer she was out there, the more she would be suffering.

Stephen's gaunt face appeared in her mind, eyes pleading at her. She knew what they both wanted her to do. What they wanted her to ask. Except to ask her, she would have to tell Sienna the truth about Nathan. Well, at least what she and Sam had discovered. It was something she dreaded.

'Did Hayley say anything about what happened? Was there any clue about who might have done this to her?'

'Oh my God. Why would you even ask that? You sound like all those wannabe detectives. Do you know that's why Hayley didn't want to leave the house? Because so many of them kept trying to talk to her?'

Libby winced. She'd known that would be the reaction, but she couldn't leave it. 'I do have a reason. There's someone else who's missing. They're older than Hayley. But it's been two days now and I know they're really scared. That's why I asked. Because even the smallest clue might help us find her.'

Sienna narrowed her eyes. 'Who is "us" and what's going on? Has it got something to do with why Sam spontaneously told you about what happened that night?'

'Sort of.' Libby tightened her grip on the steering wheel. 'There are some things I have to tell you...'

33

Three hours later, Sienna had managed to cry herself to sleep. Telling her about Gemma and her research on Colin Wallace had been excruciating; Sienna had gone through all the stages of grief like a tornado before finally wiping herself out.

Libby's bones ached as she paused on the landing and peered back into Sam's room again. He was still asleep, in the same position as when she'd last checked.

She was almost jealous and couldn't imagine her own slumber being so peaceful.

Stephen had called half an hour ago to say that it was too dark to keep looking so he was heading back to the hotel to keep searching on the Internet. Libby had been forced to admit that she hadn't found anything out, apart from the fact that Nathan's business was doing badly. She told him to come over in the morning and they'd go over what they knew.

She flicked on the light and groaned. The bed was covered with all of Nathan's clothes that she'd dragged out of the wardrobe. Her limbs had turned to lead. No way could she even think about trying to tidy up.

Then she spied the bottle of shiraz that she'd found. She snatched it up and since there was nowhere to sit, she dropped down to the floor and leaned against the bed, cradling the bottle in her hands. Maybe she should open it now and drown her sorrows.

At least it would help her sleep.

Decision made, she twisted the screw top and took a long gulp, and then another. The pepper and oak flavours teased her throat and turned her limbs to liquid. Sighing, she drank some more. Better. Much. Better. Libby leaned further back against the side of the bed, enjoying the numbness as it swept through her.

Oblivion was what the doctor ordered. Or, in this case, the paramedic. She hiccupped and giggled at her own diagnosis and treatment plan. As she held it up to her lips again, it caught in her throat. She spluttered and red wine sprayed out onto the pale carpet.

Irritation skittered along her skin. Couldn't she just wallow for one minute without disaster finding her? She watched as the ruby-red liquid sank into the thick pile. Part of her wanted to leave it. Like protecting the evidence at a crime scene. This would be the reminder of the day she discovered her marriage was over.

She managed to sit there for two minutes before her legs decided to move of their own accord. Sighing, she got to her feet and went downstairs for the salt and soda water. It wasn't her first red wine cleaning rodeo and she went straight to the laundry room where she kept her supplies. The alcohol caused her to sway and she steadied herself before bending down to the bottom shelf. Something grey was crammed in there. Giving it a good yank, she pulled it out.

It was a grey hoodie. The one she'd taken from Sam's car and washed, before hiding it away after seeing the photo Fiona had shown her. Back when she thought it might be used as evidence against Sam... or Nathan.

But that was before she'd known about Gemma.

Forgetting the salt and soda water, she rocked back on her heels and laid the hoodie down on the floor of the laundry room. Had she checked the pockets before she washed it? Just in case, she slipped her hand into one pocket, but there was nothing. Not even a lint ball. She tried the other one, but it was the same.

She ran her hand up and down the seams and studied the front and back, looking for anything that might help give them a location. But there was nothing, except the faint scent of her laundry powder. And... she pressed it up to her nose again and then stiffened. It wasn't laundry powder. It was citrus and wood. The faintest hint, which was why she'd missed it before.

Nathan's aftershave.

Disappointment churned in her belly, and she staggered back to her feet, letting the hoodie fall back onto the floor. She needed more wine. Enough to make her stop thinking about where her husband was and what he might be doing.

* * *

Libby pressed herself into the warmth of Nathan's back. Her limbs were languid as she kissed the base of his neck and her hands snaked around his waist.

'Morning, my love.' His voice was groggy, still half asleep, and Libby's heart filled with contentment. So often he was up before her, jogging or working or grinding coffee. But this morning, he'd stayed in bed, just to be with her when she woke up. These were the moments she loved best. The moments when—

Brrrring.

The harsh ringtone crashed through the languorous haze

and Libby's eyes flew open. She was lying in her own bed but there was no Nathan next to her, just the pile of clothes she'd left there last night. The warmth of the dream ebbed away, leaving her cold.

He still hadn't come home.

Fumbling for her phone in the dull morning light, she peered at the screen. It was Stephen. She didn't answer and a few moments later, a text message appeared, saying he would be there in half an hour. She managed to type *okay* and then closed her eyes as an iron band tightened in her skull. Her throat ached and her mouth tasted like mould. No, like shiraz.

She groaned, remembering last night's attempt to blot out the world. It had seemed like the world had other ideas and was now back in full force. This time, she eased herself up slowly and reached for the water bottle at the side of the bed. Careful not to drink too much, she had several gulps before attempting to stand up. Her head began to spin, and she took several deep breaths before walking to the curtains and pulling them open.

Bright light filled the room and she flinched. She was getting far too old for this. Shielding her eyes to avoid the glare and the red wine stains that were still on the carpet, she staggered over to the ensuite and turned on the shower. Fifteen minutes later, she was dressed and pulling her thick curls into a ponytail as she made her way downstairs. Harriet must've come out of Sam's room at some stage during the night and was asleep on the bottom stair as Libby walked past. The cat immediately followed her into the kitchen for breakfast, and once she was fed, Libby prepared the coffee just as the doorbell went.

It was Stephen.

He looked as terrible as she felt, but she suspected it was for different reasons.

'How did you go?' she asked, leading him back through to the kitchen.

He shook his head. 'Nothing. I spoke to the police again and they have located the rental car. It had been towed away from a car park several blocks away from the café and impounded. But are still trying to access CCTV footage from the car park itself. I've spoken to several more companies who rent lock-ups but keep hitting a brick wall. Have you heard from—'

'No.' Libby cut him off before he could say the name. It was even more difficult as the tendrils of her dream kept trying to slide through her body. She was saved from elaborating by the sound of footsteps coming down the stairs. The heavy thump, thump, thump told her it was Sam, who never walked when he could jog.

He appeared in the doorway, still rubbing sleep from his eyes as he shrugged a familiar grey hoodie on over his T-shirt. Libby froze, remembering she'd left it on the laundry floor. She'd meant to push it back into the cupboard. She swallowed.

'Morning... I think that needs a wash. It's still a little stinky. Why don't I take it from you?'

Sam stared at her through bleary eyes. 'Smells okay to me. Besides, I've only just found it again. I thought Jonathan had decided to keep it for good.'

Libby was perfectly still as white noise swirled around her, buzzing in her ears as the world stopped turning.

'W-what did you say?'

Sam tilted his head to one side and raised an eyebrow, his default mode when asked what he considered a stupid question. 'I said I'm pleased to have my hoodie back.'

'About Jonathan.' The buzzing in her ears grew louder. Was she shouting? She could no longer tell. Sam didn't seem to notice as he walked over to the pantry where the cereal was kept.

'He borrowed it a couple of weeks ago when he was around here fixing God knows what, for Dad. Said he was cold.' He took out several boxes and went in search of a large enough bowl.

'Are you 100 per cent sure that you gave it to him?' Libby's voice was urgent, her mind trying to think, despite the wretched buzz. Because if Sam gave Jonathan the hoodie, then how the hell had she found it in the back of his car? And why was someone wearing it in the CCTV footage that Fiona had showed her?

Sam frowned as he finally located a bowl and looked up at her. 'Um, yeah. I love this hoodie. It was hanging on the rack by the door and Jonathan asked to borrow it.'

Next to her, Stephen seemed to notice something wasn't right. 'Libby, what's going on. Does this mean something?'

And then, like coming out of a daze, the buzz of white noise was gone, and she seemed to come back into the room. It was like being slapped and her whole body was shaking as she met his gaze. This whole time. Right under her nose, and she'd had no fucking idea. And with it, the last little piece of her heart broke.

A sob caught in her chest. 'I know who took Gemma.'

34

Blackham Court was an ugly, purpose-built block of flats that had somehow resisted the property developers, and instead, the dull-yellow brick tower continued to blot the skyline. Libby had only been there a couple of times and it hadn't been hard to understand why Jonathan preferred to spend so much time at their house.

'Are you sure he's working?' Stephen said as they climbed out of the car.

'I am.' Libby locked the car and tightened her grip on the straps of her emergency backpack. She'd triple checked the rota and had called Denise to confirm Jonathan had turned up for his shift. He had, which meant it was safe for them to break into his flat.

Her knees buckled and she had to put out her arms to steady herself.

Jonathan. Her friend. Her colleague. The person she'd let into her life. Into her family's life. And he had been behind it all. The two weeks of torturous despair as Libby had suspected her son, her daughter, her husband. Because of Jonathan, her thoughts had gone down such dark, dark roads. And she still had no idea why.

Doesn't matter. Not right now.

She gritted her teeth. The *why* was for a later time. Right now, they needed to find Gemma. Stephen hooked his own pack over his shoulders. His jaw was tight as they walked to the side of the building and waited until a harassed-looking woman tried to herd out a gaggle of young boys, all dressed in football kits.

Stephen stepped towards her and held the door back. 'Here, let me.'

'Thank you.' The woman didn't even bother to look up at him as she grabbed one of the boys. 'Oh, no you don't, Kevin. And if you even think of crying then we'll go back inside and miss the match.'

At this point, a second boy made a break for it, and Libby darted past them and joined Stephen at the door. Jonathan's apartment was on the fifth floor and without a swipe card, they couldn't use the lift, which meant the dirty cement stairwell.

'Are you sure about the lock?' She asked in a low voice as they reached the landing. Stephen nodded and pulled out a small leather pouch.

'Most legal conferences are quite dry, but several years ago, a security consultant who was an ex-burglar ran a one-day course. It was fascinating and I joined a local club to keep my hand in,' he explained as they reached a nondescript door. Libby took a deep breath and nodded for Stephen to step back before she knocked, to make sure Jonathan really wasn't there.

After a minute, she nodded her head and Stephen lowered himself so he was eye level with the lock. He opened the leather pouch and brought out several slim picks and got to work. Years seemed to tick by before he finally twisted the handle and the door opened.

Her whole body began to shake as the rush of adrenaline set in. She knew it well. From years of being first to a scene, not knowing what heart-breaking carnage she might find. And while it never got any easier, it was something she knew how to handle. She touched his arm.

'Do you want me to go in first... in case...' she trailed off and he swallowed, eyes focused.

'No. I'm okay.' He stepped over the threshold. Libby followed him and gagged as the stench of mould and stale food hit her. The door opened straight into the living room that was barely visible underneath a tidal wave of work uniforms, magazines and takeaway-food containers. That explained the stench but not the mess. She shuddered and pointed to the hallway on the right.

'The bedrooms are that way.'

Stephen didn't even stop to look. He just strode across the detritus as if it wasn't there to the rooms. The first door was open and bright light filtered through it, but the second door was shut with a large bolt lock across it, secured with a padlock.

'Gemma. It's me. I'm here. Just hang on, okay.' Stephen's voice was strong and firm as he took a step back from the door and lifted his leg, clearly not wanting to waste any time with his lock picks. He then leaned slightly forward and brought his foot crashing into the wooden door just below the bolt lock. It was a move Libby had seen several times before as a first responder, and she wasn't surprised as the wood splintered and groaned before the door swung inwards, leaving the metal bolt lock hanging uselessly from the door frame as the sheared screws fell to the floor.

The acid stench of urine filled the air, combined with a staleness that came from darkness and despair. Libby pushed back her own revulsion, like she always did when responding to a call-out. There would be time for that later. Next to her, Stephen gagged before seeming to regain his composure.

'Gemma.' She fumbled with the light switch, but it didn't work, and so she used the torch on her phone. There was a soft moan coming from the corner and Stephen darted towards it, ignoring Libby's restraining arm. She swallowed and quickly surveyed the room, assessing it for any threats.

The last time she'd seen it, there had been an old wooden desk and magnolia paint on the walls, but now it was like a time capsule with a dull-brown floral carpet and clashing wallpaper. A standard lamp was in the corner, next to an ancient sofa, and against the far wall was a bed with a crumpled figure lying on it, held there by metal chains that had been attached to the wall.

She recognised it from the articles she'd read on Colin Wallace. It was a replica of the lock-up that he'd held Wayne Mason in over forty years ago.

Libby's vision blurred, her mind unable to take in everything all at once. Jonathan's betrayal had seemed like a shocking but arbitrary event. But this was anything but arbitrary. It was connected directly to the core. But how?

'Libby. Snap out of it.' Stephen's voice was firm, dragging Libby out of her thoughts and back into the darkened room.

'Sorry.' She crossed over to the lamp and switched it on. It worked and the room was flooded with light. She left Stephen to grapple with the manacles while she dropped to her knees in front of Gemma's huddled body and slipped the backpack off.

'Hi, do you remember me? It's Libby Curtis.' She searched for a pulse, relieved to find it was there, if a little erratic. Libby tapped her cheeks several times and Gemma's eyes flickered open; her pupils dilated. 'It's okay. I'm here to help. Stephen's here, too. Is anything broken?'

Gemma could only moan but did shake her head.

'What's wrong with her? Is she okay?' Stephen's face was pale.

'She's been drugged,' Libby said, remembering all too well what Hayley Terrace had been like. And Gemma had been here for three nights. 'Call the ambulance right now and they'll notify the police and fire department. I'm going to administer something to help keep her stable until we get her to the hospital.'

'I have to get the manacles off,' he insisted but Libby put her hand on his arm.

'No, you need to make the call.'

He opened his mouth and then shut it again, before nodding. 'Of course.' He stood up and retrieved his phone before taking another look at Gemma. Then he went into the other room and began to talk.

Libby turned back to Gemma and set up an IV before getting out her trauma scissors to cut away the fabric of Gemma's shirt sleeves and trousers. The skin around her wrists and ankles was raw and bleeding, which suggested she'd tried hard to escape. She must have been so terrified to find herself trapped in a room that must surely have been her worst nightmare. She needed to get an IV in to help with fluids and then she'd dress the wounds. But—

Crash.

The sound of shattering glass came from the next room and Stephen's muffled conversation broke off, followed by a loud thump. Libby stiffened and Gemma's hand clutched at Libby's arm.

'Don't leave me here.' Her voice wasn't much above a whisper and tears leaked out of her eyes.

'We won't,' Libby promised as footsteps came towards the room. Her fingers tightened around the scissors she'd been about to use as Jonathan stepped into the room. His blond hair was pushed away from his face and his brown eyes, which were normally full of humour, were dark with anger.

'No. No. No. You shouldn't be here.' He stalked towards her, his movements jerky and unfamiliar. Gemma let out a primal moan and Libby quickly stood up in front of her and opened the scissors to expose the blade.

'Stop.' She put as much power into her voice as she could, hoping to shock him. It worked and he came to a halt, eyes still fixed on her. But it wasn't him. Not the person she knew. Jonathan, but not Jonathan. 'Why would you do this? You wouldn't hurt anyone.'

'She's not anyone,' he said, taking a tentative step forward, his gaze now dropping to the scissors. Libby moved them forward and he took a step back, letting out a growl. 'And neither was the other one.'

Hayley?

That was him as well? Pain buried itself deep in her bones. He was with her that day at Steamer Point. He'd seen her and looked horrified. And she'd just assumed it was to see what some monster had done to her. But really, he was the monster. Had he just been horrified that she'd escaped?

'I don't understand.'

'That's because you're not meant to, Libby. Your world is good. And that's all I wanted for you and Nathan and the kids. To stay in the light. It was my job. That's why when I saw Hayley that night, I knew she deserved to be punished. All those times Sienna cried because of her. I don't even know if you saw it, but I did. It wasn't right.'

Her mind was spinning, trying to reconcile the cruel words with the friend she'd always seen him as. But she couldn't. And it hurt.

'So, you hired a lock-up and kidnapped her?'

'No.' He shook his head, eyes blinking, as if he was losing his train of thought. 'That's not what happened. The lock-up was for me. Sometimes, it's the only way I can sleep. But on the way, I saw Hayley climbing out of Sam's car, and there was poor Sienna crying again because of that girl. I was trying to teach Hayley a lesson. But I left the door unlocked. I wasn't trying to hurt her. Just making her know what it felt like to be neglected.'

He tilted his head to stare at her, as if willing her to follow his logic. But she couldn't. There was a madness in his eyes. Why had she never seen it before? But she already knew. Because her whole life, she kept only seeing what she wanted to.

'Except in the process, you set my son up. You put the hoodie back into his car.' Libby's mind tried to think. She'd already worked out the pink nail had come from when Sienna had collected Hayley from the party. But this explained the rest.

'I was returning it,' Jonathan countered. 'I would never have let anything happen to Sam. I love him. I love you all.'

'And what about Gemma? What's she ever done to you?'

'What hasn't she done?' Bits of spittle flew from his mouth as he jabbed a hand towards the bed. 'She was trying to destroy your family. I couldn't let that happen. And the cow of a woman at the factory.'

'Mo? You were the one who mugged her?' she asked.

He nodded, almost smirking.

'But why?'

'Because she was trying to betray Nathan. It was wrong of her. We've suffered enough. I had to stop them.'

'Who is "we", Jonathan?' Libby blinked and tightened her grip on the scissors. She was tired of trying to guess the answers.

'Ian and Marion... and me.'

Libby opened her mouth, but it was Gemma who spoke next, her voice low and broken. 'Wayne. He's Wayne Mason.'

'No.' Libby's hand flew to her mouth and she turned to Jonathan. This whole time, her friend had been Wayne Mason. The young boy that Colin Wallace had held captive in a lock-up until Marion had turned up and freed him, at the same time sentencing her husband to a life in prison. 'How can you be Wayne?'

'You don't get to use that name,' he snarled. 'I'm not him. He wasn't brave. He didn't know what to do. Jonathan does, though.' His eyes darkened and he lunged forward, coming at Libby with a speed she hadn't expected.

'Stay back.' She slashed the scissors in his direction, and the blade slid along his arm, drawing blood. He retreated with a whimper, clutching his arm.

'You shouldn't hurt family, Libby. That's what Marion always says. And we're all family. Don't you see? That's why she can't be here. If she tells people, then everyone will know. They'll look at us differently. Because that's what people do.' Finally, the darkness in his eyes faded and he hugged his arms around his torso and began to rock. 'We just want it to be over.'

'So do we,' Stephen's voice came from somewhere behind Jonathan and then he brought his arm up around the paramedic's neck in a choke hold. Jonathan's body spasmed in protest but Stephen held him there. 'Libby, there's rope in my bag. The police are on their way, but I'd rather restrain him until they get here.'

Libby retrieved the rope and waited until Stephen had finished tying up Jonathan before dropping to the carpet that was identical to the one Colin Wallace had used.

The tragedy of it all made it hard to breathe. Wayne had been a victim and she had no idea of the horrors he had gone through. But somehow, it had morphed and twisted him into something else. A monster. Eloise obviously knew about it. Had she helped mould him into this new version? And what about Nathan. Did he have any idea?

But she couldn't think about her husband right now. Everything hurt, and as she looked at Jonathan's limp body, the tears finally fell. She didn't understand it and maybe she never would. But at least for now it was over. Finally over.

35

'Right, that's ten minutes. It's time to put down your phone.' Stephen stood up from the hospital chair that he'd dragged over so that he could be closer to her bed. His hand was out, and his gaze was fixed firmly on her phone.

'The doctor said I was fine,' Gemma reminded him, but surrendered the phone all the same. He put it on the table next to the grapes he'd bought her. Before he could sit down, she reached out for his hand. 'Thank you.'

'For taking your phone away?' He arched an eyebrow.

'For everything,' she corrected, a lump catching in her throat. It had been four days since the police had arrested Jonathan Reid and she'd been taken to hospital. Her wrists and ankles had been dressed and the terrible nausea and headaches from the ketamine he'd drugged her with had finally passed.

But all of that paled in comparison to the news about Eloise Curtis... or should she say Marion Wallace.

Police had gone to her house after arresting Jonathan and had found her dead at the bottom of the stairs. Apparently, she'd had a bad hip and had tripped on a rug. There were no signs of forced entry but a wall safe was open and there were newspaper clippings and a key on the hallstand had led them to a small door at the back of the cellar. That's where they found the bones of Colin Wallace's many victims. Including Gemma's brother, Lucas.

Gemma's heart pounded and Stephen's fingers instinctively tightened around hers. As if knowing that's where her thoughts had gone. Tears prickled her eyes.

Forensics still needed to identify the bones but Gemma knew it was them. The terrible thing inside her that had dragged her to fulfil her purpose was gone. She'd done it, and in due course, she'd be able to mourn her brother properly.

It wasn't exactly peace, but it was something.

And Stephen had sat beside her every day as she'd ached and cried and screamed.

'Well, I was worried you might miss your train again, so I wanted to make sure you came back to Manchester.' His normally placid expression disappeared and his cheeks reddened.

'Still not what I mean,' she said, forcing him to return her gaze. His mouth opened and then closed again as something crossed his face.

'Oh.' He stepped closer to the bed, much like a swimmer testing the December waters. Gemma tightened her grip around his hand and tugged him closer. 'Are you sure?' his voice was hoarse. 'I know you haven't wanted anything serious, but that's not enough for me. Gemma, I want more.'

She swallowed. Last week was like a blur. Some kind of dream that had held her captive. And then Stephen had kicked the door open and saved her, figuratively and metaphorically. She stared at him. His blue eyes were dark and his impossibly long lashes brushed his checks when he blinked. It's all she'd thought of when she'd been locked up, and now she was free, it was like she'd always loved him.

'I want that, too.'

He nodded his head and his mouth turned up at one side. Gemma's heart expanded. Her kind, stoic friend who had been right in front of her the entire time. She returned the smile even as he kissed her, his mouth and breath warm against hers.

'Oh. Yikes. Terrible timing. Sorry, I'll come back later,' a familiar voice said and Gemma broke away to see Libby Curtis standing in the doorway. Her dark hair was loose and she was holding a large basket of what looked like cruffins.

'No, please don't,' Stephen said, also taking in the cruffins and Gemma's excited gaze. 'I've got to finish filling out some forms and Gem will never forgive me if she misses out on pastries.'

'And they're not just any pastries... they're from Maples.' Libby gave them both a shy smile and joined them. 'I hope it's okay to visit. I wasn't sure if you were up to seeing anyone yet.'

'You're not just anyone.' Gemma nodded to the chair that Stephen had recently vacated. Then she turned to him. 'You won't be gone too long, will you?'

'I swear.' He planted a warm kiss on her knuckles, then nodded at Libby and disappeared back down the ward.

Libby's mouth twitched, as if she was holding back a smile. 'Is this a new development?'

'I guess so. But in another way, it's been twenty years in the making,' Gemma admitted, though her guilt over what had happened stopped her from returning the smile. She'd thrust herself into Libby and Sam's life with a bull-in-a-China-shop approach. It had been way out of line. 'I'm pleased you came in. I've been wanting to thank you.'

'Stephen's the one you need to thank. He was persistent.'

'He's not *that* persistent,' Gemma caught her gaze. 'I know that what he asked you to do must have been difficult, given that we weren't sure if Nathan—' she broke off, more guilt catching in her throat. She pushed past it. 'I'm sorry. I should never have done that to you or your family. Stephen tried to warn me not to come down here and stir up old ghosts.'

'Definitely not the best two weeks of my life,' Libby admitted, before holding her gaze. 'But it helped get us all to the truth. We're always telling the kids that they need to do the right thing... not the easy one.'

'Still, I'm sorry. I shouldn't have tried to speak to you, or Sam, the way I did. I was so blindsided by my own needs that I handed you a live grenade.'

Libby bowed her head and inhaled, but when she looked up, her eyes were calm. 'Eloise made Nathan and Jonathan keep so many secrets that I don't think anything short of an explosion would've prised the lid off.'

Gemma studied her steepled fingers for several moments, considering her words. She knew that Stephen had been staying in close contact with Libby after police had discovered another possible victim. A six-month-old baby called Kieran Rowe.

Gemma remembered the case and she'd researched it while writing her book, but the age and date hadn't been strong enough for her to include it. But she'd interviewed Nancy Rowe. The grieving mother who had been sent to prison, accused of her own son's murder.

Of course, they'd need the DNA tests first, but if Nathan really was Kieran, then he'd been as much of a victim as Lucas and the other boys. Even Jonathan.

'H-how is he?'

Libby's brow furrowed. 'He's... doing okay. When he took off like that I panicked, not knowing where he was or whether he was even going to come back. He'd found out about Eloise and went searching for his birth mother. But he had no luck and hated being away from us. That's why he came back. We're his real family.'

'So, he's given up on finding his real mother, then?'

'No. He's going to employ a private detective to look for her. I think that's for the best. They'd know where to look. Yesterday was his first session with a therapist. I think it will help him process everything and articulate how he feels. Growing up with Colin's looming, dark shadow and Eloise's controlling personality, he didn't get to explore himself much.' Some of the worry left her face and she smiled. 'Can you believe he's started knitting? Yesterday, he finished a lopsided beanie, and in typical Nathan way, he now wants to do a surfboard cover. Who knows, it could become some strange, niche business.'

Gemma hoped so. Because he deserved peace and happiness, just like what he'd given to her and the other families.

'Well, thank him for me.' Her voice broke and Libby reached out and patted her hand. 'And if you do ever come up to Manchester, you'll have to let me know.'

'I'd like that,' Libby said as Stephen walked back into the room. Before Gemma could even protest, Libby was on her feet. The goodbyes were fast and once she was gone, Stephen turned to her.

'Good news. You can be discharged in a couple of hours, which means by tonight, we can be home.'

Home. Warmth flooded her limbs and she leaned back against the pillow. Yes, that was good news indeed.

36

A YEAR LATER

'I can't say I'm going to miss these stairs.' Stephen gave an exaggerated puff as he carried the last of the boxes of books down to the Transit van they'd hired to move Gemma's possessions into their new, three-bedroom house. It was out of Manchester in a quiet village with a back garden for the guinea pigs and a home office for Gemma to finish her book.

'I can't say I'm going to miss the vomit either. Or the lack of recycling,' Gemma looked around the ground floor landing for the last time. The guy from number three had propped his bicycle up against one wall and there was a random collection of coats and umbrellas that people left there, despite the fact it was meant to be a communal area. There was also a stack of catalogues and bills piled on top of the radiator, most of which were addressed to previous tenants.

Out of habit, Gemma sorted through them, not that she received much by mail any more. Even her book contract had arrived straight to her inbox. She smiled. For so long, she thought she needed a book deal to make sure the world heard the truth, but now it wasn't about pride. It was more of a quiet rightness.

That what she was doing was important and meaningful. And it was.

'You ready?' Stephen returned from the van and gave her an enquiring look.

'Sure am.' Gemma flipped past someone's bank statement, a flyer for dentures and a large envelope addressed to Gemma Harrington. She stared at it and then up at Stephen. 'Okay, this is weird. It's from Dalton Towers Rest Home.'

'Rest Home? We only got married last month and you're already trying to put me out to pasture. Should I be worried?'

She laughed and gave him a kiss, relishing the perfect fit of his mouth on hers. Then she pulled away and slid her nail under the flap of the envelope.

'No, you're safe for now. Dalton Towers was where Libby's mother was before she died two months ago. But why would they be sending me anything?'

'Probate could be over and she wanted to leave you something,' he said though he rubbed his chin. 'But it seems unlikely considering you've never met her. Unless you have.'

'No, never.' Gemma shook her head before gasping. 'I did contact them to see if I could ask Angela some questions about Libby. Which, I now concede, you were right. It was a little creepy.' Stephen topped his imaginary hat at this and Gemma gave him another kiss before continuing. 'But I never heard back and that was almost twelve months ago. What could they possibly be sending me?'

'I guess there's only one way to find out.' Stephen glanced down at the envelope in her hand. Gemma cautiously opened it and extracted a bundle of letters tied up in a bundle. On the top was a hasty note.

Gemma,

I found these hidden in a drawer at the nursing home where I work. One of the staff told me they must have been written by Angela Hislop. She died before I started work here, but from all accounts, she didn't have any visitors. Honestly, they look like a lot of mumbo jumbo and since the daughter had instructed us to dispose of her mother's possessions, that's what my matron told me to do. But it just seemed wrong, so I've enclosed them for you.
Carrie

Holy shit. Gemma's heart pounded as her fingers brushed across the bundle of letters and she smoothed the first one out to read it. It was a sheet of old-fashioned writing paper with a border of purple lavender sprigs. The handwriting was shaky and seemed to slide off the page as if it had been written on a rocking boat.

Nurse told me about you. Said you wanted to talk... I would like that. My name is Angela. I don't have any children and am very lonely. Could you come and visit me? No one else does. There was another girl once. She had a name, but I don't like saying it. Not nice, that one. Got mad at me. Pushed me. It hurt. The stairs hurt. Then I was broken and they sent me here. Please come and visit. Bring me some cake.

Gemma blinked. Was this real? Was Angela really saying that her daughter had pushed her down the stairs? Then she stiffened as another image superimposed itself. It was the one of Eloise Curtis – Marion Wallace – who police had found at the bottom of her stairs. The fall had been attributed to a bad hip and a rug that had upturned at the corner. There hadn't even been an autopsy.

She let out a stifled gasp as the pieces of the puzzle fell into place. How had she missed it? But she already knew the answer. All she'd cared about was that Marion and Colin's secrets had finally been revealed, meaning she and the other families were finally free to mourn their loved ones.

But she hadn't been the only one searching for justice, had she? Libby Curtis's strained face flashed into her mind, so desperate to hold her family together because of what had happened to her brother. And what was happening again to her husband and children. She started to sway and next to her, Stephen let out a concerned breath.

'Hey, are you okay? What does it say?'

Gemma steadied herself and let her fingers crumple the letter into a small ball. Then she looked up at him, this man she loved, and remembered the woman who had helped save her. Without Libby, she wouldn't even be here. She smiled at him.

'Nothing. Just a whole lot of rambling. Now, let's go. We have a new life waiting for us.'

EPILOGUE

'You sure about this?' Libby straightened Nathan's tie and stepped back to study him. He hardly ever wore a suit, but there was no denying the navy jacket and trousers perfectly fitted his broad shoulders and muscled arms.

'Yes, but only because you and the kids are with me.' He did up the button on his jacket and his gaze slid up her own outfit. It was a soft-pink dress that was nipped in at her waist and flared out around her hips as she walked. Not that she was sure how much walking she'd manage in the ludicrously high heels Sienna had talked her into buying. They were gold with straps, for goodness sake. And yet she wouldn't change them for the world.

It had been Nathan's idea to make the trip back to Yorkshire for his birth mother's seventy-second birthday. The private detective had found her easily. It wasn't the first time Libby and the kids had met her but it would be the first time for them to be around Nathan's new extended family.

'We're a team, remember.' She glanced over to where Sam was sprawled on the sofa in the house they'd rented. He'd grown since they'd dropped him off at Leeds University last month. Or maybe that was because she was adjusting to not seeing him every day. He was having a heated debate with Hayley about some movie Libby had never heard of, and he pushed his glasses back up his nose, which had become his habit. It was Danny who had worked out that Sam's slipping grades and terrible driving might be the result of eye problems and the glasses had made all the difference.

Next to him, Sienna rolled her eyes in his direction, her navy eyeliner matching the deep blue of her dress. And while it was no longer black, Libby wasn't quite sure her daughter's dark phase was over. But at least she smiled these days.

'Well, as part of my team, I need a hand with all this food,' Nathan announced as he lifted the large platter of cheeses and sliced fine meats he'd ordered from a nearby delicatessen.

'You're the one who ordered it.' Sienna got to her feet as Hayley quickly followed her and scooped up a plate of sausage rolls. 'There's enough food here for Sam's entire student hall.'

Sam stood up and surveyed it with a cynical eye. 'Maybe on a week night.' He shrugged and picked up the chocolate cake before following his sister out to the car. Libby grabbed the giant straw market bag that was filled with fresh bread sticks.

'Better safe than sorry,' Nathan told her. His eyes were gleaming though and she leaned forward and kissed him. His mouth was warm against hers but the restless, prowling energy that had once been his hallmark had gone and in its place was a calmness that had settled over him like a mantle. Or it could be because of his new career running a coffee shop.

Libby tried to imagine what Eloise would have said if she'd known her golden child now made lattes and scones for a living. But she couldn't picture it. Her mother-in-law, the woman who had denied so many people the right to know what Colin Wallace had done, had been unrepentant right to the bitter end.

She supposed she shouldn't have been surprised. Her own mother had proven time and time again that a leopard didn't change its spots. But when Nathan had written that terrible letter to her, full of his own torment and anguish, it had broken something inside her. And then when she'd been forced to see the true pain and shadows behind Jonathan, Libby knew she couldn't stay silent. So she'd gone to visit Eloise. Before the police, or Nathan, or anyone.

But her mother-in-law hadn't been home and so Libby had gone upstairs. To the second safe that Nathan had mentioned in his letter. And there it was. A single newspaper article. The thing that he hadn't been able to tell her himself because he had still been trying to accept the truth of what it really meant.

It looked like there had been more things there once but they'd been taken. Still, the article was enough. It was dated 1978. The same year that Nathan was born.

Yorkshire Police are looking into the disappearance of Kieran Rowe, aged six months. His mother left him in the house while she went to the corner shop for milk, and when she returned, he was gone.

And then it had all made sense. Libby's husband. Her beautiful Nathan and the two children that he had trusted her with, weren't related to the darkness of Colin Wallace. At least not by blood. The relief had been overwhelming.

When Eloise had returned, Libby had said all the things she needed to say. But it hadn't gone well and Eloise had refused to apologise for what she'd done to those poor families, to Jonathan, who she'd manipulated and moulded, breaking him all over again. And to Nathan. The boy she'd all but stolen from his rightful home.

Even then, Libby hadn't meant to do it. After all, once could be considered an accident, but twice...

Well, twice was something else entirely. But then Eloise had insisted on going upstairs to get the album of photos that she'd collected of Nathan over the years. To prove how much he still loved her. That she really was his mother in every sense of the word. And she had tripped on one of the antique rugs that she loved so much. Nathan had been right about that. She should have sold the house years ago and moved into a single storey. But of course, they now knew the real reason why she never would. Because of the basement of bones. The ones she'd forced Jonathan to hide away for her so that she could continue to live a double life.

And so Libby hadn't stepped in to help. She didn't really need to. The powder in Eloise's tea had done enough. The old woman was dizzy and off balance, and once she began to stumble, she couldn't catch herself or prevent it. And really, that was that. It was done and Libby had protected her family. Just like she promised she would the day that they stood together at the altar and said *I do*.

ACKNOWLEDGMENTS

We're incredibly grateful to the many people who have helped shape this story.

Thanks to our amazing editor, Emily Ruston, for your insightful contribution in turning this book into what it is today. Also, our thanks go to the rest of the Boldwood team. We couldn't do it without you.

To our families, thanks, as usual, for your support during the writing of this book.

ABOUT THE AUTHORS

Amanda Ashby and Sally Rigby are a crime writing partnership. Both authors live in New Zealand, have been friends for eighteen years and agree about everything (except musicals).

Sign up to Amanda and Sally's mailing list for news, competitions and updates on future books.

Visit Amanda Ashby's website:https://amandaashby.com/
Visit Sally Rigby's website: https://www.sallyrigby.com/

Follow Amanda and Sally on social media here:

 facebook.com/Amanda-Rigby-111632041134381

twitter.com/AmandaRigbyNZ

instagram.com/amandarigbybooks

ALSO BY
SALLY RIGBY AND AMANDA ASHBY

Remember Me?

I Will Find You

The Ex-Wife

The Stepmother

THE

Murder

LIST

THE MURDER LIST IS A NEWSLETTER DEDICATED TO SPINE-CHILLING FICTION AND GRIPPING PAGE-TURNERS!

SIGN UP TO MAKE SURE YOU'RE ON OUR HIT LIST FOR EXCLUSIVE DEALS, AUTHOR CONTENT, AND COMPETITIONS.

SIGN UP TO OUR NEWSLETTER

BIT.LY/THEMURDERLISTNEWS

Boldwood

Boldwood Books is an award-winning fiction publishing company seeking out the best stories from around the world.

Find out more at www.boldwoodbooks.com

Join our reader community for brilliant books, competitions and offers!

Follow us
@BoldwoodBooks
@TheBoldBookClub

Sign up to our weekly deals newsletter

https://bit.ly/BoldwoodBNewsletter